UNLUCKY FOR PRINGLE: UNPUBLISHED AND OTHER STORIES

UNLUCKY FOR PRINGLE: UNPUBLISHED AND OTHER STORIES

By

WYNDHAM LEWIS

Edited and Introduced by

C. J. FOX and ROBERT T. CHAPMAN

VISION

Vision Press Limited
157 Knightsbridge
London SW1X 7PA

ISBN 01 85478 013 0

CF

Printed in Great Britain by
Clarke, Doble & Brendon Ltd
Plymouth

MCMLXXIII

Contents

5

CONTENTS

General Introduction

Recalling the early stages of his career, Wyndham Lewis (1882–1957) wrote in 1935 that "the short story, as we call it, was the first literary form with which I became familiar . . . The 'short story' was the crystallization *of what I had to keep out of my consciousness while painting.*"[1] The latter part of this statement would seem to relegate Lewis's short fiction to a disproportionately secondary place in his *œuvre*. For, from the beginning of his 45 years as a visual and literary artist, Lewis was quite prolific as a fiction writer and, with the exception of the later 1920s and the 1930s, the short story figures prominently among his works in this field.

Lewis's first published stories appeared in 1909—a year after Arnold Bennett's *The Old Wives' Tale* and a year before H. G. Wells's *Tono-Bungay*—and the last stories published during his lifetime were contemporary with Kingsley Amis's *Lucky Jim* and Lawrence Durrell's *Justine*. It is not only that the time-span of Lewis's creative life makes it difficult to place him as a writer. The diversity of his fiction is also formidable, ranging as it does from *The Apes of God* (which, he wrote, paid unprecedented attention to "the externals—the *shell*, the *pelt*, the physical behaviour of people"),[2] to *Self Condemned* which, in its intensely subjective analysis of self-destruction, stands comparison as a tragic novel with Malcolm Lowry's *Under the Volcano*. Dostoyevsky, Flaubert, Gogol for the early writing; Dryden, Pope, Smollett, Swift for the satires; the Classics for *The Human Age*—few critics attempting to place Lewis into a literary tradition look to his contemporaries. In one of the earliest

[1] Walter Michel and C. J. Fox, eds., *Wyndham Lewis on Art*. London: Thames and Hudson, 1969, pp. 294–5.
[2] W. K. Rose, ed., *The Letters of Wyndham Lewis*. London: Methuen and Co. Ltd., 1963, p. 191.

reviews of Lewis's writing, Rebecca West suggested Dostoyevsky's influence on *Tarr*, and I. A. Richards, talking about *The Childermass* more than 40 years later, invoked Dante, Plato and Fielding. Like D. H. Lawrence, Lewis had no time for "novels that were copies of other novels," and both writers—in their very different ways—used fiction to embody and explore their predilections. Such formal beauties as *integritas, consonantia, claritas*—preoccupations of Joyce as well as of Stephen Dedalus —were not primary considerations with Lewis. That art is *"about* something" was axiomatic for him and, as he wrote in *Men Without Art* (1934): "Implicit in the serious work of art will be found politics, theology, philosophy—in brief all the great intellectual departments of the human consciousness."[3] Lewis's concept and practice of the fiction of ideas is nearer to the Augustan satirists, in its assertion of positives by the savagely indignant destruction of falsity, than to the varying degrees of Peacockian sophistication in contemporaries such as Norman Douglas, Evelyn Waugh and Aldous Huxley. It is much easier to say which writers Lewis is *not* like than to suggest resemblances and, in literature as well as in painting, it is as a unique phenomenon that he must finally be considered.

The present volume gathers together works of short fiction by Lewis which have remained unpublished or, having been scattered through little magazines between 1910 and 1956, were never collected for purposes of a single book. Naturally of special interest are the previously unpublished stories, most of which were apparently destined for inclusion in a volume to have been entitled *The Two Captains*. The bibliography of E. W. F. Tomlin's British Council pamphlet on Lewis (1955) mentioned an impending book of short fiction, but this book never materialized. In any event, the stories published here for the first time are part of a 1930s reworking of "The Crowd Master," initially published in *Blast* No. 2 (1915); "Junior," "The Two Captains" and "The Man Who Was Unlucky With Women" (all from the 1950s); and three tales written by Lewis during his 1940 stay in Sag Harbor, New York—"The Yachting Cap," "The Weeping Man" and "Children of the Great." Not included

[3] Wyndham Lewis, *Men Without Art*. London: Cassell and Co. Ltd., 1934, p. 9.

8

in this volume are any of the stories in the two collections of short fiction Lewis published in his lifetime, *The Wild Body* (1927) and *Rotting Hill* (1951).

All of the previously unpublished stories are not of equal literary merit. Nor are they generally on a par with the stories Lewis managed to have published during his lifetime. Yet, when grouped together with other unfamiliar Lewis material, even marginal works by the author of *Tarr* and *The Wild Body* take on added interest sufficient to warrant publication, especially if an effort is made to show how such stories blend with the general corpus of his fiction. Juxtaposed in this way with what turn out to be related works, they also enlarge the understanding of Lewis's literary aims. It should be remembered, however, that Lewis habitually did considerable revision on his writings in the "proof" stage of their production. Since none of the previously-unpublished stories apparently went to press, they lack that extra "finish" characteristic of The Enemy at his proof-slashing best. There have been additional difficulties about the text of at least some of this heretofore-unprinted material. The final typescripts of the stories seemingly to have been published in the 1950s— those of "The Two Captains," "Junior," "The Weeping Man," "The Yachting Cap," "The Man Who Was Unlucky With Women" and "Children of the Great"—were unavailable. But good carbon copies or other duplicates were found. In the case of "The Two Captains," a holograph mostly in Lewis's hand helped the editors rectify a number of imperfections, mainly dropped commas or simple typographical errors, in the carbon-copy typescript. Any lapse of a more elaborate order is signified accordingly.

The book called *Rotting Hill* was made up partly of sketches from life in the Notting Hill area of London during the post-World War II "Crippsean Ice Age" with its pervasive physical and metaphorical "rot." The stories in this present book, on the other hand, are notable for, among other things, the absence of the political preoccupation prevalent in *Rotting Hill*. But obviously there are similarities, quite apart from the drive and sparkle of Lewis's prose at its best. The *Rotting Hill* ambience of the bedraggled Britain of the 1940s obtrudes somewhat in "The Two Captains," and Lewis's life-long fascination with

9

rooms and flats as microcosms is as apparent in "Unlucky for Pringle" as it is in the *Rotting Hill* sketch called "The Rot." The historian Paul Eldred in another of the *Rotting Hill* tales is as much a "celebrated ruin" exploiting forever afterwards the temporary visitation of a muse as is Thaddeus Trunk in "Doppelgänger" (1954), a story included here.

But the stories in this new collection are more closely related to *The Wild Body* than to *Rotting Hill* if only because, as a whole, they are in the category of what might be called pure fiction as opposed to semi-fictional reportage. *The Wild Body*, a modern classic, is a book which, like *Rotting Hill*, brings together works sharing a common theme. In the former collection that theme is the primitive human breed, like "big, obsessed, sun-drunk insects,"[4] which fascinated Lewis as painter and writer in his early years. As such, *The Wild Body*'s inspiration comes closer than that of most of his other books to drawing on themes simultaneously at work in his pictures. Lewis's pre-World War I drawings abound in strange, ritualized figures. But Bestre and Brotcotnaz in *The Wild Body* are as much "executants of a *single* ritual" (the phrase is Walter Michel's) as are the figures in such drawings as "Indian Dance" and "Courtship" (1912). "Their enormous vitality," writes Michel, "is in the service of an obsession."[5] Lewis observed humanity like an anthropologist scrutinizing a newly-discovered species of homunculae, at once unbelieving and delighted by their absurdity. These wild bodies, driven either by demoniacal *idées fixes* or the vagaries of a perverse autonomic system, cavort over the canvases and through the stories of the young Lewis.

In *The Wild Body* Lewis defined his theory of the comic as rooted in "observations of a *thing* behaving like a person."[6] This is an idea to which Lewis adhered throughout his career and it is evident in most of the stories here collected. Polderdick ("The King of the Trenches"), for instance, is as mechanical as his "flying pigs," and Kipe in "The Yachting Cap" is a tatterdemalion Canute as elemental as the ocean he defies. Similarly,

[4] Lewis, *Rude Assignment*. London: Hutchinson and Co. Ltd., 1950, p. 117.
[5] Walter Michel, *Wyndham Lewis: Paintings and Drawings*. London: Thames and Hudson, 1971, p. 49.
[6] Lewis, *The Wild Body*. London: Chatto and Windus, 1927, p. 246.

Monsieur Chalaran in "Unlucky for Pringle," with his "animal-like selfishness and self-absorption," is very much in this Lewis tradition and that story as a whole is a tale merely transposed from the French or Spanish settings of the original *Wild Body* universe into an English scheme of things. "Unlucky for Pringle" has been chosen as the title story of this collection because, though written while Lewis was still in his twenties, it provides a precocious demonstration of virtually all his gifts and attitudes as a writer. With hindsight, the critic might see in this story an uncannily accurate premonition of the fate that awaited Lewis in the subsequent five decades of Anglo-Saxon literary history.

All of Lewis, it can be said, is in "Unlucky for Pringle." There is, for instance, the presence of the rootless connoisseur of rooms from Brittany to Morocco, via frigid Canada, Bayswater and Chelsea; there is the "gusto for the common circumstances of his life," and the ability to infuse the lowliest objects with a bizarre and exciting vitality. But there is also, embodied in Pringle, that "mysterious power of awakening hostility" which Lewis later ascribed to Rousseau in *The Art of Being Ruled* (1926) and which he felt in himself. From his position "outside," Lewis persevered all his life in starkly recording—through his social and literary criticism as well as in his fiction—what in *Self Condemned* (1954) he called "the madhouse of functional character." But like Monsieur Chalaran, this malignantly insane element does not relish the presence of a recording mind. In "Pringle" the crash of a looking-glass, customarily an omen of misfortune, should have warned the hero of the consequences of his "mystic contentment." Like the ultimate fate held for René Harding by the Hotel Blundell in *Self Condemned* and that reserved by the Anglosaxon cultural establishment for Lewis himself, the destiny of Pringle's lodging house was to "vomit him forth; it could not assimilate him . . . its inhabitants became filled with mysterious hatred for him."

Together with "Pringle," the other writings in the first section of this book give a preliminary display of how Lewis worked from the raw material of life, whether it was the Roland-centred domestic constellation of "A Breton Innkeeper" or the fictional presentation of an actual salon event under the shadow of war in the "Crowd Master" story. The rest of this collection exemplifies in an even more positive way the main themes evinced in all of Lewis's literary work. It is these themes, to the extent that they manifested themselves in the stories that follow, which determined the form given to this book as a whole.

First there is world war, a twentieth-century fact of life which, in Lewis's case, makes itself powerfully felt not only in the auto-biographical *Blasting and Bombardiering* (1937) but also, if more obliquely, in later books such as *Self Condemned* and *The Human Age* (1955). Lewis called the war of 1914–18 "a cyclopean divid-ing wall in time: a thousand miles high and a thousand miles thick, a greater barrier laid across our life."[7] However, as C. H. Sisson has suggested, Lewis was intellectually steeled, as his Georgian contemporaries were not, to absorb a shock of these proportions. "The Lewisian apocalypse was a pre-war affair," says Sisson. "It was not an excitement borrowed from events but an intellectual performance of his own."[8] Perhaps as a con-sequence of this, Lewis's most fascinating fictional insight into what the war was doing to Western Man came in a story written prior to his initial taste of military action. In the words of a *Rotting Hill* character created years later, Rob Cairn in "The French Poodle" (written 1915) swiftly finds himself "forcibly, violently, reborn" once he becomes a soldier on the western front. This whole story is a subtle analysis of that shell-shocked rebirth and also of the war's wider implications. Even in 1915, when martial enthusiasm on the home front had still not given way to weary disenchantment, Lewis's Cairn, with grim prescience, sees the great conflict as "the beginning of a period, far from being a war-that-will-end-war." In "The King of the Trenches," on the other hand, the focus is on mad Captain Burney Polderdick for his own sake rather than for purposes of any general exploration of the meaning of the war. This is, *par excellence*, a cracking good front-line yarn, although Burney shares some of the characteristics of the hollow-men protagonists found elsewhere in Lewis's fiction, being "a sort of prolongation" of his old self. As monarch of "the terrible narrow Kingdom" of his madness, he merits a prominent place in the galaxy of gargantuan puppets which

[7] Lewis, *The Writer and the Absolute*. London: Methuen, 1952, p. 38.
[8] C. H. Sisson, "The Politics of Wyndham Lewis," *Agenda* (London), Autumn-Winter, 1969–70, p. 109.

remain impressive monuments to Lewis's distinctive literary powers.

Unlike Polderdick, however, with his typically modern addiction to mass, mechanized violence as an outlet for pent-up savagery, some of Lewis's characters find their release in metaphysical battles and on another front : against Woman as personification of "the devil Nature." The fictional Benjamin Richard Wing in Lewis's "The Code of a Herdsman" proclaims, for instance, that "women, and the processes for which they exist, are the arch conjuring trick : and they have the cheap mystery and a good deal of the slipperiness, of the conjuror."[9] In most of his literary depictions of women, Lewis fell far short of the ease and grace that typified his portrayal of them in scores of paintings and drawings. In his fiction there is a degree of the deliberately grotesque, but also of genuine awkwardness, about the presentation of his female characters. At the same time, a number of his main male *personae* ridicule their women companions rather in the manner of the "propagandist indictment of the feminine" brilliantly paraphrased by Lewis in *The Art of Being Ruled*, where the female physique is pilloried as a "chocolate-cream trap to catch a rustic fool."[10] Describing the projected theme of *Self Condemned* to a publisher seven years before the book's appearance, Lewis wrote : "Woman has been called 'the eternal enemy of the absolute' : so our perfectionist (René Harding) must encounter immediate difficulties when he comes in contact with woman."[11]

The central male characters in "Cantleman's Spring-Mate," "The War Baby" and "Junior" are by no means perfectionists. Instead—except for John Leslie in "Junior"—they are self-styled *übermenschen*. Leslie differs from his two forbears in that he is not aggressively intent on dominating Woman but, like a debased Cantleman figure, flees from an overbearing and over-fecund femininity which he both fears and despises.

Yet there is a strange beauty about some of the very images of derision heaped on characters like the pregnant Tets in "The War Baby" who is "softly sculpting a Totem, whereas others

[9] Lewis, "Imaginary Letters: The Code of a Herdsman," *The Little Review* (New York), July, 1917, p. 6.
[10] Lewis, *The Art of Being Ruled*. London: Chatto, 1926, p. 276.
[11] *The Letters of Wyndham Lewis*, p. 410.

had not had that art—or craft." Gestation—"the toad-life at the bottom of the tank"—is a central, indeed menacing fact in all three of these stories just as, along with creation and nativity, it served as an important theme for Lewis's painting during that arduous period of exile, the 1940s. The women portrayed here, however, emerge as anything but defeated parties from the contests into which they are plunged. Tets, for instance, scores a vicarious victory, and a contemptuous Perdita is able to hurl the epithet "insane" at John Leslie in "Junior". "Insane" (though also heroic) is the description René Harding too might merit. "She has the effrontery to set herself up as my defender against myself," complains Kell-Imrie in bewailing the machinations of the much-lampooned Val in the novel *Snooty Baronet* (1932).[12] It could be said that this was also the role of Hester in *Self Condemned*, and Lewis had René suffer a living death as the penalty for ascribing to the protective Hester nothing more than an "effrontery" meriting only haughty rejection. In "Pish-Tush," the bluff Lionel Letheridge learns the price of unduly crossing womanhood. His actions arouse the virulence of that "volatile aura" which necessarily is all Constance-the-Spook retains of the redoubtable female life-force, with its "mysterious indomitable will."

As do many of Lewis's stories, "Pish-Tush" ends with an eruption of violence. To Lewis, violence was of the essence of human personality. "Within five yards of another man's eyes we are on a little crater, which, if it erupted, would split up as would a cocoa-tin of nitrogen," he wrote in *The Wild Body*. This explosiveness lurks beneath the surface of personality and "the finest humour is the great play-shapes blown up or given off by the tragic corpse of life underneath the world of the camera."[13] Memorable "play-shapes" swarm through Lewis's fiction and elsewhere in his work. He revelled in close-ups of such elephantine grotesques: Bestre and Brotcotnaz in *The Wild Body*, Kreisler in *Tarr*, the Bailiff in *The Human Age*, Jack Cruze in *The Revenge for Love* (1937), Charlie the janitor in *Self Condemned*, Augustine Card in *The Red Priest* (1956), Borzo the hotel-keeper in *Filibusters in Barbary* (1932) and Brandleboyes in

[12] Lewis, *Snooty Baronet*. London: Cassell, 1932, p. 308.
[13] *The Wild Body*, pp. 238–9.

America I Presume (1940). In the present stories there is "Bob" Allen Crumms racked by the same "convulsions of meaningless mirth" as shook Harding when he pondered the hotel fire and the "absurd" extinction of Affie, the wily but lovable hotel manageress in *Self Condemned*. Or there are the Card-like fighting transports of Dickie Dean in "The Man Who Was Unlucky With Women," or the superb anti-oceanic posturings of Kipe, the bum *à la Beckett* rendered with a flamboyant Lewisian twist in "The Yachting Cap."

Finally there is another Lewis speciality represented in the pages that follow. This is The Impostor. The American academic faculty to which René retires at the end of *Self Condemned* was unaware that this celebrated British historian had become by that time "a glacial shell of a man," the authenticity of whose work was by now merely a delusion. Far more deliberate and relentless in his activities as Impostor was Vincent Penhale in *The Vulgar Streak* (1941), whose bourgeois mannerisms were as carefully counterfeited as his false fivers. In the present book, "The Two Captains" explores the idea of The Counterfeit not only in its characterization but also, as in *The Vulgar Streak*, in its Social Credit-like ruminations on the subject of money. As for "Children of the Great," it in part is an elaboration of a concept later broached again by René Harding when he remarks: "The children of the great are their deeds. Their biological offspring is generally the dullest or vilest."[14] But, beyond this, "Children of the Great" provides another variation on the Impostor theme in the person of Derek Gilchrist, a living "libel upon the great." An authentic reincarnation of the Genius of whom Derek is a cruel parody ultimately takes shape in the story, just as a similar personification of The Real materializes in "Doppelgänger," the third and finest study of an Impostor figure included here. Thaddeus Trunk is a great poet who has been transformed by his clamorous, adoring public into a publicity figure. It is Thad's folly actually to *become* this figment of his fan-club's imagination. As a pioneer student of Publicity—a subject dealt with at length in such books as *Time and Western Man* (1927) and *Doom of Youth* (1932)—Lewis was well qualified to probe the techniques of "image-building" responsible for

[14] Lewis, *Self Condemned*. London: Methuen, 1954, p. 261.

15

sundry forms of star status in contemporary western society. "A man's publicity is a caricature of himself," says the narrator of "Doppelgänger." "It is really how the public sees 'greatness.'" The destiny of Thaddeus Trunk, majestic word-man consumed by his "publicity scarecrow," has obvious parallels in the real-life world of letters, which—under the logic of twentieth-century civilization—tends to be as dominated by the star system as is show business.

Thus this collection ends with Lewis re-emerging from the realm of fiction and assuming once more his equally characteristic functions as sociologist. His command of this latter genre forms a natural whole with his gifts as fictionist, especially as short-story writer. *The Art of Being Ruled* draws on the same masterly sense of group rhythms as does "A Breton Innkeeper"; or, in the category of travel writing, the account of film-star absurdities in *Filibusters in Barbary*; or, among the novels, the microcosmic goings-on at the Hotel Blundell; or, even in Lewis's painting, the abstract of mob dynamics represented by the great 1914–15 oil, *The Crowd*. In the crowd, yet not *of* the crowd : this is the quintessential Lewisian position. Lewis "manœuvres in the heart of reality," with a voracious eye alert for any new "stylistic anomalies" worthy of satiric note. Lewis called his *Wild Body* stories "essays in a new human mathematic" and spoke of wanting "to compile a book of 40 of these propositions, one deriving from and depending on the other."[15] In a sense, *The Art of Being Ruled* might qualify as that book. In any event, as Geoffrey Grigson once wrote, "all Lewis's work is one work."[16] And it is with this unity in mind that the reader should approach the stories here collected.

The editors have taken it upon themselves to insert commas, apostrophes or other punctuation marks where these seem to have been accidentally dropped during the transcription of such stories as "The Two Captains." Occasionally a word was found to have been omitted from the original text or from a printed or typewritten version. In any case of this kind, the word has been

[15] *The Wild Body*, p. 233.
[16] Geoffrey Grigson, *A Master of Our Time*. London: Methuen, 1951, p. 18.

inserted but within square brackets to indicate that the editors were responsible for its presence in the text published here. A square bracket has also been used where an obscurity in the original text obliged the editors to clarify an illegible phrase in a heavily-corrected passage.

Acknowledgements

The editors wish to acknowledge the help and encouragement given to them by Mrs. Anne Wyndham Lewis, widow of the writer. She also granted permission for publication of these stories, which are in her copyright.

Preparation of the book would have been impossible without the invaluable help and information unstintingly supplied by library assistant Mary Daniels and her colleagues at the Department of Rare Books, Cornell University Library, Ithaca, New York, where many of Wyndham Lewis's papers and manuscripts are now kept. Permission to examine stories, through photocopies of typescripts and holographs in the Cornell collection, and eventually to publish those included here from that rich archive was given by the Cornell University Library Board. The editors wish to acknowledge this permission in connection with "The Countryhouse Party, Scotland," "Junior," "The Yachting Cap," "The Weeping Man," "The Man Who Was Unlucky With Women," "The Two Captains" and "Children of the Great." A typescript from Cornell was also used as an aid in the preparation for publication here of "The King of the Trenches."

Another source of great help in the editorial work was Bernard Lafourcade, Lewis's French translator and a redoubtable authority on the life and works of The Enemy. Much encouragement too came from Walter Michel.

Further acknowledgements go to Calder and Boyars of London for permission to reprint "The King of the Trenches," "Cantleman's Spring-Mate" and "The War Baby," all of which appeared in that publishing firm's 1967 edition of *Blasting and Bombardiering*; to *Encounter* magazine, London, for "Pish-Tush" and "Doppelgänger," which first appeared in its pages; and to *Shenandoah* magazine of Washington and Lee University, Lexington, Virginia, U.S.A., original publisher of "The Rebellious Patient," which is a story quoted at length here.

SECTION I

The Common Circumstances
of Life

Sectional Introduction

The stories in this first section are all—except, to some extent, for one—from the initial phase of Lewis's literary career. All three stories have autobiographical overtones. "Unlucky for Pringle," published in *The Tramp* (February, 1911), was written after Lewis's return in 1909 to England from mainland Europe. His stay of several years on the Continent had been a period of study and travel on which he was to base the novel *Tarr* and the stories which, set in Brittany and Spain, appeared ultimately in *The Wild Body*. Like his character Pringle, the young Lewis lived in the area of Chelsea around King's Road, where the first story in this collection is set. *The Tramp* was a periodical edited by Douglas Goldring, an associate of the then Ford Madox Hueffer (later F. M. Ford). As its subtitle "An Open Air Magazine" implies, accounts of wanderings, tramp-like or otherwise, seem to have been a stock-in-trade of Goldring's magazine, though it also published a poem by Lewis.

In 1910, *The Tramp* had published "A Breton Innkeeper," which was more in line with the writings by Lewis appearing in Hueffer's celebrated literary magazine, *The English Review*. The stories which Hueffer brought out were fresh from Lewis's experiences on the Continent. On the other hand, the section of "The Crowd Master" story printed here—subtitled "The Country-house Party, Scotland"—is a development deriving from a work which first appeared in Lewis's own *Blast* magazine in 1915. A portion of the larger work emerged in revised form as part of the 1937 autobiography *Blasting and Bombardiering*, reissued with extra material in 1967 by Calder and Boyars of London. "The Countryhouse Party" should be compared with pages 56–59 of the 1967 *Blasting and Bombardiering* as an example of how Lewis created a fictional canvas from a "real-life" original, with Ford here portrayed as the character Leo Makepiece Leo.

20

Relevant in connection with this work also are pages 414–417 of Ford's own autobiographical volume, *Return to Yesterday* (New York: Horace Liveright Inc., 1932). "The Crowd Master" as a whole was, by the 1920s, the basis for a projected novel about the period of the First World War and it is obvious that this book would have been heavily autobiographical. But Lewis apparently was put off the idea by an editor who warned him about the glut already created by the plethora of war novels then coming on the market. "The Countryhouse Party" in typescript form possibly dating from the 1930s and is included in a larger block of material in the Wyndham Lewis archive at Cornell University, Ithaca, N.Y., which also includes re-worked versions of the *Blast* "Crowd Master" story, additional material about Cantleman's London adventures and a section telling of his relations with a literary character named Mordkine. The material ends with a version of "The Code of a Herdsman," a declaration of principles ascribed in this instance to Cantleman. The whole typescript contains numerous corrections and interpolations in Lewis's hand and often the hand-written additions persist in spelling the central character's name "Cantelman."

If "The Countryhouse Party" can be construed as historical fiction, in view of the menacing sense of the impending First World War which it conveys, it is only one example of how Lewis could turn actual situations or events to his own creative purposes. Another instance of this was his use of a ferry steamer disaster now virtually forgotten as an event but likely to endure as part of a classic Lewisian paragraph. This eminently deserves to be quoted here even though the story to which it forms a prelude—"The Rebellious Patient"—turned out to be an anti-climax. As printed on page 3 of the special Lewis issue of *Shenandoah* (Summer–Autumn, 1953), the reference to the ship disaster runs as follows.

It had been a great Winter. It had not allowed anyone in England to be warm, for however short a time, since it began in October. Until January was passing into February, it had contented itself with low temperatures, but then it began to blow. The Atlantic has waves which are loftier than any cliff, but it does not often show them. However, a ferry steamer called the *Princess Victoria*, which ran uneventfully between Stranraer,

Scotland, and Belfast, Ireland, came out as usual into Atlantic waters on January 31st, to effect the routine crossing to Ireland. The moment she did so the blowing began. She found herself in the middle of waves greater than had ever been seen before by people who had looked up at waves all over the world. The top part of the ship slid away from the underpart, and they sank separately. The captain went under the waves stiff-armed and steely-eyed at the salute upon his bridge; practically all the passengers, with a mass of automobiles, sank higgledy-piggledy, rushing down among the fishes to the shocked surprise of the public. Was it the fault of the ship? Or was the Winter too violent for the scale of precautions against Nature which is usually found adequate by man? It was an un-British wind which had blown at that spot, out of the mouth of a Winter which turned out to be a dragon.[1]

[1] "The Rebellious Patient" appeared as part of a special Wyndham Lewis issue of *Shenandoah* magazine. Reprinted here is the first paragraph of the story, the whole of which appears on pp. 3–16 of the magazine. The special issue of *Shenandoah* also featured writings about Lewis by Ezra Pound, Hugh Kenner, Marvin Mudrick, T. S. Eliot, Peter Russell, Roy Campbell and Marshall McLuhan, together with reproductions of paintings done by the artist-writer during his wartime stay in Toronto. This excerpt is Copyright 1953 by *Shenandoah*, reprinted from *Shenandoah*: The Washington and Lee University Review with the permission of the Editor.

Unlucky for Pringle

(First published in *The Tramp: an Open Air Magazine*, London, February, 1911)

"Apartments to let." That sign never lost its magic for James Pringle. For others a purely business announcement, for him it appeared a soft and almost sensual invitation. It was the pleasant and mysterious voice of innumerable houses. A street with many of these signs almost agitated him. To install himself in the midst of somebody else's life, like a worm in a wall, was a luxury and delight, a little vice fostered by migratory circumstances. Perhaps the ideal vocation for Pringle would have been that of a broker or sheriff's officer—an affable, rather melancholy one. As it was, he was a landscape painter, whose circumstances confined his occupation of houses to rooms at ten or fourteen shillings a week, with north lights. If not certain about the length of his stay, it would be furnished apartments; otherwise he would move in his own furniture. "Rooms to let" meant that a warm, obscure, and typical life—that of the letter of the rooms and her possible daughters, husband, family, and friends—was free to be entered into and peacefully invested.

There for ten shillings a week he might inhabit that area, thickened, as it were, by their special personality into a wide, sluggish, and warm wall of Self. On the very frequently recurring occasions on which he set out to look for rooms he would savour the particular domestic taste of each new household he entered in the course of his search with the interest of a gourmet. Smiling strangely, as she thought, at the landlady who answered the door, he would at once go to her parlour—come for a debauch that she would never suspect.

On July 2nd of a recent year, at one o'clock in the afternoon, James Pringle walked down Beaufort Street, Chelsea, scanning the houses with characteristic interest, and in the course of a characteristic occupation. He was looking for a room. But he was depressed. He knew Beaufort Street very well, and that he would find nothing there. It was true there still remained in the West End many streets in which he had so far culled no room. But then he was wearily reminded that Beaufort Street, Smith Street, Margaretta Terrace, had all been, once upon a time, avenues charged with fanciful hopefulness for him. He had long learned to look on Beaufort Street as an interesting street, but of no practical interest to him; in Margaretta Terrace he had gathered two grimy and dubious flowers of lodging, which he had been compelled to throw away almost at once; he had not been happy in his dealings with Smith Street. Many will not understand how difficult it was for Pringle to find a room. But he understood. He said to himself that he had practically exhausted the resources of London. Vast as it was, he had taxed it to the uttermost in the matter of lodgings; it had given him all it had to give. (Any other city would have broken down long before.) In a year or so a new supply would no doubt have come into existence. The gradual decay of a generation of landladies was an almost imperceptible process. Still, the sleepy and musty mass would, in a year or two, have some way shifted—a chink the size of a pin's head have appeared where Pringle could creep. But, as it was, he would probably wander about all day and all the next and find nothing. Then hope set in again. There *were* tracts. It was one o'clock, and lunch time. He gave way to a suggestion that had presented itself to him many times already, and that he had experienced certain difficulty in resisting. "I'll go there; I suppose I must. I'll get it over at once."

Pringle had just arrived in London after a year or so spent in Paris. He felt, in its new strangeness, as if he had returned to his London of five years previously, and not that he had left only a year before. When that morning he had set out to look for rooms the various places he knew of were marshalled in his mind. Every time that he was at a loss where to turn, and had rejected one idea after another, Marchant's house—in which he had sworn never to live again—presented itself in its inviting probable emptiness, low rents, and accommodating landlord. He seemed fated to go there, and unable to escape it. Had there been nothing

24

else against it, the fact of its facility and the wearying solicitation of its emptiness was enough to repel him.

He felt that going there was a stale compromise, and that it had something insufferably ready-made, lax, and roomy about it. But now at one o'clock he gave way, but somewhat in exasperation, determined, as he said to himself, to "get it over."

Then this would be *something* to begin with. He would have seen *something*, anyhow; and then, perhaps, the thing he wanted would turn up more easily.

All he had to do was to cross the King's Road, pass through a few short streets, and there was Deisart Grove. The grove was gruesomely bowery—presumably its hirsute appearance had kept at a respectful distance those bent on "improvement"; it would, in fact, be a messy job to pull up and rebuild Deisart Grove.

No. 2, where Marchant lived, an old house resolutely decaying behind its allotment of shabby trees, looked as though it had stepped aside there to die. There was a strange air of wilfulness and menace about it, as though, disgusted with existence, it had determined to take its fate into its own hands, and if its owner refused to pull it down and went on demanding service of it, to tumble to pieces of its own accord; an air, in fact, of natural suicide about the whole place, a sullen revolt of inanimate things against the importunities of man, who would not leave them alone.

Here lived T. A. Marchant. His business in life was to exploit poor old ramshackle houses that could be obtained cheap. He would install himself in them, let every available cranny, and live there till they fell to pieces. One felt that this one might at any moment take a terrible revenge. He was standing in his doorway as Pringle approached, as though undecided as to whether to go out or go in—his front door was an almost insuperable barrier for Marchant. He would get as far as that, and there remain, becalmed in his porch for considerable periods, until some exterior motive force, a lodger or errand boy, moved him in one direction or the other. Pringle acted as a blast driving him in— eventually, indeed, driving him up the stairs into several of his rooms, vacant and eligible.

"Well," he sniggered, "you back again? Where've you bin?

25

Bin to France?" He had an educated cockney accent. He was very familiar, but chiefly through timidity, as though not only not daring to be distant, but not daring to be anything but familiar, or to withhold a single scrap of himself for fear it should be snatched from him. To avert the stringency of more heroic manners, the *timide* will sometimes affect this *sans gêne*, invoking "our common humanity." Humour is called in to help in these systematic belittlements. Marchant was a very humorous dog. He was always sniggering and joking.

"Yes," said Pringle to his inquiries. "Have you got any rooms to let? But I'm not sure whether I'll take unfurnished rooms this time. Do you know anybody who has a furnished room to let, and who'd do my cooking?"

"Yes," Marchant replied truthfully; but he did not say *where*, or any more about it, and continued :

"I've got rooms under yours—*yew* know—to let. 'Ave a look at them?"

And then they went upstairs, both of them, without any enthusiasm, and looked at several rooms. Marchant did nothing to induce his former lodger to take them, and when they had both depressed themselves with the sight of the empty rooms for some minutes, Marchant said :

"The people next door—well, it's the same house, but separate, they're French—*they* 'ave a furnished room to let, and would do anything you wanted, I expect."

On hearing they were French, Pringle at once determined to go round. He liked the French, although as a nation "furnished apartments" are unknown to them—and wanted practice in the language. The great question now was whether it were *really* next door or not. It had a different number—2B—whereas Marchant's was 2. Pringle had always regarded 2 as a particularly unlucky number. "What about 2B?" he reflected. "Does the addition of a 'B' really neutralize the horrible effects of 2?"

Two years ago, in helping the men to carry in his furniture, he had let a looking-glass fall. It had broken to pieces, and the man he had been helping with the lighter articles gazed for some minutes at him in pitying silence, and then said :

"Seven years, mister!"

Seven years' ill-luck seemed so ample a spell that there was no immediate anxiety. But that night, sitting in the midst of his furniture, this ill-omened accident on the threshold had its effect. His furniture was arranged more or less as it always was, a restricted and symmetrical scene he had sat in the midst of for several years in different districts of the city. This furniture moved with him like a gloomy cloud, in the heart of which he dwelt, with periodic returns to its garage, or the store-room, as mentioned. Only its contours changed slightly in the course of its slow progress. This last contour it had taken, that of Marchant's rooms, he had looked at dubiously. He looked out of his window, out of his cloud, and surveyed the Cockneyfied trees. Moving into new rooms was invariably accompanied by a period of depression and restlessness with him, and doubt as to their suitability. This was strengthened and perpetuated in the present case by the breaking of the mirror. At the end of a month he had left, going to Paris. And so Marchant's French tenants had against them their connection with Marchant, and the fact that they lived under the same roof.

"Do you mean that little place round there at the side?" he asked.

"Yes, round there. I'll show you."

So he went round a narrow slabbed walk, and knocked at the adjoining door, Marchant retiring with a guilty nod and a snigger to his own threshold, as though he had put Pringle up to something naughty. A bearded and languid little man, the colour of a Chinaman, answered the door.

"Yes?" he asked, staring at the ground; then, as an afterthought : "You want see rooms?"

He seemed to have been expecting Pringle, or, to be quite exact, somebody rather like Pringle. He stepped aside and ushered him into a back room. Once there he lost all interest in his visitor, and wandered restlessly about, as though seeking to take up a listless life at the exact point where he had dropped it to answer the door. Pringle had hardly time to notice his new host's relapse, for he was superseded by an elegant, youngish woman, who advanced towards Pringle as if she had been waiting her "cue" in this back room, and now approached as though from the wings of a theatre into the gaslight.

"Good morning. You want rooms? I suppose Mr. Marchant

27

recommended you? I'll show you what we have. Will you come upstairs?" said in very careful and respectable English.

There were two rooms adjoining each other at the back of the house, suitable in the subtlest sense. Pringle was elated. He looked at his guide. A constant, plaintive break in the high-pitched voice, which was precise, resigned, and distinguished, an obtrusive, plaintively challenging sincerity and hint of pathos, but, above all, sincerity, in the eyes, which were quite black, and the elegance of the lady's *mise* were the dominant points for Pringle. That plaintive break or quaver he had heard before. Had his experience been wider he would have connected it inevitably with the particular *âme* developed in Geneva.

He took the rooms, and it was half an hour afterwards that he met me, I finishing, he beginning, lunch at the "Copper Gate" public-house, just off the King's Road.

The foregoing narrative is, no doubt, in every essential detail exact, as it is compiled from facts and impressions then directly noted and received, and from my exhaustive intuitive knowledge of Pringle.

Pringle has always remained the strangest of my friends. He is like the passion of the book collector or amateur of furniture and practical arts. Only his taste is for the accidental—just whatever life brings. One might almost say that the chief value of anything for Pringle is its accidental quality, its inevitability in the succession of the accidents of life—the fact that just *that* thing turned up (whatever it be) and no other. He is as much elated, in his way, by the shabby furniture in the rooms of some London lodging-house as another would be over a room full of Louis Quinze. In the case of a man of genius the mediocrity of his daily life —his lodging, however mean, with the rest—takes a warmth and vitality from him. No doubt Goethe felt somewhat the same glamour in living in his own house in Frankfurt-on-Main as any educated man would feel if he suddenly became the tenant of Goethe's house. An exhilaration, almost excitement, is reflected back to the artist from anything. Pringle, not possessed of exceptional gifts, had been strangely endowed with his gusto for the common circumstances of his life; or, rather than definitely "endowed with," I should suppose it to have developed in the following way. Originally seeking merely for suitable conditions for his work, etc., but conceiving of these conditions too fastidiously and morbidly, gradually this got the upper hand, as it were, so that it seemed almost—as I have described my friend—that his sole preoccupation consisted in sampling those conditions.

There beneath the somnolent chimney of the "Copper Gate," with a laconic eloquence, he told me about his "find," and discoursed generally of the difficulty of discovering rooms. The existence of any eccentricity in Pringle was not so much as hinted at between us, or, for that matter, often realized by him. Every thing was translated into commonplace psychical formulas. For instance, his delight in the landlord or landlady would appear as a gleeful or humorous "interest in character." As to the details of the rooms, they would be referred, in his description, either to his requirements as a painter or comforts as a man. But I, having the key to my friend's strangeness, had no difficulty in casting this back into its original and veritable idiom.

I left Pringle in Sloane Square, he being bound for Charing Cross, where he had left his boxes. I did not see him again for six weeks. Then one day I found him drifting along in front of me. I followed him the length of Oakley Street. His eyes were cast up at the ground floor windows and the glassy spaces above the front doors. Being more or less in the neighbourhood of the "Copper Gate," we repaired there, and I learnt of the following extravagant conclusion of Pringle's second tenancy in Deisart Grove.

"I hate looking for rooms," said Pringle.

But I could not transcribe his words on this, or any other occasion, because frankly I have not the vaguest recollection of them; and although his bulging eyes and easy gestures are very familiar to me, lacking invention, I could not reconstruct our interview, memory having deserted me.

On the other hand, I have a quite distinct picture of the Pringle of the six weeks in Deisart Grove. That is why I always consider him the strangest of my friends. I always forget the Pringle before me to see the Pringle he is telling me about, or who appears in his words. I seem to see the intimate Pringle, the soul of Pringle, in its favourite pursuits and experiences. When I think of him I never think of the man I have sat with in the "Copper Gate," but of the man he has given me glimpses

29

of in his talk. So it would be simpler for me at once to describe how, having got his boxes at Charing Cross, he hurried back to No. 2B Deisart Grove, his conversation with his landlord, and even his most secret reflections, than what passed between us in the bar of the public-house.

Pringle sent for some of his furniture the same afternoon, to supplement his new room's exiguous contents. On driving up with his boxes, he felt the customary rank depression—the indigestion of Reality. The reality always overwhelmed him at first; then came an Homeric struggle with it, usually ending in its assimilation. He was very fond of reality; but he was like a man very fond of what did not at all agree with him. When he at last found himself—the things deposited on the floor, the door finally closed upon him—alone with his new room, nothing short of horror descended on him. To undo and let loose upon the rooms his portmanteaus' squashed and wrinkled contents, like a flock of birds and pack of dogs, the brushes dashing to the dressing-table, the photographs crowding to the chimneypiece, the portmanteaus, boxes, and parcels creeping under the bed and into corners, was a martyrdom for him. The unwearied optimism of these inanimate objects, how they occupied stolidly and quickly room after room, was appalling. Then they still had the staleness of the former room about them, and the souvenir of a depressing hour of tearing up and packing.

On this particular occasion he at once descended into the back-parlour on the ground floor, and thence into the kitchen beyond, to seek consolation in his French host.

The parlour, windowless, and lighted from the kitchen, found the bedroom preferred to it on the one hand, and the kitchen on the other. The kitchen in a certain sense took advantage of its position, abused it, for it was extremely dirty, and did not attempt to make amends for its smallness by being tidy. It lay in the full glare of day, with its glass door and large window; a slut of a room, dribbling at the sink, full of unsavoury pails, garishly dirty. A dresser occupied one side—an Alps of a dresser, with gloomy glaciers of unused plates, rifts of mouldering tarts, and a crowding landscape at its base; the outer side was the glass door and window and the ribs of the dresser; the opposite side the gas-stove and shelves.

Pringle, not quite used to his new quarters, entered and tentatively remained in the parlour, opening a conversation with his host. It did not take him long to discover the position this room held in the house, however, and he moved into the kitchen, with an obsequious leer at the sink. Monsieur Chalaran continued to take Pringle quite as a matter of course. It was only later, indeed, that he appeared to become less used to Pringle, and to regard him as it is natural for human beings to regard each other at the first. The result of this inverted order of things was that Pringle became an "inmate" in the full sense of the word, remarkably quickly. In fact, when I met him, he appeared rather dazed with the suddenness that had marked all the stages of his stay with the Chalarans. For it is the *becoming* in things that bulks out, so to speak, and leaves behind it a substantial impression of a lapse of time. And I, in telling his story, now I come to think of it, only have a few almost abrupt "states" to record, and not a series of "becomings," as should be the case.

Here, anyhow, we find him seated in front of Monsieur Chalaran, and at once engrossed in a first and superficial examination of the latter's health. Monsieur Chalaran's familiarity was of another order to that of Marchant. "One's sure to be at ease and comradelike with this person in a couple of days—why not at once? One pays a man too great a compliment in being distant," he would seem to have said. Then it was pathologic; the listlessness and indifference caused by his disease had its share in it; also democratic sentiments.

He had been a chef.

"I tried to go back to work," he told Pringle; "in fact, I had no idea I was finished, first of all. I got four or five places; in each I had to leave after a day or two. I've been here four years;" he said in answer to Pringle, who was surprised on reflecting that only four years ago his host had been an active worker. Monsieur Chalaran sat with his eyes affectedly staring, his bearded lips thrust out, and desperate amusement painted on his yellow face.

As to the nature of the disease, Monsieur Chalaran said *he* knew very well what it was. Madame Chalaran also would say sometimes that *she* knew very well what it was. But they neither of them liked to hear the other say this.

31

"If I've seen specialists!" he said on this occasion to Pringle. "But they don't know what it is. One said it was probably something or other, but he didn't know. For me it's rheumatism!"

He always called it rheumatism in his brighter moments, but when he had his headaches he was willing to call it anything he could lay his tongue to—even paralysis. What it exactly was Pringle never knew, except that the poor man suffered a great deal, and took morphine all the time.

His wife "earned good money" as a milliner near Sloane Street. Meantime, left alone in this little house, he was converting everything within his reach into something else—the flower-beds into a lawn, one of the outhouses into an aviary, an old trunk into a sort of ping-pong game, etc. These activities corresponded to bursts of energy, he seeming more or less to gauge the probable extent and duration of each of them at its advent, and to undertake something that would occupy him for just so long as it would last.

Pringle left Monsieur Chalaran, recovered from his depression. and the terms of his stay arranged. He should have his meals in the kitchen with the Chalarans—at least, one meal a day. In the end he had all his meals there. Everything turned out *à souhait*. In a week Pringle was savouring the delights of "lodging" as he had never done before, having lost less by actual inhabiting than usual. On the next stage of his stay in this house I got a unique picture of Pringle. It was a scene of almost patriarchal peace, Pringle being the patriarch. There in the small, garish kitchen he spent the greater part of his days, sheltered from the world by the encompassing personalities of Monsieur and Madame Chalaran, occasionally also Marchant, and all the other objects and details of his new life in this household. His meals were cooked by a first class chef, whose operations he could watch and discuss. He would sit smoking in the kitchen, gazing at M. Chalaran tossing up potato cakes, arguing with him about the respective hanging of French and English meat, obtaining an insight into the life of a large, populous kitchen, hearing of the chef's perquisites and tradesmen's canvassing, etc. Then he would enjoy the luncheon *à trois* with the Chalarans, contending with madame that the hats she made were unbeautiful, as was all modern dress, with the threadbare arguments of "the classic nude."

"C'est un jeune homme fort intelligent, je trouve," Madame Chalaran said to her husband. He said nothing, not being by nature addicted to praise.

Pringle's cup of content, in short, was full. And this, in my opinion, was the trouble. Perhaps he showed his satisfaction too much. This mystic contentment of his may have been registered by the acute nerves of the invalid, and in some way resented. Perhaps the latter realized that he was being enjoyed, without understanding how. Pringle, in his delight, could not apparently keep his hands off things—with difficulty even off persons. Monsieur Chalaran's saucepans, among other things, were touched.

The ex-chef's professional pride suddenly awoke. And Pringle's account of the first slight friction was Monsieur Chalaran finding him peering into one of his pots—coming up brusquely—whisking the saucepans about, clashing them down and saying, his eyes averted :

"Je n'aime pas qu'on touche à mes outils ! Je n'aime pas ça, Monsieur James. I don't like that !"

Then, after a pause :

"I don't like that !"

But this was certainly not the first of it. Pringle, too, felt that. Monsieur Chalaran's animal-like selfishness and self-absorption hardly revealed any new element in his inner life until it was ripe. The realization of a peculiarity in Pringle, and of its nature—a "contentment," a gloating, even—must have taken a considerable time in sinking through his torpor, and then, having done its work, in emerging again.

Pringle, still absorbed in his sensations of an almost enervating peace and well-being, was oblivious to this little cloud the size of a man's hand.

The natural pathos of Madame Chalaran's manner, the restrained nobility she preferred, fitted in with her present unfortunate situation. Still, it was possibly more of a chance than she would have asked for; her husband's illness was like a malicious and mocking gift of Fate. But Pringle was not fastidious in matters of this sort, and Madame Chalaran's "heroism" pleased him along with everything else. Monsieur was a "brave garçon," and liked by Pringle.

On coming down to breakfast one morning, Pringle found Madame alone, her face rather drawn, and thrown back as it always was when something unusual had occurred.

"My husband has had a very bad night. I've not closed my eyes once. His groaning keeps me awake."

Pringle, concerned, asked for further news.

"Oh, I expect he'll be up in an hour or two. He'll cook your lunch for you. He was very bad last night; he has not been so bad for a long time."

A certain curtness in madame's speech struck Pringle, as though she hardly trusted herself or hardly had the patience to say any more in this restrained and conventional way, and that indignation and the truth were very near her lips. What Pringle noticed was something *sullen* about her. "Something has gone wrong," he thought.

Pringle himself did eventually see through all this, and, retrospectively, grasp how things had stood. He would never have arrived at this point of clairvoyance had it not been for his personal sufferings. The pain it caused him to leave the Chalaran's roof at the last moment threw a vivid light on the whole situation.

So Pringle, in his later and enlightened state, thought he could detect the germ of this first additional indisposition of monsieur's. This germ was a conversation over the supper table two days earlier. This, he had no doubt, had caused Monsieur Chalaran's relapse. But (characteristically) it had taken two days to grip and finally become manifest in his organism. For two days Monsieur Chalaran had been visibly ailing. He did not even know what was the matter himself. No specialist could have helped him. But he, and Pringle, too, became, shortly, wiser than a specialist.

The conversation had been sustained by madame and Pringle alone, monsieur being compelled to remain silent for some time. It had dealt with a sex question. Pringle had enjoyed the frankness permitted by the calm and scientific nature of the discussion, especially as it was with French people. Had it been *legère*, or even *grivoise*, Chalaran would probably have seen no particular objection. But there was something almost uncanny to him in this way of handling nakedly such a delicate question. Pringle, for his part, seemed to think he was giving these French people, noted for their ribald and indecent frankness, a specimen of English *sans gêne*.

Monsieur Chalaran had shown his displeasure and discomfort by eating up hastily everything within reach; as a man might stop his ears, Monsieur Chalaran stopped his mouth.

Madame held her own wonderfully. She kept her head raised, her eyes became almost heavy with sincerity and intelligence. She "understood," of course. Her husband was twice reproached with a hushed and weary dignity for gobbling up his food.

"Emile, don't bolt your food like that! We're not going to take it away from you," she drawled.

In any case, what his indisposition succeeded in doing was definitely to enlighten him as to his feeling for Pringle. He rose from his bed implacable. He had had enough of James Pringle.

When that evening—Chalaran's indisposition passed—they were all three at table again, a change had evidently come in the relations of husband and wife. Madame was dangerously considerate.

"I shouldn't drink so much coffee, Emile. You know it's not good for you."

"Oh, je m'en foue pas mal. If it kills me."

"Yes, but it doesn't kill you : it's apt, though, to make you pass bad nights."

Further, she told Pringle of her husband's sufferings in the past, discussed his illness, etc. Monsieur Chalaran quite naturally looked moved and sorry for himself at this talk. He took it all to himself. His careless and matter-of-course invalid's greediness was evidently a source of intense irritation to his wife. She was manufacturing this pathos for her own consumption, but half anticipating her husband's attitude; and now she remained ironically and venomously starving. Pringle, by this time somewhat shaken out of his beatific state, noticed so much, puzzled.

Chalaran felt the steady, invisible sirocco of his wife's indignation. He sullenly bowed his head. His usually bent head aided in this mental picture. Pringle and his strange passion was now appearing a stirrer up of strife, and divider of wife and husband. He vaguely realized his new *rôle*. On the fourth day, however, Chalaran completely recovered from his relapse, and in a burst of energy that lasted two afternoons built a summer-house at the bottom of the garden. The summer-house, no doubt, saved Pringle. But had Pringle grasped then the at once compact and elemental character of these bursts of activity, and his own position as regards Chalaran, he would have shaken in his shoes. For who could say whether the next time a storm of such violence as to build a summer-house might not seize on some more substantial and apposite object?

During these days of doubtful relationship Chalaran resorted often to a violin, to give voice in a sort of abstract and peculiarly exasperating way to his dissatisfaction. He would not look at Pringle once during lunch time. But the moment he had gone upstairs to work Monsieur Chalaran would take his fiddle out and begin playing at him underneath in the kitchen. The violin appeared afflicted with exactly Monsieur Chalaran's disease, and its "rheumatism" found expression in the same way. He could not be ill himself the *whole* time. It was the complement of his own malicious relapses. Pringle felt the intention; and it was possibly noticing this connection that first put him on the road to the truth of the situation.

One evening madame took on a very good-natured expression, and began bantering Chalaran on his sluggishness and silence. Pringle, not understanding, joined in a little. His host looked so near breaking forth into some unusual and quite *inédit* passionate state that he desisted, and retired soon after. Then the final stage was reached. No two days to take effect this time! A half an hour later it happened. With a howl Monsieur Chalaran flung himself on the bed, come to the end of his patience or torpor. No more Pringle! He meant it this time. He cast himself down with a howl. A doctor had to be sent for, and by the next day he had succeeded in dragging himself to the edge of the grave.

There is nothing more to be told, for there was only one course for Pringle—once more to quit Deisart Grove.

He had passed like a ghost, in one sense, through a hundred unruffled households. Scores of peaceful landladies, like beautiful women caressed in their sleep by a spirit, had been enjoyed by him. Their drab apartments had served better than any boudoir. But at last one of the objects of his passion had turned in its sleep, as it were, its sleep being the restless slumber of the sick—

had done more than that, had cried out and chased Pringle away. His late landlord no doubt gave the sleepwalker or spirit in Pringle a considerable shock. I found him very much shaken.

He could only judge of the intensity of madame's indignation and the treatment that awaited monsieur on his recovery by the way in which *he*, Pringle, even, had been implicated. When she came upstairs to speak to him about her husband's condition she was not uncivil, but she *looked less sincere*. The significance of this could not be exaggerated. She had come with the intention of uprooting Pringle there and then, as she felt, no doubt, how firmly he was fixed, and the need there would be of loosening the roots.

"I have written to my young sister at Bexhill to come and stay here and look after my husband during the day."

This was the first wedge. There would be nowhere to put the sister unless Pringle vacated his room. Then the wedge was worked about and Pringle's roots disturbed, prodded, and tugged at.

"I can't ask her to come if I don't provide some accommodation for her," etc.

Pringle stood quite still—too still—under the operation, and watched the face of the operator.

"I'm afraid you'll find it very uncomfortable here, Mr. Pringle," etc.

Pringle did not wince; but when he felt that finally the ground had been taken away from under his feet, and, in fact, that there was not a square inch, which had not been accounted for in Madame Chalaran's cutting and clearing operations, he pulled himself together. He said that in the circumstances perhaps he had better look for another room.

"You know, Mr. Pringle, I wouldn't turn you out," she said. But he saw with surprise how he had suffered even in her estimation. Perhaps his defeat by her husband may in some unseizable way have contributed to this. Just at the last she may even have realized that there was something strange in Pringle. Anyhow this house *would* vomit him forth; it could not assimilate him. Glasses crashed down at its doors as he was entering; its inhabitants became filled with mysterious hatred for him.

Pringle found a room remarkably soon. But this was not a

good sign. Also he inhabited it alarmingly long. I felt for many months after this that Pringle was living *anywhere*. But now he has quite recovered, become a great believer in Pimlico, and is changing his rooms with perfect regularity. His hygiene, in short, leaves nothing to be desired.

2

A Breton Innkeeper

(First published in *The Tramp: an Open Air Magazine*, London, August, 1910)

He has been a gentleman's servant – though how this restless and vociferous mass can have been contained in any well-behaved diplomatic household is more than I can imagine. Before settling down here in Brittany as innkeeper he was five years in Vienna with a German *Chargé d'affaires*. I suppose, once he got there, they were so dismayed at his size and appearance generally that they lost their heads for the moment—hesitating to send him right about turn back again, after such a long journey. When some days after his engagement by letter, hailing from a distant registry office in France, Roland invaded, like the waters of a bursted reservoir, that consternated household, prompt action was needed if ever it were. They tried without doubt every *diplomatic* means of getting rid of him; but all their subtlety proved of no avail. I should have the gravest apprehensions for the peace of Europe if I heard that Roland was beneath the roof of a great and responsible official. Himself the very incarnation of method, he carries anarchy and chaos anywhere he goes outside his own walls.

By his stature and physique generally, although *not* by nature, a loud bullying person, he retains and even exaggerates a certain bullying tone and demeanour : cracks jokes in which he threatens "to get angry," and, in fact, puts in evidence the bully in himself, the brute strength, that his clients may have the exquisite sensation of the proximity of this bellowing, menacing force, but *their* heads he always spared.

And, indeed, this immunity he extends to everybody down to the boy in buttons that he keeps in the bar—for I have never seen him forsake his farcical manner with any one. He rages often, cries *nom de Dieu*, stamps and fumes when the aforementioned youth does something that displeases him. And doubtless there is some *nuance* in this that touches the brass-buttoned boy—doubtless there is in that youth's exquisite instinct for Roland many a shade in this rough voice imperceptible to a stranger—some inflection that makes him scamper more hastily about his business. But outwardly it is the same heavy and desperate geniality.

So Roland, even with his staff, never departs from his *rôle* of buffoon. If the bull could suddenly be rendered avaricious, and were given a brutal cunning to direct him, he might not forsake his appearance of sullenness and fierceness, still reminding man that he retained his original and dangerous character, and so induce humanity to pay him to behave himself. Or, as Roland does, pretend to be angry, to butt people—Roland slaps people on the back and thumps them playfully sometimes—and people would quail deliciously beneath the impact of this murderous force, assured the while that (for his own ends) the bull would not desert his playful restraint. One of the most intense pleasures of childhood is being frightened, and made to quail physically, assured the while that no harm will ensue. Children's greatest favourites are those that procure them this pleasure : to be thrown up in the air, chased and roared at by a booby uncle—with real physical shrinkings, but reassured all the same by experience and custom. This makes them crow or giggle more feverishly than any other entertainment. What sends a boy out apple-stealing is the desire to taste this pleasure of fear. But this sensuality is universal, how universal will be best seen by drawing a simple picture of one of the most homely and familiar scenes in our national life. While the owner of the house is burying his head in the bedclothes, transfixed with a delightful horror, and sweating as much with pleasure as with fear at the burglarious sounds arriving from below stairs, the burglar for his part is perhaps passing some of the most exquisite moments of his life, tingling with a delicious apprehension : while the policeman outside, gazing at the parlour window ajar and the many other signs of infraction, feels his flesh creeping all over with the familiar and cherished emotion of fear. Does a special aptitude for experiencing to the full this pleasure, and a natural though perhaps unconscious desire to multiply the occasions for doing so, induce so many stalwart fellows to adopt this profession? I do not say, however, that Roland's customers relish this form of amusement placed at their disposal. No doubt there are some who do. He is not a very popular *hôtelier*, although not at all unpopular.

Roland owns one of two hotels immediately in front of the station. It is extremely important and yet a thing demanding the utmost cunning to get past his hotel on arriving at St. Pol. I have never succeeded in doing so, and am one of his best customers. It is not only strangers that are in jeopardy. The peasant on his way to market sees to his horse's condition, tightens the girth, and sets his own teeth with an oath on approaching Roland's.

A characteristic *geste* of his on a market day this summer caused a good deal of talk. He had been drinking copiously. Drink stimulates inordinately Roland's commercial obsession, affecting him only in this way and inducing him to pursue more blindly and indefatigably than ever his methods and dreams. Two peasants were driving past, intending to put their cart up at his rivals', the neighbouring inn. Roland shouted to them, they slowed down, and he came up with a shower of pleasantries and greetings, grinning reprovingly, as though to say, "I know where you're going." He then, pursuing his customary tactics—applied to this especial case—began with gentle force to lead them, horse, cart, occupants and all, towards his stable door. Caressingly and with mirthful coaxing, he insinuated that they were going to stop with him this time, his momentarily trebled enthusiasm for his own methods lessening his capacities for nice observation. And indeed, after the first moment's acceptance of the joke, the two farmers showed signs of great unappreciativeness, and then began swearing. Or, rather, as they never speak without swearing, suddenly and with vehemence immensely increased their vocabulary, calling up that group of oaths, jealously preserved pure and undebased from common use, and reserved to lead the forlorn hope of Expression ere Action be resorted to. At this Roland, with the true impatience of the idealist, treating them as cyphers of his imagination and ruling passion, saying "No! you *shall* come and stop!" ran them into the stable in their cart, and began unharnessing their horse. They sprang down and a noisy struggle ensued, Roland fighting with a somnambulic

41

tenacity, and as a dog disturbed in the discussion of its bone—he prevented in the pursuance of his master idea, and they with the indignation and brutality of men that the dreamer has attempted to incorporate in his dream, or the enthusiast too importunately to win over to his theory. The police had to be sent for, and Roland, dazed, staggered back to his door, and his opponents went on to the adjoining inn.

Roland is like one of those "eccentric musicians," as they are called, that tear about in front of a row of different sized bottles, playing "Rule Britannia" with inconceivable agility. His perpetual verbosity and ubiquity are appalling. Rather than relapse into anything approaching calm, he will talk to his own wife, or to a little ragged boy that has stopped in the street to stare at the boy in buttons. He is capable of banging on the back of a saucepan or rattling the dishes to "keep things going."

This is his method. Economy of energy by a constant output of mere mechanical and empty force; and thereby disarming that bane of innkeepers, the customer requiring information and personal attention. Of course, in a hotel there are always people lying in wait for the Proprietor : they are often very difficult to detect, these customers. Often a man of an extremely shy and reserved appearance, taking advantage of a lull in the unwary innkeeper's activity—who thinks he at least may allow himself a rest in the presence of such a mild-looking man—will rise up and pin down his unfortunate host for three-quarters of an hour with swarms of unexpected questions. So innkeepers have to be constantly on their guard.

His wife is a fit mate for him in size. She is a shade more human, and a little more approachable. You are afraid with Roland to pose him any questions; there is a feeling that he is not to be approached with impunity, as with the wheels of a machine in motion. With Madame Roland you can speak as with a horseman or cyclist, who does not stop but will nevertheless listen to you—beside whom, as long as your breath holds out, you may run and converse, although obliged to quit him in the middle of a sentence, he shooting ahead.

Roland influences his staff in an uncanny way, and everything on his premises breathes *his* energy and no other, and takes colour from him. Chiefly remarkable are the two maids who wait in the restaurant, and the boy in green uniform who serves in the bar. This boy also goes over to the station at the arrival of each train, to attract customers into the hotel. I say "to attract them" advisedly, for when the travellers arrive at the station, he seldom addresses them, but stands in their way, seeming to think that the Roland magnetism will be sufficient to draw them after him without any words or solicitations.

The large Roland's mechanical rolling gait becomes in one of these maidservants a rhythmical, lurching trot, in the other a keen little stumbling roll. They seem drawn or impelled along, or suddenly left idle or listless, left stranded as though suddenly deprived of an exterior motive force. This ebb and flow of energy corresponds to Roland's approach or distant withdrawal, although they may not be aware of his movements. They generally go about in silence, and it is when addressed that they become suddenly and startlingly verbose. They each take somewhat of Roland's personal *cachet* and manner, adapting it unconsciously to their own physical characteristics. If you succeed in breaking through Roland's spell they become nonplussed and bewildered.

But as Roland is the sun of this system round which all revolve, they also are affected to each other. The lesser members of this household are doubly servient and satellite, circling in turn round that member that possesses most of the Roland fire, and most negative moral magnitude. One of the servants is a little round-shouldered girl with a fox-like face, insignificant chin, head thrust forward, and eyes shining with what would seem at first a continual roguish amusement. But this is a light left shining while he to whom it was entrusted is no longer there. I dare say she was, poor creature, a girl of "infinite jest" before coming into Roland's service. I once, that she might discover her witty spirit, asked her what she was amused about. Grinning maliciously, and with a glance of wounding sarcasm—that she meant to be a smile of menial courtesy and a discreet glance of amiable respect —she completely rearranged everything on my table, salt-cellars, spoons, mustard-pots, eatables, so that I, who had got used to the first arrangement, could subsequently find nothing when I wanted it. My remark had evidently moved her, but she had not grasped its meaning. Roland was too strong in her. The other servant is a blonde, very fair; her expression is blank, astonished, with a shade of distress. She is heavier than her companion in body, and gyrates clumsily but swiftly round her, morally.

The boy is very curious. He is seventeen years old, and appears fourteen, both in manner, size, and expression. This retardation of his growth morally and physically is surely due to the fact of his having served in Roland's hotel for the last three or four years in this particular atmosphere. One thinks of him sometimes as being half-witted. He is rather like one of those dwarfs who have the appearance in middle-age of a dissipated boy in his teens. They arrived at the age, size, &c., of a boy of fifteen; why did not they, at least approximately, attain the growth and shape of a man of twenty-five? A question that, with no special scientific knowledge, it is difficult to answer, unless one should happen to know that at the age of fifteen they had met with Roland. This for me at least would be conclusive. In the case of the boy one knows his history, and that at thirteen he entered Roland's service. Any additional growth he may get will be nothing but Roland—has been nothing but Roland for the last four years. But always that charming nature of the boy of thirteen mixed into it, the freshness of his thirteenth year embalmed as it were beneath the beds of Rolandism. Roland descended on him like the cinders of a volcano, and occasionally we are given glimpses of his nature as it was when this calamity overtook him. His small body rolls with Roland's steady, rolling, occasionally stumbling gait. His forehead is seamed as his master's is with the constant elevation of his eyebrows : this wrinkled forehead being a characteristic of the whole household, by the way. These foreheads all seem puckered up in readiness for thought, whenever it may be the customer's good will to provoke it. Also there is an expression of wistful profundity over all their faces at times, largely contributed to by this. In conclusion, this youth speaks heavily, slowly, and somewhat nasally, as Roland does : and has the strangest little rough, bullying way imaginable —and a reassuring girl-like softness that is quite charming.

3

The Countryhouse Party, Scotland

(Previously unpublished. Excerpt from unfinished *Cantleman-Crowd Master* novel, begun 1914 and worked on further in the 1920s and 1930s)

Cantleman was in the North. He was at a countryhouse with an American, just across the Border, with a large party, because he had just become a celebrated writer. There was a writer there as well who had long been celebrated, who had followed him there with his wife, because he had become famous from associating with other celebrated people, and he attached himself to this rising star.

This was Leo Makepiece Leo: through his mother he was related to Thackeray. Leo's wife had come with him: she had been celebrated an even longer time than he: she was a great woman novelist. The American hostess desired to be celebrated, and to be a novelist. In their different rooms they were all writing books, sketches, or articles about each other. The great woman novelist said, "Leo is a diplomat." She always said this. She had converted him now into an earl (Lord Raymond Mount Maurice —Leo had chosen his own christian name), she had peopled the stables of the hired countryhouse with hunting horses (though in fact only occupied for this let by a single Rolls Royce), extended the lawns, provided a male staff of footmen, chefs and valets (there were no men-servants in the house except the chauffeur) and was well away towards a very brilliant Victorian piece, in her most renowned manner. Her celebrated husband Leo's pen did not lag behind. He filled the atmosphere with crafty "diplomats," laboriously adulterous. He placed them as he found himself, only more so, in surroundings of extreme luxury. He hemmed them in with obsequious valets, and provoked them to interpret

45

the most spectacular traditions of Anglo-Norman landowning society. They had an unaccountable touch too, a florid touch—a thwarted "inhibited" gusto for the flesh-pots of sex, but always the flesh-pots of others (hence the adultery) which they may have picked up on their long diplomatic missions to Vienna, in contact with exotic pathologists; and they possessed a dull and heavy lip, a fishy and inscrutable, welt-political, eye, they did not get in the English county—but that did not matter. All these things in due course passed into currency. Men dislike true portraits. So all was well, the romantic pen was busy on all sides. Cantleman stored up the stories of the aged-famous. They flowed in an adenoidish nasal low-voice twanging from the wet hanging lips of Leo. The house became peopled with a century of English greatness. Cantleman, the celebrated "futurist," swam sullenly against this historical tide. England he patronized : "victorianism" he exploded against in glib contempt. Leo humoured the young lion, the young lion tolerated Leo : they were "high contracting parties." "Diplomacy" was called in and did its work. Leo read the papers in the morning.

"A war is coming," he piped nasally one day at breakfast, the big naif fat-boy, his hair untidy and tie crooked, a smile bulging one pink shining cheek, one wet azure eye cocked above it at the company.

"You don't really mean to say that, do you, Leo? You don't mean there's going to be a European war?" the American hostess asked in passionate expostulatory waves of rising and falling sound.

"I'm afraid that's what it means," his [. . .]¹ pipe (pitched for the alarm) replied, *The Times* put down beside him, open at the leaders.

"But England will never go to war," she said. "A Liberal government, anyway, will never declare war. If it were a Conservative government, then perhaps *they* might."

"What do you bet?" croaked Leo, the jolly sporting gentleman-journalist.

"Oh I'm not betting, Leo !"

"I'll bet you anything you like that the Liberals will do it. They

¹ Word, written in Lewis's hand and part of revision by him to typescript at this point, illegible.

will go to war more easily than the Conservatives. They always have."

"I don't see how they can."

"Well, I know all of them, several are my intimate friends," he quavered and snuffled. "If you knew them as well as I do you'd know they would. I hope I'm wrong."

Leo was of German nationality. He had several eminent Liberal friends, whom Cantleman had met at his house.

"I don't believe Asquith dare declare war."

"You see!" croaked Leo.

Cantleman did not understand. He knew nothing about Liberals or Conservatives. "War" conveyed nothing to him. He was totally ignorant of what these people were discussing. The "future" was the province of his election. It was a Utopia of course. War was not a part of it. Other countries went to war, not his.

They went on talking about war. What was war? He had no idea. Cantleman took up *The Times* and read what Leo had been reading. He could not understand. His father had been a soldier. That was a reason to misunderstand war, or think little about it : what his father had done he would not do. He would never be a soldier, since his father had been one : so why consider war?

"Leo's body is a sluggish colony of massive blond segments," Cantleman had registered in his notebook. "Those are worms that are his arms—also his legs. I regard him as a gigantic annelid. His body is probably a red-blooded earth-worm, white at the extremities of the segments." After this was written : "*Note*. This disgusts me, but evidently this is not the case with most people. (Worms breathe by their skin, as they do not possess any special respiratory organs. The two sexes are united in the same individual, but two individuals (same sex) pair together. This sounds like Leo.)"

Leo's attitude to his body was that it was very large and fat. Cantleman put down his heavy breathing to adenoids. He did not understand his gasping. He did not understand Leo.

Next morning Leo sighed and gasped as he read the newspaper. It sounded as though he were in a bath. He kept raising his thick eyelid up and depressing his cheek; an eyelash had not

47

got into his eye; he was acting as his body dictated. That made him prop his eye open, whose blue disk was painted upon a reddish egg, the size of a small fowl's.

"What's the news, Leo?" asked the hostess.

"Oh—there's going to be a European war," Leo said looking up from his paper. He had said that already : but there was nothing else to say. He passed his large protruding wet blue eye impassively over the faces of these children—absorbed in their luxury, eggs, fish, bacon, marmalade and porridge, their self-satisfied eras of sheltered peace.

"I hope you're wrong, Leo," said the American hostess.

Cantleman watched Leo in silence. Leo looked at him and returned to the paper. Cantleman took one up, and read the news. After breakfast Leo read the other papers in the hall. Cantleman came down from his room going towards the main house-door. Leo put down his paper and held out his hand.

"Help me up, there's a good chap!" he panted with a pained discomfort, a bitter slightly quivering mouth, that appeared to be suffering from the sensation following a rebuff.

Cantleman pulled him up out of the chair. Leo liked being helped up from chairs by people over whom he exercised any authority, by nobodies or by juniors. He got on his feet with a limp, as though he had stuck together. He shook. He stood still, his large feet pointing flatly to right and left, his legs fat cylinders clinging at the knees as though still adhering.

"When will the car be ready?" he asked, in his soft panting "diplomatic" nasal undertone.

"I'm just going to see."

"I'll come with you," said Leo.

The car was outside the door. Leo lit one eye, his jagged teeth appeared through his walrus moustache, he nodded, and went and had a jolly companionable talk with the chauffeur. Soon the guests had collected. They went to play golf. Cantleman left them near the small county town, and went into it alone to get the latest papers. The *Northern Dispatch* had a poster : in large letters, violet on a white ground, was the announcement :

MORPETH OLYMPIAD. RECORD CROWD

48

Wonderful crowds, gathering at Olympiads! What is the War to you? It is you that make both the Wars and Olympiads. When War knocks at the door, why should you hurry? You are busy with an Olympiad?—Cantleman looked at the perfidious poster and reflected as above.

This crude violet lettering, distillation of suffragetic years, of minor violences. He was a suffragette. He now felt eager for news. He bought a London Edition of the *Daily Mail.*

GERMANY DECLARES WAR ON RUSSIA.

With the words came a dark rush of hot humanity in his mind. An immense human gesture swept its shadow across him like a smoky cloud. "Germany declares War on Russia" seemed a roar of guns. He saw active mephistophelian specks in Chancelleries ("diplomats" like Leo). He saw a rush of papers, a frowning race. With innate military exultation he regarded it. The ground seemed swaying a little. He left the paper-shop swallowing this tragic morsel with stony dignity.

The party at the golf links took his *News, Mails,* and *Mirrors,* as the run home commenced. Each manifested his gladness at the bad news in his own restrained way. Would England declare war? Leo said "Yes"—simply, "quietly" and with a fatigued patience. "She" would, he said. He knew what "she" would do, if "she" didn't know herself.

The closing of the Stock Exchange, announced, suggested a host of fascinating changes in life. What would happen as to the Banks? Food supplies had better be laid in. What of invasion?

The excitement and novelty of life foreshadowed pleased this group of children. Leo, also, in his way, appeared satisfied. The general satisfaction showed itself in various disguises. The next few days was a gay Carnival of Fear, or conventional horror. The Morpeth Olympiad poster was secured, and pinned up in the hall. It appeared an adequate expression of the greatness of the English nation.

Then all London newspapers began to be bought up in Edinburgh, and none ever got as far as this countryside. Cantleman left the house-party and returned to London.

SECTION II

The Cyclopean Dividing Wall

Sectional Introduction

"The French Poodle," published in *The Egoist* in March, 1916, was probably written in 1915 at a time when Lewis was suffering ill-health—as does James Fraser in the story. Harriet Weaver—"that admirable and self-denying Quaker lady," Lewis called her—was editor of *The Egoist*. But, as Lewis recalled in *Blasting and Bombardiering*, "you would rather have supposed that it (the magazine) belonged to Ezra Pound." *The Egoist* began serializing Lewis's *Tarr* in April, 1916, after completing the serialization of James Joyce's *A Portrait of the Artist as a Young Man*. T. S. Eliot was also amply represented in the magazine. Richard Aldington was the periodical's literary editor at this time. *The Egoist*'s printing of "The French Poodle" was adorned with a portrait drawing of Lewis by Roald Kristian. The drawing shows Lewis with his characteristic pipe and the accompanying story has many touches typical of its author. But it is probably unique among his works because of its feeling—almost worthy of his fellow painter Franz Marc, killed on the German side in the First World War—for animal life in the face of the ravages of Machine-Age Man.

With the £50 fee he received for the serial rights to *Tarr*, Lewis settled his affairs and, having recovered his health, enlisted as a gunner in the Royal Garrison Artillery. His experiences at the front both as an artillery man and as a war artist with the Canadian Army, are recorded in the autobiographical *Blasting and Bombardiering*. "The King of the Trenches" appeared in the second edition (1967) of this book. The printing here was based on a typed carbon copy now at the Cornell archive of Lewis material. Readers contemplating Capt. Polderdick should perhaps recall that Lewis's father, Charles, was a captain on the Northern side in the American civil war—"eccentric almost to the point of madness," as the son once described him.[1]

[1] See "The Do-Nothing Mode: an Autobiographical Fragment," *Agenda* Lewis issue, pp. 216–221. The quotation here appears on p. 219.

The French Poodle

(First published in *The Egoist*, London, March 1, 1916)

I was reminded of another man's fate when I saw Peter yesterday, in khaki, with his dog. The dog appeared rather confused by Peter's newly resumed uniform. It fell in behind other people in khaki : even when keeping in orderly proximity to its master, it followed a certain indifference or contempt.—Peter's destiny had nothing sultry in its lines : his dog was a suburban appendage. It was the khaki and the dog brought me to the other story.

It appears the following things happened to a man called Rob Cairn, during a long sick-leave. The time was between July and October 1915. I can tell the story with genuine completeness : for James Fraser, the man he saw most of then, told it to me with a great wealth of friendly savagery.

Rob Cairn was drifting about London in mufti, by no means well, and full of anxiety, the result of his ill-health and the shock he had received at finding himself blown into the air and painted yellow by the unavoidable shell. His tenure on earth seemed insecure, and he could not accustom himself to the idea of insecurity. When the shell came he had not bounded gracefully and coldly up, but with a clumsy dismay. His spirit, that spirit that should have been winged for the life of a soldier, and ready fiercely to take flight into the unknown, strong for other lives, was also grubbily attached to the earth. It, like his body, was not graceful in its fearlessness, nor resilient, nor young. All the minutiæ of existence mesmerized it. It could not disport itself genially in independence of surrounding objects and ideas. Even as a boy he had never been able to learn to dive : hardly to swim. Yet he was a big red-headed chap that those who measure men by redness and by size would have considered fairly imposing as a physical specimen. It requires almost a professional colour-matcher, as a matter of fact, to discriminate between the different reds : and then the various constitutional conditions they imply is a separate discovery.

Cairn, then, was arrested in a vague but troublesome maze of discomfort and ill-health : his sick leave, after he had left the hospital, lasted some time. As an officer, therefore more responsible, he had more latitude. He was an architect. He went to his office every day for an hour or two. But he was haunted by the necessity to return once more to the trench-life with which he had been for some weeks mesmerically disconnected, and which he felt was another element, with which he had only become acquainted in a sudden dream. This element of malignant and monotonous missiles, which worried less or more, sleeplessness and misery, now appeared to him in its true colours. They were hard, poisonous and flamboyant. A fatiguing sonority, an empty and pretentious energy : something about it all like the rhetoric of a former age, revolted him. It all seemed incredibly old and superannuated. Should he go back and get killed it would be as though the dead of a century ago were striking him down. Cairn must have been a fairly brave man, considering all things, before his tossing. It was now with him rather sullen neurasthenia at the thought of recommencing, than anything else : renewed monotonous actions and events, and fear not of death but of being played with too much.

James Fraser, his partner, who because of heart-trouble had been unable to join the Army, heard all this from his friend, and cursed "the whole business" of bloodshed in sympathy with the recriminating soldier.

"I'm sure there's something wrong, Rob. How do you feel exactly; physically, I mean? What can happen to a man inside who is blown up in the air? What do the doctors exactly say?"

"They can find nothing. I don't believe there is anything. But I don't feel at all well. It's something in my brain, rather, that's dislocated : cracked, I think, sometimes. I shall never be any good out there again."

He read a great deal, chiefly Natural History. The lives of animals seemed to have a great fascination for his stolid, faithful thoughts. When he got an idea he stuck to it with unconscious devotion. He was a good friend to his ideas.

One of the principal notions to which he became attached at

this time was that human beings suffered in every way from the absence of animal life around them. Pigs, horses, buffaloes, snakes, birds, goats : the majority of men living in towns were deprived of this rich animal neighbourhood. The sanity of direct animal processes : the example suggested constantly by the equilibrium of these various cousins of ours, with their snouts and their wings : the steady and soothing brotherhood of their bodies; this environment appeared necessary to human beings.

"Few men and many animals!" as he said to Fraser, blinking dogmatically and heavily, light red eyelashes falling with a look of modesty at the base of eyes always seeming a little dazzled by the reds all round them. "That's what I should like; rather than *men* and nothing else. It is bad for men to beat and kill each other. When there are no patient backs of beasts to receive their blows men turn them more towards their fellows. Irruptions of the hunting instinct are common in cities. Irruptions of all instincts are common and inevitable in modern life, among human swarms. Men have taken to the air; they are fighting there almost before they can fly. Man is losing his significance."

Fraser had an objection to make.

"You suggest the absence of animals.—Did not men in every time kill and beat one another?"

Cairn twisted as it were archly in his chair.

"Men loved each other better formerly; and—they at least killed other animals as well. I have never killed any animal; never a bird; not a mouse; not knowingly an insect; but I have killed men."

He said this staring hard at his friend, as though he might be able to discover the meaning of this fact in his face.

"And I did not mind killing men," he proceeded. "I hardly knew what killing meant."

"You do now?" his delighted partner asked him.

Rob looked at him with suspicion.

"No; possibly because I have never killed anyone I could see properly."

"Yes; your gunner's scalps are very abstract. But, again, I do not see what you mean. Do you think that a butcher, because of his familiarity with the shambles, would have more compunction in killing a man?"

"No. But it would do him no harm to kill a man or anything else, of course. Then he's a professional murderer."

"But why did you never kill birds?" Fraser asked him with uninterested persistence.

"I should have if I'd lived among them.—Do you think men would eat each other if there were no succulent animals left?"

"Very likely." Fraser laughed in accordance with the notion. "They might possibly at all events eat all the ugly women!"

Rob Cairn discussed these things with a persistent and often mildly indignant solemnity. The trenches had scarred his mind. Swarms of minute self preservative and active thoughts moved in the furrows. Little bombs of irritable logic appeared whirling up from these grave clefts and exploded around his uneasy partner. Fraser wondered if Cairn would be able to take up his place in the business again, if nothing happened to him, as usefully as he had occupied it before the war. He seemed queer and was not able at the office to concentrate his mind on anything for more than a few minutes.

As to the war, his ideas appeared quite confusedly stagnant. He wondered, arguing along the same lines of the incompleteness of modern life, whether the savagery we arrive at were better than the savagery we come from.

"Since we must be savage, is not a real savage better than a sham one?"

"Must we be savage?" Fraser would ask.

"This 'great war' is the beginning of a period, far from being a war-that-will-end-war, take my word for it."

So Cairn was a tired man, and his fancy set out on a pilgrimage to some patriarchal plain. He had done his eight months' stint, and was exhausted. His bounce into the air had shaken him out of his dream. He was awake and harshly anxious and reflective.

It was at this point that he bought his French poodle.

In answer to an advertisement in two papers for a fairly large dog, a lady at Guildford answered that she had such an animal to sell. The lady brought the dog to his flat in a street off Theobalds Road, and he immediately bought it. He was very shy with it at first. He was conscious of not being its first love, and attempted to bribe it into forgetfulness of its former master by giving it a great deal to eat. It shortly vomited in his sitting-room. It howled a great deal at first.

But the dog soon settled down to novel life. Cairn became excessively fond of it. He abused a man in the streets who insulted it. It was a large fat and placid brute that received Rob's caresses with obedient steadiness, occasionally darting friendship back at him. As he held it against his legs Cairn felt a deep attachment for this warm bag of blood and bone, whose love was undiluted habit and an uncomplicated magnetism. It recognized his friend-liness in spasms of servile good nature, as absent-minded as its instincts.

Cairn noted all the modes of its nature with a delighted care. Its hunger enthralled him; its ramping gruff enthusiasm at the prospect of the streets filled him with an almost Slavic lyricism and glee. He was calm in the midst of its hysteria; but there was a contented pathos in his quietness. Its adventures with other dogs he followed with indulgence. The amazing physical catholicism of its taste he felt was a just reproach to his fastidiousness and maturity. It would have approached a rhinoceros with amorous proposals, were it not for elementary prudence.

He called his dog Carp. He loved him like a brother. But it is not at all sure that in the end Carp did not take the place that some lady should have occupied in his heart, as many of the attachments of men for girls seem a sentiment sprung up in the absence of a dog. Cairn had had one sweetheart; but after several years of going about together she had seemed so funny to him— she had seemed settling down like an old barge into some obscure and too personal human groove—that he had jerked himself away. The war had put the finishing touch to their estrangement.

"Dolly's lurch is becoming more pronounced," was his Monday morning's bulletin at the office. She appeared to remain an incredible time on each foot, while her body swung round. In following her out of the restaurant he felt that she was doing a sort of lugubrious cake-walk. He could hardly help getting into step. She became more dogmatic every minute : and rheumatism made her knuckles like so many dull and obstinate little faces.

"You're getting tired of her at last." Fraser advised him to take advantage of his mood and to say good-bye to her.

He had done so and had regretted it ever since. He felt superstitious about this parting : he regarded her in this conjecture, as a mascot abandoned. He blamed his partner and the war for this. Somehow his partner and the war were closely connected. In many ways he found them identified—a confused target for his resentment. When he found himself cursing the war he found himself disliking his partner so much the *next* minute that it seemed the *same* minute. Fraser did not approve of Carp, either : although Carp appeared to like Fraser better than he did his own master. Cairn noticed this, and his humour did not improve. Towards the end they did not see him so much at the office as formerly. Once or twice a week he put in an appearance, rather primed with criticism of the conduct of the business in his absence. Then he turned up one day in khaki again : he was going back to the Front in a couple of days. Fraser and he got on better than they had done of late. He was much more open and good-humoured, and had seemingly recovered his old personality entirely. This may have been due somewhat to his friend's sentimental spurt of pleasantness under the circumstances.

"What are you going to do with Carp ?"

When Fraser asked him this he seemed confused.

"I hadn't thought about that——"

They did not say anything, and there was the illusion of sudden groping out of sight.

"Are you going to take him to the Front ?" Fraser suggested, and laughed impatiently.

"No, he might get shot there," Cairn replied, screwing up his nose and recovering his good humour, apparently. "I must give him away."

Fraser knew how fond he was of the dog, and attributed his awkwardness to his dislike at the notion of parting from it.

"Let me keep it for you," he said, generously.

"No, thanks. I'll get rid of it."

Fraser saw his partner on the following day at their office. The next thing that he heard was that Cairn was ill in bed, and that his return to France would have to be again postponed. On going to his friend's flat he crossed at the door two men carrying out a small box. The charwoman was very mysterious. He asked what the box was.

"It's the dog," she replied.

"Is he sold then?" Fraser asked.

"No. 'E's dead."

He looked at her melodramatically unconcerned and bloated face for a moment.

Rob Cairn was alone in his bedroom. He was very exhausted, and faintly bad-tempered.

"What's up? Have you had a relapse?"

"Yes—something : I'm not well."

"Can I do anything for you?"

Cairn was lying on his back and hardly looked at his visitor.

"No, thanks. Listen." He turned towards Fraser, and his face became long and dulled with excitement. "Listen to this. You know Carp, the dog? I killed it yesterday.—I shot it with a revolver; but I aimed too low. It nearly screamed the place down.—Poor brute!—You know——"

He suddenly lurched round, face downwards, flattened in his arm, and sobbed in a deep howling way, that reminded Fraser of a dog.

When he looked up his face was a scared and bitter mask.

"What a coward I am! Poor beast! Poor ——. How could I——"

"Nonsense, Rob! You're not yourself. You know you're not yourself! Have you seen a doctor? Don't worry about this ——."

"I'm only glad of one thing. I *know* I shall pay for it. That thought is the only one that quiets me. I know as surely as I am lying here that my hour is fixed! I have killed my best living luck. Not that I wanted the luck! God, no! I care little enough what happens to me! But that poor beast!——"

"Damn you and your mascots! You are the slave of any poodle——!"

Fraser remembered his detestable lady-love, and the perpetual threat of an idiotic marriage.

The doctor came into the room.—He told me that he fancied more had happened between Cairn and Carp, at the dog's death, than his friend had cared to tell him. Cairn was another fortnight in London, then went to France. Two weeks after that he was killed. He understood the mechanism of his destiny better than his partner.

The King of the Trenches

(First published as part of *Blasting and Bombardiering*, expanded 1967 edition, Calder and Boyars, London)

Why was the lieutenant pale? Why did he gaze so fixedly from beneath his new Gor'-Blimey? Because his mother came from Lima. That was also why his face was serious, and his nerves removed to a plane of reasonableness seldom reached by heat and shock. He had a certain gentle lisping breathlessness. Sandhurst had not curtailed his charm, which reached back to civilized Savannas.

He was astonished on the 4th May to see an unusual figure standing near him in the Trench. It was staring at his Flying Pig,[1] and twirling a stick. It twirled and twirled the stick and looked at the Flying Pig. Then it gave the fascinating siege ordnance before it a blow and exclaimed "Ha! *Ha!*"

That Ha! *Ha!* was a new note in Menzie's life of war. Lieutenant Donald Menzies (Lima, London and Linlithgow) absorbed the new sound that he recognized at once as belonging to this outlandish life, and temporarily placed it in what he supposed must be its proper position among the ejaculatory and explosive noises by which he was surrounded. That trench where they were had never heard of it as far as he knew. Perhaps it came from another trench? Or it might be that except when uttered by that figure, it never occurred at all anywhere. He had never heard it before in any case. He noted and placed it with military tidiness. A breath of bald absurdity, a new comic gas, had entered Menzies' trench with that figure, however. Menzies looked at him again. Then with a delicate smile of recognition, he took in the situation. This figure must be his newly-posted commanding officer.

[1] Trench mortar.

With politely sarcastic câlinerie he approached the new biped, with the new noise, dropped from some strange Christmas-tree into his trench.

"Good morning, sir."

"Good morning. Good morning!"

The gentleman was whistling.—"*How-do-you-doodle oodle-oo. Oh fancy meeting you!*" was what he whistled. Meantime he lazily struck the gun with his stick.

"Captain Polderdick?"

"Polderdick! How did you know my name?" Polderdick's mouth grew round and slushy : the military moustache over it was a fierce camouflage for hiding "Ha *Ha's*!" The ribbon of the D.C.M., the Military Medal, the usual South African medal and many others jostled each other, two deep, upon his advancing chest. A drawling, extremely circumspect and ponderous delivery, suggested that language was not without its pitfalls for him. The old ranker swelled with the officialdom and diaphragmatic pomp of all those promoted across that portentous gulf which separates officers from men when the change of worlds comes after a life-time of habit.

"How did you know my name?" he screwed his eyes up cunningly, his name, like his rank, was for him an object, a thing secured, perhaps by means of some stratagem, by this stranger.

"I supposed it was you, sir, who had been posted to us."

"You were quite right my lad, quite right. It *was* me! Here I am! And there you are. And here *we* are! What next, my lad? Ha! *Ha!*" He twirled his stick round, imparting supple movements to it till it appeared to flex and waggle like a fencing sword. He prodded the Flying Pig, repeating his war-cry "Ha *Ha!*"

Then fiercely and quizzingly he wheeled round on Menzies, like a ruffled dog. With a fresh flourish of the stick, and a guttural "Ha! *Ha!*" he lunged, prodding Menzies in the stomach.

"Oh sir!" exclaimed the lieutenant, carrying his gloved hand to the region affected. After this initiation Polderdick wandered off, followed by his new subaltern, to inspect the rest of his stock.

"Handsome pieces of ordnance, my lad!" he exclaimed as

61

they came upon one. "Fine handsome pieces!" Then sinking his chin down into his historic chest, with the object of fixing his roaring mouth like a funnel over the lung where the deep sound comes from, he began chanting, one hand over his ear in the orthodox fashion.

> "Won't you buy, oh won't you buy
> My sweet lavend-er-er,
> Fifteen branches one penny-y-y"

"Burney" was known for leagues, all over the Line. Polderdick was known as "Burney". He had a great name for intrepidity, and as an able gunner. Menzies grew accustomed to the spectacle of his O.C. (on the scene generally a little late) coming down the trench whistling a few bars of "Won't you buy my sweet lavender" or "Goosie—Goosie—Gander," making facetious passes with his stick. When he met an infantry soldier, he would, to this Tommy's dismay, if it were his first meeting with Polderdick, twirl his stick, with his "Ha *Ha!* my lad—How's that? If you never get anything worse than that, my lad, you can thank your lucky stars. Nickwar? Pass on! To your post!"

It was also his habit to poke his stick into all shelters and dug-outs that he passed, blessing them or banning them with his "Ha! *Ha!*" He stirred up many a figure in some damp black hole, who thought it was a visiting general being funny, and cursed under his breath.

When Polderdick arrived the Line was quiet. A few days afterwards the Trench was constantly shelled. Polderdick was there. They began shelling with shrapnel. At the first patter of the shrapnel Polderdick dived headlong into a dug-out, but his tin-hat crashed with great force against the tin-hat of an infantry captain who was darting out at the moment. They both disappeared, Polderdick's buttocks revolving as he fell inside. Menzies crouched against the side of the Trench, which was spouting earth a few yards higher up from the last burst, and was full of the momentary wasp-music of hurrying splinters.

"No sir, I'm a flying pig!" Menzies heard his commanding officer exclaiming. "You got in the way, sir!"

"You silly bastard, you nearly broke my neck. Let me get out. What are you doing? Get off my leg!"

"Stop here, my lad, and keep me company. Outside all is war. Don't go looking for trouble, my lad. Gently does it."

Two shells swooped and buried themselves like furies in the earth above Menzies' head, and a moment later two red fountains of earth poured down deluging him from head to foot. The infantry captain appeared and hurried past him down the trench. Polderdick's head peered out, looking to left and right. There was a considerable noise coming from every direction, and Polderdick shouted to Menzies:

"Keep those pigs barking. Give Fritz hell! Give him hell! Where's all this stuff coming from do you suppose?"

There were two cracks overhead, Menzies flattened himself against the side of the Trench, and the shrapnel spattered everywhere for a moment. Polderdick's head appeared again.

"My head's rotten!" he exclaimed. "Did you hear just now how I knocked it? It's rotten. I shall go to the rear. You carry on, sergeant! I'm off."

"Have you hurt yourself?" asked Menzies.

"Rotten!" said Polderdick. He scrambled out, shook himself and stumbled quickly away, watched by the gunner corporal.

" 'Burney's' got the wind up," said the corporal.

"He banged his head," said Menzies.

"Ah! so I saw!" said the corporal.

A stunt had been announced. It was the morning of the attack. There had been a good deal of shelling. Menzies, in coming up with the relief, met in the support lines a figure being borne upon a stretcher. It's eye, as he passed, appeared aware of him; the head remained facing the sky. A solemn eye swept over him as they passed in placid recognition, nothing more. Menzies felt it was his O.C., though he had not noticed the face as he passed him. He ran back.

"Are you hurt, sir?"

Polderdick's eye settled down in the corner of his head to observe his subaltern.

"My rheumatism's something cruel this morning. It's laid me out something proper. They're taking me back.—You carry on, my lad. Pass on! It's downed me this time properly."

He spoke in the quiet voice of one in pain. Menzies got used, likewise, to this. Whenever a stunt was coming off, Polderdick disappeared, on a stretcher, if he could get one, to the rear, or he kept away till the worst was over.

Menzies and Marshall, the other subaltern of his section, talked over the situation. Marshall was resentful. He had been sent to Trench Mortars with death in his soul. A month of them had developed in him a hatred of everything in this inferno. Menzies did not entertain a severe view of Polderdick, however. He explained to the sullen Marshall the advantages, as he saw it, of the cane. Also he excused him. He pointed out that Polderdick had been wounded in the temple. Before that—who could doubt, who had glanced casually at his left breast?—he had certainly been a very brave man. But also, of course (it was to be supposed) he had not then exclaimed "Ha! *Ha!*" He had not prodded people in the stomach with his stick.—For Menzies there were two lives, where Polderdick was concerned. There had been one in which he had been a madly-brave soldier in the ranks (look at his ribbons, consider his record!). There he got his crosses, his nickname, his prestige. Then there was the other one in which he was just *mad*, without however being brave. He was charming, but no longer brave.

Much of his madness, Menzies proceeded to argue—as they sat at the tin-table of the café in Bailleul where they had gone in a lorry for the afternoon to get tobacco and condensed milk for the officers' mess—much of his peculiar wildness, had gone into, had been absorbed by, his physical daring, about that there was little doubt. It had had to go somewhere. It had gone into that. Then the wound in the temple stopped that up, brusquely. You see? (Marshall did not see: he cursed the metaphysical Scot, he yawned, he stamped, he lit cigarettes, he glared.) The wound, for whatever reason, prevented his madness from any longer flowing into the moulds of physical heroism. It found other outlets. He became a different man. He did not forget his past bravery, however. His new incarnation was its distorted child. The "Ha! *Ha!*" itself drew the gusto of its note from the cold, cruel, almost intellectual courage of the former Polderdick. Physical strength remained with him. Could he not take one of the heaviest and least willing of his men in his arms, lift him kicking and howling until head and shoulders stuck up over the

parapet? "Ha! *Ha!* Look over there, my lad!" he would cry.
(Menzies and Marshall had both witnessed this episode.) He still
liked, in a sort of prolongation of himself, to look over the top
through the eyes of a reluctant subordinate. So Menzies discoursed, with his mild persuasive southern eyes wandering about
the busy square. Marshall transferred all the feelings one by one
that he had had about Polderdick to Menzies. Menzies was mad!
Menzies was balmy! He was madder than Polderdick. He had
always disliked Menzies. He had been right. No one could help
disliking a man who could talk such cock as that! Also he was
evidently inclined to suck up to the O.C. He said nothing. He
stood up and stretched.

"Well, shall we beat it? Come on, you bloody philosopher!
There's a lorry, let's get that." He started running.

Polderdick was not popular with his men. Like most ranker-
officers, he was extremely exacting; it was his tendency to make
them work if anything harder than he had worked for so long
himself.

At the point of the English Line where his battery was placed,
a stream had once flowed and still took a little water across No
Man's Land, bisecting the German front-line and the English.
In the English Line (as in the German) a foot-bridge had been
built inside the trench where this happened, with a parapet of
sand-bags continuing the face of the Trench across the little
gully.—On two occasions his men pushed "Burney" off this bridge
into the water, alleging accident, assuming dismay. The first
time he clambered out. As a clown, his indignation was circum-
scribed. He protested and swore. But it happened again shortly
afterwards. The second time he said nothing. But the men
responsible for it had a good deal of work in the ensuing week.
When in future he had occasion to approach the bridge he
looked carefully round before crossing. If he was with men of
his own he allowed them to pass first. He even would not cross
when an infantryman was behind him.—His chief objection to
falling into the water was that he believed a German sniper had
his rifle trained on this spot. Menzies gathered this from his
guarded inquiry: "Many Tommies fall in there, my lad? It's a
dangerous spot." As the water did not make it dangerous, it must

c

be that. And once, when a man was missing, he asserted that the man had fallen into the stream, been sniped, and had subsequently been borne down its waters to the rear. The corpse would turn up in the end, it seemed, beneath the windows of Corps Headquarters, which he appeared to conceive as situated on the brink of a pool, by this time practically full of men who had lost their lives in that manner.

He was not always beneath the shadow of this dream. Probably, as an outcome of his aquatic experiences, he one day said to Menzies:

"The British Army when I first joined was some Army! It was small, but it was a pukka army, second to none, my lad. There was initiative. Initiative is what you want. This is a rag-time army. Look at it!—It's a ragtime war, my lad, from what I can see of it. I should like to be in civvies again. No! straight I would, that's right!"—Menzies had a puzzled look. "Burney" stared at it a moment: then he became more normal. "It breaks my heart to see chances lost, as I do every day.—A soldier should be on the lookout for opportunities. That's what a soldier should be." He turned suddenly upon Menzies. "Now, why don't you jump into that stream; swim up it, swim up it!"—He fixed Menzies violently with his left eye—"and bomb Fritz from the water? He wouldn't see where it came from.—You can swim, my lad, can't you?"

"Yes, sir. But there's not enough water to swim in. And the Boche has it under observation all the time."

"Rot! That's rot what you're saying there, my lad! Don't tell me you couldn't.—No! But you're like me. You've lost interest in this ragtime war, is that it? No? Well you must be a B.F., if you haven't, that's all I can say!"

"I never have been interested, like you sir. You are a soldier."

"Me! A soldier!? Get along with you! I'm not a soldier! I *was*!"

Menzies smiled affectionately at his chief.

But Polderdick, soldier or no soldier, grew depressed. This was really a necessary exploit, that the stream had been placed there to make possible. The consciousness of the things he no longer did weighed heavily on him. It was stupid to have to ask another man. He had never refused such occasions. How could they? *Yet he understood how they could*, that was the most depressing part of it. A world in which he was a major, surrounded by nothing but soldiers who were not soldiers, wholly given over to war that was not a war, was a ragtime world.

This restless spirit of haunting adventure would sometimes make him mischievous. He would come up from his billet into a quiet world, a local truce reigning throughout the stagey ditches and melodramatic crypts and holes of the landscape, of which he was a notable faun. A few lonely shells sang or creaked along overhead, bursting in the remote distance, like the noisy closing of very far-off doors. Butterflies drifted here and there. German and English, Fritz and Tom, read the newspaper, slept, wrote to Gretchen or the lovely Minnie.—Polderdick would gaze round at this idyllic scene with a dissatisfied and restless eye.

On one of these occasions Marshall was on duty. He was sunning himself on a stretch of wet mud. One gunner was asleep, another writing a letter. Polderdick appeared and fixed his eyes upon Marshall. Blankly with sudden unction he declared :

"Ha! *Ha!* Mr. Marshall! An excellent opportunity for Trench Mortars! What do you think? Is that right?" He put up his periscope and peered into it. "I see a Hun's back in what is evidently a post, an advanced post. The Fritzes in that sap to the left seem to have got it into their heads that this part of the line is a branch of the Millennium! Swelt my bob if I don't see two having a shave, the bastards, as large as life!"

As fast as they could be loaded, he sent his Flying Pigs hurtling in all directions. All the peaceable warriors in the trenches were filled with amazement, which rapidly turned to fury when they realized what was happening. A raucous murmur, a tenuous hubbub of alarm and inquiry, floated across No-Man's Land. This was quickly succeeded by a fusillade of every description of missile and projectile on which the enemy could lay his hands quickly. A black cloud of anger surged along our trench. Infantry officers rushed up to Polderdick, shaking their fists in his face. But flourishing his stick mysteriously, he hastily retired down the communication trench, and was seen no more till the next day.

Meantime the *riposte* had come and a furious bombardment had fallen on the trench. In the rear the Field started, the Heavies joined in, layer behind layer, until the enormous guns right back on the old ramparts of Ypres were shattering the air with their discharge, and for a short time all was confusion. On both sides everyone stood by, expecting an attack. Marshall was wounded in the lung. Two gunners were killed. Menzies was telephoned for from the trench by the breathless telephonist, and as he was hurrying up he met his O.C. retiring hastily along the duckboard track.

"Is it an attack?" he asked.

"An attack? No-o, attack be buggered! It's as quiet as Heaven up there!"

"Marshall's wounded. Didn't you know?"

"Marshall wounded? Who said so?"

"The telephonist. They're probably attacking. Look at all this coming over!"

There was a line of black stumps on a low ridge to their left, and every few seconds an immense impressive chocolate black burst rose up and spent splinters flapped in the mud on either side of the duckboard track.

"Yes, it's not over healthy here, I agree," Polderdick said starting anxiously forward, his eye on a line of burst on the road ahead, that he would soon have to cross. "I'm going to get back. My rheumatism's something awful today. But it's quiet enough up in the Line. I came away because there was nothing doing. You can go up there if you want a nap."

Menzies left him : by the time he reached the trench all again was as Polderdick had described it, very quiet, except for a few restless guns that still continued slamming on both sides. But there had been a number of casualties.

"Where's that son-of-a-bitch of an O.C. of yours? If he comes back here I'll put him under arrest! He ought to be shot! Is the man mad? Where is he?"

Informed at Battalion Headquarters of what had happened, the O.C. Infantry was on the spot. Stretcher bearers were passing along the trench. The bodies of three gunners lay near the Flying Pig, the leg of one two yards away and another beheaded. Marshall had been taken to the dressing-station.

"Burney" Polderdick prepared his story of this event. So well did he know his way about in the professional military mind, and so high was his military reputation, that his bluff soldierly

view of what had occurred was accepted at Headquarters.—
Shortly after this, his four Flying Pigs were moved to a neighbouring divisional front.

For anything below a General, as things stood, Polderdick had a
sovereign contempt. In the new world in which Polderdicks were
majors, this perhaps must of necessity ensue. His obsequiousness
in the presence of a General-Officer was no doubt the complement
of his wounding attitude to those below that rank. Lieut.-Colonels,
for instance, he looked upon frankly as so much dirt.

A feud instantly sprang up in the new position between a
Company Commander and himself (a company-commander
under the Derby Scheme—*justes cieux*!).[2] It was to do with the
site he had decided upon for the operations of his Flying Pigs.
Secretly Polderdick obtained a written order from Brigade Headquarters to say that "Captain H. H. Polderdick has permission to
dispose his 9.45 Battery wherever he considers it will be most
useful." That morning he set about the installation of his guns
in the position in the trench to which the Company-Commander
particularly objected. A sergeant hurried up to say respectfully
that "Captain Nixon had given strict orders that Trench Mortar
Battery was not to use that spot," Polderdick came up and drove
off the sergeant. Then Captain Nixon, cold leisureliness of an
officer and gentleman, arrived. "Burney" Polderdick stuck the
written order under his nose. With the usual "Ha! *Ha!*" he
followed up with the regulation lunge towards the belly with
his circling stick. Nixon concertinaed, avoiding the exultant prod.

"Ha! *Ha!* my lad! Pass on!"

Nixon passed on hurriedly, going for help. But now Polderdick's
enemies gathered against him.

An unfortunate thing occurred in the rear, at his billet. His
landlady, or rest-billet-lady, became restless and anxious. On
one of those mornings when he woke up very much his new self,
Polderdick asked her to come up to his room. When he had got
her there, he locked the door behind them, and taking up his
stick, twirling it, stamping his foot, he began prodding her in the
stomach, with delighted "Ha! *Ha's!*"—The woman escaped and

[2] Lord Derby (1865–1948) was British war secretary from 1916 to 1918,
as well as subsequently. He was an advocate of conscription and this may
account for the coupling of his name here with a career officer's contempt
for the new breed of citizen's-army company commander.

complained to the A.P.M.[3] She refused any longer to billet him. The crowning peculiarity of this ex-sergeant was that he very rarely drank anything more than lime juice. A vine seemed to grow within his skull. No one would have believed that he was not intoxicated when, issuing from the Mess one dark night, and finding a Sunbeam not far from the door of the billet, he sprang in and expected it to go. Some A.S.C.[4] men loitering there, who knew him, got behind and pushed it. When it was in the middle of the road, they peered round at him, and in the voice of Harry Tate's Eton-collared assistant,[5] whined and bawled "It will not *go*, Pa-paa! There is something wrong, Pa-pa! It will not go, Pa-paa!" He sat there snorting fiercely. It was the owner of the car, just then arriving, who refused to believe that he was not tight. He disarmed and confused this official by a deft stroke with his stick (which never left him) just below the region of the wind. But his guns, although in position, and firmly cemented by written authority, were not so secure as they seemed. The infantry gathered for the attack. On a fine afternoon, when, in fact, Polderdick was on the point of exclaiming "Ha! *Ha!* an excellent opportunity for Trench Mortars!" a suave, hirsute and old Colonel arrived on the scene, and made straight for the Flying Pigs. Polderdick, with a dramatic leap, intercepted him, stick in hand, twirling and feinting. He appeared to take it for granted that this interloper had designs upon his fat little ordnance.

"Are these your guns?" The intercepted Colonel fixed him severely with his veteran eye, that noted the Ranker's ribbons, and sought to quell the life-long "common soldier" beneath the new Sam Browne. Polderdick, on his side, saw nothing but a Lieut.-Colonel in this hostile person.

"Yes. Yes.—Yes. My guns. My pigs. My little pigs, sir."

"I don't think that is a very good position for them."

"No? No!"

"You must see that dug-out——"

"I see the dug-out. I've had my eye on it from the first. And if you know of a better hole, sir—well, you know what to do!"

[3] Assistant Provost-Marshal.
[4] Army Service Corps.
[5] Harry Tate (1873–1940) was a music-hall entertainer. Part of his act was a display of long-suffering patience in the face of his "assistant's" exasperating behaviour, followed eventually by an eruption of wrath.

"Yes, but that dug-out——"

"Yes sir, that dug-out.—But you can't attack Fritz with a dug-out, sir. You fire nothing out of a dug-out, sir. You might fire Captain Nixon a hundred yards or so, with a big charge. But I'm accredited to these 9.45's, these 'flying pigs' as they call them. I have no order, sir, as regards Captain Nixon——"

"Stop this tom-foolery please. Your guns are in the way where you have placed them. And they are not well-placed either——"

"I beg your pardon, sir?" Polderdick grew suddenly one harsh blotch of red, as though he had been slapped. "Are you aware to whom you are speaking?" He drew himself up, and flung his chest out, the mad-soldier entering into him again for a moment, following this direct affront to his professional pride. His voice too got its wild and shouting note. "Do you know my name, sir? Captain Polderdick is my name, Polderdick. 'Burney' Polderdick."

He continued to glare at the Colonel for a moment; but his eye gradually filled with the peculiar light of the transformed "Burney," though more wild even yet than usual.

"I am the King of the Trenches!" he shouted. "Didn't you know who I was? Yes! I am Burney Polderdick, the King of the Trenches!—Ha! *Ha!*" He flourished his stick, twirled it lightly, lunged forward, and dug the Colonel in the middle of the stomach.

"Ha! *Ha!* The King of the Trenches!" he shouted in triumph, as the Colonel hastened away, his fingers convulsively grasping his stick, not venturing to give further utterance to his thoughts.

That afternoon Polderdick decided it was "an excellent afternoon for trench mortars," and inaugurated this phase of his reign by a few unexpected salvoes. But the divisional commander in this new section was not the man for him. He took a disobliging view of the events reported to him.

Polderdick a few days after this was removed from his command. He was sent back to the Training Depot in England.

"I think, yes, we will have a bottle of wine!"

Burney Polderdick's last lunch with his subalterns was enlivened by this sudden decision. A bottle of Ordinary Wine was obtained. Menzies, who was Mess-secretary, was curious to see if "Burney" would pay for it. He supposed that he would not. But at the last moment the now exiled King of the terrible narrow Kingdom his madness had caused him to be expelled from, that he would probably now never see again, fumbled in his pocket and produced the necessary ninepence. He had evidently meant to pay all along.

When the twirling stick receded, and passed the bend in the smashed and dilapidated street, although still, like a perfume, he could faintly hear the whistling of *Won't you buy my sweet lavender-er-er*, Menzies returned to the Mess with a regret at this personal loss.

SECTION III

Chocolate-Cream Traps
and Rustic Fools

Sectional Introduction

The first two stories in this section have a similar wartime setting
—training camps or military billets—with subsequent transfers
to widely-separated fronts. "I am writing a story for an American
paper," Lewis wrote to his mother from Roffey Camp, Horsham,
in about August, 1916. "All dull dogs," was how he described his
soldier companions,[1] just as Cantleman in "Cantleman's Spring-
Mate" found that "it had seemed impossible that there were any
duller men than those in the mess of this particular battalion."
As Lewis told his mother, Ezra Pound was placing the new story
and it seems indeed to have been "Cantleman," which appeared
in *The Little Review* in October, 1917. Pound was foreign editor
of this celebrated pioneer magazine of the modern movement,
which was edited in America by Margaret Anderson. But the
American post office refused to handle the October issue, alleging
that the "Cantleman" story was obscene. Margaret Anderson
appealed but Judge Augustus N. Hand upheld the ban. The
judge found that the young woman Stella and her relations with
Cantleman were described with a wealth of detail that did not
seem necessary for communicating whatever message Lewis
intended, or for telling a story of some artistic value, or for
arousing a praiseworthy emotion. The affair served as a prelude
to the trouble Miss Anderson was to have later with the U.S.
Mail over her printing of James Joyce's *Ulysses*.[2] Pound wrote
to Lewis, by then serving with the Canadian army in France as
a war artist : "You will be grieved to know that *The Little Review*

[1] *Letters*, p. 82.
[2] *Cantleman's Spring-Mate—Cantleman et la Saison des amours* (English–
French bilingual edition), introduced and translated by Bernard Lefourcade.
Paris : M. J. Minard, 1968. Lafourcade's excellent introduction sets out
Judge Hand's evaluation (pp. 12–13) and also notes that Roffey Camp
was situated on Salisbury Plain, "the geographic centre of Hardy's Wessex."

lost its case, despite J. Q.'s (lawyer and art patron John Quinn's) noble defence." Pound quotes Quinn as arguing that "the man who wrote *that* story can *not* be a sensualist."[3] Meanwhile, however, "Cantleman" was reprinted along with a short play called "The Ideal Giant" and "The Code of a Herdsman," the three being privately issued as a slim volume, with a striking Lewis cover design, for the London office of *The Little Review*. The name Cantleman is variously spelled in the two *Little Review* printings. Even in making handwritten corrections to a typescript in the 1920s or 1930s, Lewis used the spelling "Cantelman." But in the actual typed sections and in published print, the spelling by then had definitely become "Cantleman," which is adhered to here.

Also adhered to is the text of "Cantleman" found in the 1967 edition of *Blasting and Bombardiering*. Drawn from a typescript in the possession of Mrs. Wyndham Lewis, this text was somewhat more elaborate in crucial places than either the version printed in *The Little Review* or the slightly different one printed in the booklet edition.

No such problem of texts occurs in the case of "The War Baby" which originally appeared in *Art and Letters*, edited by Herbert Read and Frank Rutter. Lewis had known Rutter before the war when the latter was curator of the Leeds Art Gallery, and he met Read in 1917. Years later, Lewis and Read were to be antagonists, with Read attacked in *The Demon of Progress in the Arts* (1954) as "a Mister Abreast-of-the-Times for Everyman who paints or sculpts." But at this early stage of their careers, they were friends. *Art and Letters* lasted only from 1917 to 1920 and published visual work by Lewis as well as his "War Baby." At the time of the story's appearance in the Winter, 1918–19 issue, Osbert Sitwell was literary editor of *Art and Letters*, which in the same number with "The War Baby" published poems by Ford Madox Hueffer, Richard Aldington, Osbert, Sacheverell and Edith Sitwell, Aldous Huxley and Siegfried Sassoon, and contained reproductions of work by Picasso, Gaudier-Brzeska and Lewis himself. Writing to Read on December 17, 1918, Lewis seems gratified that "The War Baby," with its "Cantleman"-

[3] D. D. Paige, ed., *The Letters of Ezra Pound, 1907–1941*. London: Faber & Faber, 1951, p. 187.

like theme, had encountered no censorship complications in reaching the public.[4]

"Junior," on the other hand, has never reached the public, in any form. It was seemingly due to have appeared in the projected 1950s volume *The Two Captains*. The version used here comes from a carbon typescript in the Lewis archive at Cornell. The references to the fugitive spies Burgess and Maclean help date the story somewhere between 1951 and the 1956 appearance of "Pish-Tush" in *Encounter*. This latter work too was to have been included in *The Two Captains*. In all, *Encounter*, with its Anglo-American dual editorship, published two stories by Lewis. "Here, in England, there is a chronic absence of [magazines]," he wrote in a December, 1954, letter. "A short-story, when written, remains in my drawer —except for *Encounter*, which is half American."[5] The idea for "Pish-Tush" came from a chance anecdote told about her London neighbourhood by a woman friend of the Lewises, an indication of how the writer—almost to the end of his days—remained constantly alert to all forms of news about the world which, by late in his life, lay beyond his visual ken.

[4] Lewis, *Letters*, p. 102.
[5] *Letters*, p. 558.

Cantleman's Spring-Mate[1]

(First published in *The Little Review*, London, October, 1917. This version
based on text in the Calder and Boyars edition of *Blasting and Bombardiering*)

Cantleman walked in the strenuous fields, steam rising from
them as though from an exertion, dissecting the daisies specked
in the small wood, the primroses on the banks, the marshy lakes,
and all God's creatures. The heat of a heavy premature Summer
was cooking the little narrow belt of earth-air, causing everything innocently to burst its skins, bask abjectly and profoundly.
Everything was enchanted with itself, and with everything else.
The horse considered the mares immensely appetizing masses of
quivering shiny flesh; was there not something of "je ne sais quoi"
about a mare, that no other beast's better half possessed? The
birds with their little gnarled feet, and beaks made for fishing
worms out of the mould, or the river, would have considered
Shelley's references to the skylark—or any other poet's paeans to
their species—as lamentably inadequate to describe the beauty
of birds! The female bird, for her particular part, reflected that,
in spite of the ineptitude of her sweetheart's latest song, which
he insisted on deafening her with, never seemed to tire of, and
was so persuaded that she liked as much as he did himself, and
although outwardly she remained critical and vicious: that all
the same and nevertheless, chock, chock, peep, peep, he was a
fluffy object from which certain satisfaction could be derived!
And both the male and the female reflected together as they
stood a foot or so apart looking at each other with one eye, and
at the landscape with the other, that of all nourishment the
red earth-worm was the juiciest and sweetest! The sow, as she
watched her hog, with his splenetic energy, and guttural articu-

[1] The story title appears in the 1967 *Blasting and Bombardiering* as
"Cantleman's Spring-mate" in one instance.

lation, a sound between content and complaint, not noticing the untidy habits of both of them, gave a sharp grunt of sex-hunger, and jerked rapidly towards Him. The only jarring note in this vast mutual admiration society was the fact that many of its members showed their fondness for their neighbour in an embarrassing way : that is they killed and ate them. But the weaker were so used to dying violent deaths and being eaten that they worried very little about it.—The West was gushing up a harmless volcano of fire, obviously intended as an immense dreamy nightcap.

Cantleman in the midst of his cogitation on surrounding life, surprised his faithless and unfriendly brain in the act of turning over an object which humiliated his meditation. He found that he was wondering whether at his return through the village lying between him and the Camp, he would see the girl he had passed there three hours before. At that time he had not begun his philosophizing, and without interference from conscience, he had noticed the redness of her cheeks, the animal fulness of the child-bearing hips, with an eye as innocent as the bird or the beast. He laughed without shame or pleasure, lit his pipe and turned back towards the village.—His fieldboots were covered with dust : his head was wet with perspiration and he carried his cap, in an unmilitary fashion, in his hand. In a week he was leaving for the Front, for the first time. So his thoughts and sensations all had, as a philosophic background, the prospect of death. The infantry, and his commission, implied death or mutilation unless he were very lucky. He had not a high opinion of his luck. He was pretty miserable at the thought, in a deliberate, unemotional way. But as he realized this he again laughed, a similar sound to that that the girl had caused.—For what was he unhappy about? He wanted to remain amongst his fellow insects and beasts, which were so beautiful, did he then : Well well! On the other hand, who was it that told him to do anything else? After all, supposing the values they attached to each other of "beautiful," "interesting," "divine," were unjustified in many cases on cooler observation;— nevertheless birds were more beautiful than pigs : and if pigs were absurd and ugly, rather than handsome, and possibly chivalrous, as they imagine themselves; then equally the odour of the violet was pleasant, and there was nothing offensive about most trees. The newspapers were the things that stank most on earth, and human beings anywhere were the most ugly and offensive of the brutes because of the confusion caused by their consciousness. Had it not been for that unmaterial gift that some bungling or wild hand had bestowed, our sisters and brothers would be no worse than dogs and sheep. That they could not reconcile their little meagre streams of sublimity with the needs of animal life should not be railed at. Well then, should not the sad amalgam, all it did, all it willed, all it demanded, be thrown over, for the fake and confusion that it was, and should not such as possessed a greater quantity of that wine of reason, retire, metaphorically, to the wilderness, and sit forever in a formal and gentle elation, refusing to be disturbed?—Should such allow himself to be disturbed by the quarrels of Jews, the desperate perplexities, resulting in desperate dice throws, of politicians, the crack-jaw and unreasoning tumult?

On the other hand, Cantleman had a more human, as well as a little more divine understanding, than those usually on his left and right, and he had had, not so long ago, conspicuous hopes that such a conjecture might produce a new human chemistry. But he must repudiate the human entirely, if that there were to be brought off. His present occupation, the trampling boots upon his feet, the belt that crossed his back and breast was his sacrifice, his compliment to the animal.

He then began dissecting his laugh, comparing it to the pig's grunt and the bird's cough. He laughed again several times in order to listen to it.

At the village he met the girl, this time with a second girl. He stared at her "in such a funny way" that she laughed. He once more laughed the same sound as before, and bid her good evening. She immediately became civil. Enquiries about the village, and the best way back to the camp across the marsh, put in as nimble and at the same time rustic a form as he could contrive, lay the first tentative brick of what might become the dwelling of a friend, a sweetheart, a ghost, anything in the absurd world! He asked her to come and show him a short cut she had indicated.

"I couldn't. My mother's waiting for *me!*" In a rush of expostulation and semi-affected alarm. However, she concluded in a minute or two, that she could.

79

He wished that she had been some Anne Garland, the lady whose lips were always flying open like a door with a defective latch. He had made Anne's acquaintance under distressing circumstances.

On his arrival at Gideon Brook, the mighty brand-new camp on the edge of the marsh, he found that his colleague in charge of the advance party had got him a bed-space in a room with four officers of another regiment. It had seemed impossible that there were any duller men than those in the mess of his particular battalion : but it was a dullness he had become accustomed to.

He saw his four new companions with a sinking of the heart, and steady gnawing anger at such concentrations of furious foolishness.

Cantleman did not know their names, and he disliked them in order as follows :

A. he hated because he found him a sturdy shortish young man with a bull-like stoop and energetic rush in his walk, with flat feet spread out to left and right, and slightly bowed legs. This physique was enhanced by his leggings : and not improved, though hidden, in his slacks. He had a swarthy and vivacious face, with a sort of cunning, and insolence painted on it. His cheeks had a broad carmine flush on general sallowness. The mind painted on this face for the perusal of whoever had the art of such lettering, was as vulgar stuff, in Cantleman's judgement, as could be found. To see this face constantly was like *hearing* perpetually a cheap and foolish music.

B. he disliked, because, being lean and fresh-coloured, with glasses, he stank, to Cantleman's nose, of Jack London, Summer Numbers magazines, bad flabby Suburban Tennis, flabby clerkship in inert, though still prosperous, city offices. He brought a demoralizing dullness into the room with him, with a brisk punctiliousness, several inches higher from the ground than A.

C. he resented for the sullen stupidity with which he moved about, the fat having settled at the bottom of his cheeks, and pulled the corners of his mouth down, from sheer stagnation. His accent dragged the listener through the larger slums of Scotland, harrowing him with the bestial cheerfulness of morose religion and poverty. The man was certainly, from every point of view, education, character, intelligence, far less suited to hold

80

a commission than most privates in his platoon.—Alas that the stock of gentlemen, even, was so limited.

D. reproduced the characteristics of the other three, in different quantities : his only personal contribution being a senile sing-song voice from the North, and a blond beam, or partially toothless grin, for a face.

When ten days before, Cantleman had been dropped into their midst, they had all looked up, (for it was always all, they having the inseparability of their kind), with friendly welcome, as brother officers should. He avoided their eyes, and sat amongst them for a few days, reading *The Trumpet-Major*, belonging to B. He had even seemed to snatch Hardy away, as though B. had no business to possess such books. Then they avoided his eyes as though an animal disguised as an officer and gentleman had got into their room for whom, therein, *The Trumpet-Major* and nothing else exercised fascination. He came among them suddenly, and not appearing to see them, settled down into a morbid intercourse with a romantic abstraction. The Trumpet-Major, it is true, was a soldier, that is why he was there. But he was an imaginary one, and imbedded in the passionate affairs of the village of a mock-county, and distant time. Cantleman bit the flesh at the side of his thumb, as he surveyed the Yeomanry Cavalry revelling in the absent farmer's house, and the infantile Farnese Hercules, with the boastfulness of the Red, explaining to his military companions the condescensions of his infatuation. Anne Garland stood in the moonlight, and Loveday hesitated to reveal his rival, weighing a rough chivalry against self interest.

Cantleman eventually decamped with *The Trumpet-Major*, taking him across to Havre, and B. never saw his book again. Cantleman had also tried to take a book away from A. (a book incompatible with A.'s vulgar physique). But A. had snatched it back, and mounted guard surlily and cunningly over it.

In his present rustic encounter, then, he was influenced in his feelings towards the first shepherdess by memories of Wessex heroines, and the something more that being the daughter of a landscape painter would give. Anne, imbued with the delicacy of the Mill, filled his mind to the injury of this crude marsh-plant. But he had his programme. Since he was forced back, by his logic and body, among the madness of natural things, he would live up to his part.

The young woman had, or had given herself, the unlikely name of Stella. In the narrow road where they got away from the village, Cantleman put his arm round Stella's waist and immediately experienced all the sensations that he had been divining in the creatures around him : the horse, the bird, the pig. The way in which Stella's hips stood out, the solid blood-heated expanse on which his hand lay, had the amplitude and flatness of a mare. Her lips had at once no practical significance, but only the aesthetic blandishments of a bull-like flower. With the gesture of a fabulous Faust he drew her against him, and kissed her with a crafty gentleness.

Cantleman turned up that evening in his quarters in a state of baffling good-humour. He took up *The Trumpet-Major* and was soon surrounded by the breathing and scratching of his room-mates, reading and writing. He chuckled somewhere where Hardy was funny. At this human noise the others fixed their eyes on him in sour alarm. He gave another, this time gratuitous, chuckle. They returned with disgust at his habits, his peculiarity, to what he considered their maid-servant's fiction and correspondence. Oh Christ, what abysms! Oh Christ, what abysms! Cantleman shook noisily in the wicker chair like a dog or a fly-blown old gentleman.

Once more on the following evening he was out in the fields, and once more his thoughts were engaged in recapitulations.— The miraculous camouflage of Nature did not deceive this observer. He saw everywhere the gun-pits and the "nests of death." Each puff of green leaves he knew was in some way as harmful as the burst of a shell. Decay and ruins, it is true, were soon covered up, but there was yet that parallel, and the sight of things smashed and corrupted. In the factory town ten miles away to the right, whose smoke could be seen, life was just as dangerous for the poor, and as uncomfortable, as for the soldier in his trench. The hypocrisy of Nature and the hypocrisy of War were the same. The only safety in life was for the man with the soft job. But that fellow was not conforming to life's conditions. He was life's paid man, and had the mark of the sneak. He was making too much of life, and too much out of it. He, Cantleman, did not want to owe anything to life, or enter into league or under-standing with her. The thing was either to go out of existence : or, failing that, remain in it unreconciled, indifferent to Nature's threat, consorting openly with her enemies, making war within her war upon her servants. In short, the spectacle of the handsome English spring produced nothing but ideas of defiance in Cantleman's mind.

As to Stella, she was a sort of Whizzbang. With a treachery worthy of a Hun, Nature tempted him towards her. He was drugged with delicious appetites. Very well! He would hoist the Unseen Powers with his own petard. He could throw back Stella where she was discharged from (if it were allowable, now, to change her into a bomb) first having relieved himself of this humiliating gnawing and yearning in his blood.

As to Stella, considered as an unconscious agent, all women were contaminated with Nature's hostile power and might be treated as spies or enemies. The only time they could be trusted, or were likely to stand up to Nature and show their teeth, was as mothers. So he approached Stella with as much falsity as he could master.

At their third meeting he brought her a ring. Her melting gratitude was immediately ligotted with long arms, full of the contradictory and offending fire of Spring. On the warm earth consent flowed up into her body from all the veins of the land-scape.

That night he spat out, in gushes of thick delicious rage, all the lust that had gathered in his body. The nightingale sang ceaselessly in the small wood at the top of the field where they lay. He grinned up towards it as he noticed it, and once more turned to the devouring of his mate. He bore down on her as though he wished to mix her body into the soil, and pour his seed into a more methodless matter, the brown phalanges of floury land. As their two bodies shook and melted together, he felt that he was raiding the bowels of Nature : he was proud that he could remain deliberately aloof, and gaze bravely, like a minute insect, up at the immense and melancholy night, with all its mad nightingales, piously folded small brown wings in a million nests, night-working stars, and misty useless watchmen.—They got up at last, she went furtively back to her home : Cantleman on his walk to camp, had a smile of severe satisfaction on his face. It did not occur to him that his action might be supremely unimportant as far as Stella was concerned. He had not even asked himself if, had he not been there that night, someone else might have been there in his place. He was also convinced that the laurels were his, and that Nature had come off badly.—He was still convinced of this when he received six weeks afterwards in France, a long appeal from Stella, telling him that she was going to have a child. She received no answer to that or any subsequent letter. Cantleman received [them] with great regularity in the trenches, and read them all through from beginning to end, without comment of any sort.—And when he beat a German's brains out it was with the same impartial malignity that he had displayed in the English night with his Spring-mate. Only he considered there too that he was in some way outwitting Nature, and had no adequate realization of the extent to which evidently the death of a Hun was to the advantage of the world.[2]

[2] The two other versions of this story read at the end "to the advantage of the animal world."

The War Baby

(First published in *Art and Letters*, London, Winter, 1918. Reprinted 1967 in the Calder and Boyars edition of *Blasting and Bombardiering*)

The West Berks Hotel dominated a Military Avenue. Fifty yards from its door was the Guard Room of the Flying Corps. A boy sentry marched up and down its twenty yards of covered porch. When an officer passed, he faced the front with a series of stamps, stepped forward, and slapped the pistol holster at his side. At the conclusion of this rumpus, at which he did not look, the Officer would raise his hand languidly in front of his right eye. The boy sentry then stamped loudly as though in anger, and walked fiercely up and down for several minutes as though to work off his discontent. He then stood at ease and waited for the next Officer, when the same scene was repeated.

The Hall of the West Berks Hotel was like a theatrical store. It contained a variety of military properties. There were airmen's leather helmets, perpendicular Russian infantry caps, swords of all sorts, airy khaki forage caps. The Russian army air students were as proportionately more picturesque than their slogging earth comrades as our airmen are more picturesque than more venerable corps. But with the Russians it was veritably a plumage. Long cavalry swords and scimitars hung from pegs by slender slings in gorgeous braid and bead work, with dazzling and sinuous silver tassels. There were Circassian dirks, with jewels about the handles. The gay medals, of course, were not in the hall, but hanging all over the breasts of the heroes.

Hurried bursts of expostulatory buzzing came from behind some curtains, where a lounge was, a language that was like a new situation to unfamiliar ears. Impetuous or dilatory forms left now the door leading to the dining-room, now the curtains, and took vociferously or softly the road to the Bar, the bedrooms or the smoking-room. At the back of the hall was a large office, in the middle of which sat a sulkily handsome elderly flapper of twenty-four summers. A mass of dark juiceless hair hung pompously over her eyes. She was swarthy, sophisticated and robust; sat like a big delicate watch-dog in her illuminated dug-out in the body of the Hotel. Whenever the front door opened she shot a black glance of inquiry in the hall; sometimes rang a bell. At present she had two glances, though; the dark one, and a soft variety like a furtive cuddle, which she cast a yard to the right and some fifteen yards nearer than the door, at a long stout figure lounging at the window of her room. A subaltern remained leaning on a ledger, his round head stuck well inside the Hotel office, his spurred field boots at an angle of 30° with the vertical without. He was quietly sniffing the fragrance that her handkerchief and person filled the office with, and conversing on topics likely to fan the second of the two glances. His eyes ran steadily and blandly over her figure, returning from its round, that is from her ankles up to her face again, almost always in time to absorb her recurring glance, burning lighthouse-like, its regulation moment. Their conversation picked its way more or less among the visitors' accounts which she was checking.

"I can do figures with anybody now," she said. "It's funny, because when I was at school I was always bottom of the class. I was very bad at arithmetic."

She breathed little airy numerals all over an immense page, and then gathered them up in aggregates with attentive eye, registering the result at the bottom of the column.

"I think your mathematical accomplishment is wonderful," the artillery subaltern said, looking at the centre of her loose high-waisted skirt at the back, trying to disinter the Kirchner beneath it: especially one Kirchner pinned to the wall in his room, a concession to the military life, not a diagnostic of the commonness of his mind.

"I wish I could play with figures like that." With hopeless intensity he gazed at her figure, the incommensurable feminine chiffre, which also he considered it desirable to master.

But despite her tardily acquired skill, she got into difficulties, seemingly, at the bottom of each page, until at last she was about a couple of pounds out. She hunted back through the columns for the slip or slips.

86

"What margin of error do they allow you?" her admirer asked, delicately, lisping a little.

"Oh! nothing, none. We are supposed to get it——"

"You just stick it on to somebody else's bill?"

"Yes!"

The young man wondered if he might take it as a hopeful sign that the little airy figures for once had bested her: or whether the old arithmetical incompetence really still lingered on in the prestigious accountant.

A woman's occupation was important in deciding her quality as a sweetheart. These millions of little blue figures that she dwelt among were, he decided, quite wholesome; an abstract and inoffensive sort of gnat. They, after all, had only attacked her comparatively late in life.

"Oh! I've got Major Kirkpatrick's bill wrong! D'you know, I'm terrified of that man!"

"It's his name I expect."

"Yes, that's it, I expect!"

A small man with a hairy, deeply fresh-complexioned, spectacled face came into the front door and drifted quickly across the hall, then towards the drawing-room, taking his coat off as he went. He wore an infantry coat, but artillery cap badge. This was probably in order to have red edges to his shoulder straps in addition to his two gold stars. Richard Beresin—the figure adhering to the ledge of the office—knew him, through having seen him at the hut where he worked with regard to a batch of men in his battery down with measles. He had a permanent job at Paynes.

"I hate that man," the young lady had followed him with a surly eye. "I hate that family. I don't know why."

"It's his mother, isn't it: and his wife?"

"No, it's his mother and sister. They seem to think that we have nothing to do but run after them. I'll tell you how, for instance. All their letters come here together to the office in the morning. The sister will come down and ask for the letters. She'll say, 'Oh, these are my brother's—keep them for him.' She'll put them down and take her own away. The mother does the same. And the mother won't take her daughter's letters either! It's so silly. Why can't they take all their letters together? They're one family. Oh, I don't know. I hate people like that. Then they go to the front door with him at night and see him off. 'Good night, my *darling* boy,' for fear he should go to the *left* when he ought to go to the right! You'll see: here they are! No, it's my *darling* this, and my *darling* that. I'm sure he does not like it. Could a man?"

"I don't know."

"Oh, but that's *different*."

The mistress of the Bar came into the office and sat down, saying "Swish!"

Her elderly figure was emphasized by a slack silk jersey. She stared with an energetic smile at the subaltern.

"Perhaps I am *de trop*?"

"Don't be silly," her colleague said.

"Of course I know I am not young and *attractive*." She drawled the last word. The watcher at the window was surprised at the strength of her voice.

"She is always saying that! Why are you always saying that?" the other lady asked her.

The Bar lady looked down, and affectedly picked at her dress.

"Why do you part your hair in the middle?" the subaltern asked.

"Because it's straight : like yours."

It was black and straight, and he saw the resemblance too. Also he thought she looked rather like him in other ways. Her good-natured aggressiveness, her straight mouth, the dark creases under the eyes, were points of resemblance. He did not say this, however, because he thought that the younger woman would then also see it, and that he would not benefit by this comparison.

He had been leaning there for an hour and ten minutes, he found, on pulling his sleeve back. It was twenty past ten. Gathering himself up, he walked with the least unsteadiness—a few glasses of whisky taking advantage of his stiffness—towards his hat, cane and coat. Over his shoulder, as he left, he said "Tra-la-la!" He went upstairs to the left.

Ten minutes later he was standing in a slack attitude, a long white bulk in front of a large glass, stroking his sides and thighs, and wondering whether to immerse himself across the passage, or roll his hot, unclothed body in the sheets and cool gradually into sleep.

Next day Richard Beresin considered whether he could afford to remain at the West Berks. He found that he could not. Yet he wanted to live out of camp. The Mess was bad. A passion for civilian ease grew in him daily. Three months previously he had left hospital and was at the most boring period of the training of a new battery.

Beresin was the son of a well-to-do city merchant, and had only left Haileybury one year before the outbreak of war. His father had sent him to Paris to learn the French language. The public-school idea, its tenacious middle-class snobberies, had held him with a poor slouch and drawl for some months. Then he had grown Parisian, but kept the Anglo-Saxon prerogatives of gait and manner somewhat for the prestige they had among his French companions. In England, after six months on a holiday, he was very parlez-vous. On the other hand with the Frenchman he was a little bleak, dumb and ironical.

In the midst of a captivating and increasingly careless life, in which he had begun to cut a figure, begun to sleek himself in front of the mirror of his fellows, discover with a nimble science the resources of his civilized spots, particular physique, the war harshly and suddenly burst on him. It received a mixed welcome at his hands. He saw at once that it was no friend of his. Patron of some, bloody Father Christmas to many a Spartan child, bringing hundreds of little lead soldiers to drill and damage, toy guns and sabretaches, it was bringing him nothing, with good instinct he felt, as he first saw it. Certain things were expected of him, he was in the home of noisy Gallic nationalism—although it was, in other moods, the home of his dream of cheap elegances and pleasures. He became a soldier early in the war. Paris soon grew distant, and he looked towards it even with a grudge and a grimace. France became the "France" of the sentimental soldier song, with its inseparable sententious "somewhere," the romance country of death and naïf steadfastness. France with all its pageant of history was less important than this intense localized France of four years, of the English imagination, with its belts of graves and trenches; this narrow gash of a France, five-miles-deep incredible landscape developing an ephemeral species. To belong to this male, elect, death-facing genus he accepted dourly as a consolation for his vision of desirable life foregone. He took all that on, as he had affected Paris. But he wasn't so sure a man and his reactions became of a more original type, more experimental. His struggle with this endless adventure that did not suit set him spinning sometimes rather wildly. Meantime the years went on, and he was young enough to thrive, although thwartly, on his new destiny. In this idle, hectic existence he made the most of his short past, and developed its more flattering veins. He became a little literary—snubbed, in a schoolboy way, with an impermeable contempt, his fellows with less fortunate histories. He wore a bracelet, read Huysmans in his dug-out, wore mufti whenever opportunity offered, acquired a settled consciousness of the aristocratic idea. He began to visualize himself as a young blood—he sought in his ancestry for the bluest seeming streams, courted imaginary ghosts. His Nietzschean illusion almost broke the heart of his subservient soldier-servant. The leather of riding-breeches pipeclayed, buttons burnished, no spot on boot or belt neglected, ever, in the line, even—during pulling out or pulling in, weeks of battles, even, when all stores were lost in a retreat? He was liked all the better for that. He was a gentleman. Both he and his soldier-servant saw the same popular image of a perfection.

But war grew more and more a sinister phantom. The death-line was always there, crackling, thumping away. He could not take his aristocratic ideal to his bosom, and luxuriate with it, so near to a harsh extinction.

Enteric took him to hospital for some time, however; now he was experiencing a tantalizing lease of leisure. So extravagant were his tastes that it had its stoppages and drags.

Beresin had fixed nicely his sense of what dwelling he should choose : how comfortable, spacious, and above all, not disgustingly suburban! South fronting (gaya scienza, of course) with mulberry bushes, laurels, and one rose if possible.

The village of Paynes had had its camp for a long time. A dismal barrack look pervaded it. Beresin knocked at last at the door of a decent, but very, very mediocre house, whose rooms, he was sure, contained nothing colossal or comfortable. It was the best that presented itself. The landlady appeared a precarious creature. She was almost certainly never warmed by the sun. All the windows were at the front, which faced north. He made many arrangements, inquired about this and that : then surprised her by saying he "would come back when he had considered what she had told him." What had she told him? She did not know! She stared at his back with fear.

He left too bored to continue further, and put off his search until the following day.

At the Hotel his groom was waiting for him. It was a question of leave for this soldier necessitated a walk down to the Battery office. Back from that, three-quarters of an hour separated him from dinner. Stripping, the evening process to which he had accustomed his orderly began. Two bath-mats, a bristling loofah, a jug of scented and tepid water arranged by Misrow, awaited this young, apolaustic patrician of theory. The orderly was a sleepy-looking boy with a face like an artist. He wore a truss, grumbled at military duties. Beresin lay stomach down, his white fat springing into luminous strawberry pink beneath the massage. Misrow used to grooming horses, as he got to the back of his master's thighs his free hand seized the leg behind the knee from instinct.

"What are you up to, Misrow? Are you afraid I shall kick?" Misrow had tickled his master.

"No, sir." Misrow smiled his quatro-cento smile, and sleep seemed to be pumped out of his eyelids, like a stagnant mist, having the effect of a barber's spray, but redolent of delicate demarcated life. Beresin rolled over. The front of his body was a series of close drifts of dark hair, with a wide central vein of dull verdure. Terminating this hairy column, raised on the best thing about him, a rather rigid and disciplined neck, his round, closely-knit head was exquisite, harsh and stone-like, reminding you of a snake's sling-like extremity. The muscles gathered up beneath the skin as he moved, like the hundred parts of a child's block puzzle coming together by cinematographic magic. He scratched his close-cropped head, slowly hissed a rag between small opaque teeth. Particularly unaffected by experimental disquiet of the senses, he yet enjoyed the rather anomalous figure of Misrow. It was incumbent on him to live up to the Nietzschean, the Greek, picture, have this what might be decadent panel occur

91

somewhere in the series of his day's tableaux. Excuses had to be found, with subtleties to explain the rather degrading scene where we first have seen him figuring.

That night at dinner Beresin's crowing laugh reached to every corner of the extensive room. It darted like an insolent mask among the voices and sounds of all the other diners. Everyone objected to it except the Russians, who objected to nothing that wasn't Russian : several people administered the glance of annoyance. This caused him a real satisfaction. He had the mania of shocking, the love of facile challenges. Let the aristocratically-minded display at least, by a suitable arrogance, by a flouting of the bourgeois hush, that a master was present. Let no human apprehension within reach enjoy its meal until it had bitterly noted, scowled, paid its tribute.

"Richard! Richard! your howl freezes my nerves," his companion said, not so seasoned in the insolent life as he.

"I like laughing like that. D'you know, I always feel a better man when I laugh. If I didn't laugh for a fortnight, I believe I should grow so inhuman and wicked that I should be—a criminal without a crime!"

He brought this out with eager surprise, overlapped by a doubtful and critical moment. However, it was only Nicky. When Beresin wrote, it was always on the model of pen, pencil, and poison. Charlie Peace was of course in the first rank of his heroes. The Brides in the Bath, in those sinister houses especially designed by the Great Architect of the Universe to entrap the innocently cunning, was a case he much liked discussing. Crime—as an artist he appreciated crime! For those above the law the only mates within it are those who break the law in the grip of some beautiful folly! Madness alone may mate privilege; but it must be an evil (or a pretty) madness. The saint breaks out at the opposite end, loaded with more villainous chains than any central drudge. Wilde, the philosopher of the English dandy and fashionable frigid oligarch, the flower of West European democratic life, he liked better but respected less than Nietzsche. Beresin, after all, was *not* a Prussian! He had a far cunninger brand of Junker than any Nietzsche knew on which to model himself.

Now, as regards his connection with Nicky, it is necessary to say that Beresin was not a broadly comic "aristocrat" : that is, his discourse did not divulge with a farcical grossness the hobby of his mind. You might converse with him for half an hour and not suspect him, unless you were very acute, of being an aristocrat in any way. He had good sense : bonhomie, disastrous quality for his dreams, complicated his romantic humours. On this occasion he gave Nicky, as it happened, a brief lecture, designed to improve him; to free him, as it were.

"Besides, I like getting amongst these beggars with my laugh. I made that man at the next table there purple with anger. He's getting red again now : that's because he's listening to what I'm saying! It's so stupid of him to listen! You see, Nick, here you have a lot of glum-looking cattle. You want to stir them up : show the whole mob what you think of them! If they don't like what they hear, well, Nicky, they can do the other thing! If that gentleman there wants to know what I think of his unprepossessing countenance, why shouldn't he, bless him ?"

The gentleman at the neighbouring table was prodding his wife with apoplectic sentences, to avoid listening to Beresin. A rupture would hardly arrive from him, although red. Nicky grinned. He had had his first definite lesson in the school-boy creed, and had grasped the cunning truth behind Beresin's simple exposition. This truth consisted in the perception of the impunity of the bold : of how much fun and swank could be compassed without so much as a black eye! Who would not be a "blood" on these terms, indeed, who not?—the eager, rather vain but cautious soul of Nicky considered! Beresin imparted this with the glee of life's unfortunately wasted morning, as some new-found infallible "tweek." Beresin had not found out these things for himself, either. A real live prancing young noble of his acquaintance had initiated him into the fine subtleties and sub-limities—so cheap as really to be within the reach of the poorest —of insolence and disregard. However humble a gentleman, you need not even be able to pass for that, once you have the trick, there will always be at least a million unenlightened souls on whom to practise. You know: they don't: an accident. Therefore you have the trickster's glee, you satisfy your eternal mood —which would be exactly theirs had they the tip, not you— and your hilarity. Is it ever necessary, Nicky might heedfully have inquired, to pay with violence on your body, or with money ?

Yes, his noble mentor would have been compelled veraciously to reply. For instance : you have to maintain a certain style : your tips to commissionaires, to servants and so on have to partake of that redundant quality that must characterize you. In everything you are really checkmated. That must be borne in mind. You *need* the anger of the shopkeeper as much as the opinion, or imagination, of the commissionaire. It is because you are fundamentally like, as like as two peas to, your less informed, less polished brother, that you have need of him. You need to be seen by him, to keep close to or far from him. You are always a pea disguising itself from a million other peas. The other peas all know you are a pea, and love to think of a pea like themselves being a soft, subtle, clever, insolent pea! But your identity is precarious. Yes, you must be lavish; otherwise—you will receive that deadly look that one pea gives another when pretence is laid aside. You must furthermore be careful never to touch, mingle with or attack anything before first convincing yourself that it be, in fact, *a pea*. Do not be so fatuous as to interfere with a melon! It might not result in harm, but it is no fun!The whole game is constructed, all its rules made, for bodies roughly speaking, identical in volume and potentialities.

This is taking the lesson farther than Beresin would have done, and to a conclusion, or by means, too unflattering, perhaps to have furthered his end—in the event of so much instruction being considered desirable for Nicky. But had you said to Beresin with sufficient authority and the credentials of a newer or more ancient time, that all political philosophies were for the herd, one herd or another, big or little; that a man who was indeed fastidious, or superior, was not so liable to think of himself as an "aristocrat," whether he were or not, you would soon have reversed his discipleship. He would have been a ready apostate to the romance of the junker. For all he required was an illustrious segregation, a superiority. He would imitate any figure that would satisfy the natural vanity of a young animal with an acute sense of its personal life, without worrying much about the details of your argument.

Having developed the correct atmosphere of hostility in the surrounding hotel guests, he naturally paid no further attention to them.

"I have been looking for fresh quarters."

"Oh! Why! Isn't this all right?"

"Well, the food here, as you can judge, is abominable. The expense is appalling. I am on the way to a fresh overdraft."

"You are leaving Miss Brunker?" That was the name of the secretary. Beresin looked towards the hall.

"I spend half my time with my head inside that jolly old window. Snow use! She's the only civilized being here. Well, I have found nothing up till now."

"I should have thought there were plenty of rooms—"

"Ah!" Beresin animated himself, and drawled the word at him with a vigorous, argumentative cunning. "Ah, yes—s! But not the rooms I want. I must, my dear Nicky, have a deep, sunny, *square* room." (He was all for a bit of cubism, was Richard.)

"A deep, elastic bed, that reminds you of the vaulting, the velvet ocean! Spongy blankets, quite new, two inches thick. I like a large mirror on slender supports. I like everything top-heavy! Then a double-basined basalt wash-hand stand."

Nicky's face grinned hospitably for these absurdities. Beresin stopped and looked at him, encouraging his grin to keep going as though to announce that something even better were about to arrive. It arrived at the end of a minute-long repression.

"I must have a girl, too! I have needed a girl now for three weeks. It is a scandal. Just consider: for three weeks I have wanted a woman! But I want a particular kind of woman!"

"Are you as particular about her as you are about the room? And do you want a top-heavy one, by any chance? Because if you do, I know just the thing for you. She is a waitress down in the Flying Corps Mess——"

"No; no. I want none of your air-scullions. I want a woman so shy that she can hardly bear to be looked at. To undress her would be like tearing a shell off a living crab. Her nudity would be so indecent that I should rush out of the room, at first, in horror. She would at the same moment faint on realizing that she was there——"

"I can see you're in a bad way, old chap. Why don't you run up to London for a few days?"

"I haven't got any money. Besides, it is here, in Paynes, that that woman exists."

"Ah, if you know that——"

"If, if——?"

Beresin laughed once more and duly disturbed the diners.

When he was with a friend and crowing, Beresin never approached a woman. He did not go near the office of the hotel on leaving the dining-room. He went and scandalized and deafened the lounge for an hour or more.

Nicky left the camp on the following day. Beresin had grown accustomed to the hotel. But, once more examining the record of his expenditure, he was forced to the conclusion that this tendency must be discouraged.

In the hour between tea and nightfall the sun appeared bitterly and mechanically above the wet landscape, and created a dreary illumination unfavourable to hope. Richard hurried out, struggling inefficiently with inconsequent regrets, disinherited tendencies, all sorts of bleak, jabbering ideas. The unlucky sky, the squalid regularities of the town, his legs' exasperating shapeliness in their lemon puttees, his isolation in this apricot-coloured damp, severe evening; this was *so* unsuccessful a "pocket," if thinking of flying in the air, or barrage of melancholy, if turning to land war for your analogies, that it damped the very recesses of his spirit. He would have to overhaul everything because of it.

It was in Tewksbury Avenue and in a villa named after the god of Paynes that he found his room. Mars Villa did not face the south; it stood shamelessly, squabbly aligned with other villas, as ignorant of its more than relative bestiality as the Hottentot photographed in a row with his scowling kith and kin. But it contained what most of even such houses contain—a woman. And was not a woman what Richard wanted?—boasted that he wanted and would get. Here she was right enough. She was a particular description of woman; he was fortunate to have found her. Her lips at all times in a lurid pout of love, set in a stagnant dream, lay at the opening of the cooing cavities of her contralto physique. She appeared generally in a dull glow of extinct passion, receding from life, or some moment of early eruption, and burning away harmlessly in Mars Villa. Could she be retrospectively amorous? Had she always glowed like this with a kind of empty heat? Had her parents watched very swarthy dying queens, and been familiar with volcanoes? By all means with volcanoes!

Whatever answers might be found to those questions at once presenting themselves along with her like a well-trained suite, Beresin now put himself in a posture of seductive aggression. He had not liked hanging on the counter of the office at the hotel like a string of sausages, nightly. Sex and his dignity—or should you say his imposed character—were at war. He gazed and gazed at Miss Brunker, and was too afraid of his ideas—his boon companions really—to act. Here was something accessible, not encompassed with commerce, in a cheaper dwelling, materializing his boast to Nicky, approved by the fleshly poet within him.

The camel, however, he also has his thoughts. The young lady of Mars Villa thought her thoughts in the discomfort of her cramped female thinking space—merely so full of subterfuges and practical business of sex. She thought her thoughts rather, too, like the crew of a retreating tank, huddled in a vulnerable and by no means swift vessel, as she ascended the stairs, pursued by his blandishments, bombarded by his bark. He barked at her, delightedly and repeatedly. It impressed her very much. "What a funny laugh!" She dreamt of it.

He took the rooms, paid in advance, and left to bring his things round without delay. That night he was scrubbed by Misrow in Mars Villa. He also kissed Titsy when he came in after dinner, she pressed against the wall, her face tastefully averted, her hands clutching his in an evidently not unfriendly spasm.

"Don't! Mr. Beresin! Please! you mustn't kiss me."

Tets' languor welled into his room when she brought his tea. He concluded that his first impression of retrospective smouldering must be due to race: by some accident a clear and unimpeded descent on one spot or town. Everything that she felt had been felt in precisely the same way so often before by her ancestral replicas (same conditions, same chemistries and atmospheres) that its mean point of energy was considerably displaced into a past not properly hers: and also her own combustion was grown

D

97

mechanical and unconvincing. But still she brought with her into the room something like a rich aura of generations of passion. When he kissed her he felt as though he were at play with a fat and sceptical ghost. She blushed in a heavy sudden way, her wet lips expanded and closed, and expanded again on his lips, like some strenuous amœba. If he looked into her eyes they appeared to open and receive him like some extremely remote stranger. Any part he attacked, then, awoke to half life, with gentle and deliberate responsive spasm. He felt that she could lie on his breast for hours or months as naturally as a plum on its stem against a wall, without restlessness. For he still had the sensation of her consuming herself constantly. All that happened when their bodies were pressed against each other was that she appeared burning away rather more quickly.

Meantime, as regards conversation, which they had when he was not playing at the sun, or more local agency of heat, they talked very much as he had talked on the window-ledge of the West Berks office. When she came in at seven o'clock to light the lamp, he would say, "Tet, come and sit on my knee."

Titsy, as she was called, was a diminutive of Lutitia. Tets appeared to Beresin to sum her up.

She would look at him with a smile and slowly shake her head. He displaced himself and put his arms round her waist. She immediately became the plum on the wall, hanging heavily and ripely. The fruit of her breasts, which were large, was like a symbol of her entire flesh, hanging warmly and idly on the wall of her body. When his hand pressed these, her eyes fluttered and grew heavy. They were much more the essential part of her than anything else. And his enterprise was confined to that.

"Why do you kiss me?" she said one evening. "I don't like those French kisses."

"Are those French kisses?"

"Yes."

"I kiss you because I don't believe too much in individuals."

"Go hon!"

"I want to know what you taste like, and I want to keep fat."

"You're quite fat enough."

"Kisses take one back six thousand years. It is a delicious journey."

"Don't be so silly."

"But I promise you——! That's it. Kiss a woman and you become naked at once." His talk of the crab's shell and the swooning nudity had got no farther. "You are running wild once more and light-hearted."

"You do say funny things sometimes."

"Kiss me now; you will find that you are no longer in this room! It takes you much farther back than it does me."

"Are you often taken like that?"

The "finest story in the world" took him no further. The cheap sententious mysticism of the imperial bard recoiled before the deaf reality of this rather psychic, rather Eastern, young lady. So far did the brave Beresin get and there he unaccountably stuck. Just as the jolliest romances are apt to draw up abashed before too naked realities, so presumably his light-hearted lechery had been damped and cowed to its nursery by the contact of a full being. Then came the bolt from the blue of his marching order. He was to leave Paynes camp all at once, and to be hurried with his battery to Pitport, a two hours' journey the other side of London. They were for the East. It was the time when Batteries were rushed out before their scheduled training was complete, and before the final push overseas, they were hurried from spot to spot, saw much of England, the routine displacement retained.

Before leaving he arranged with Tets that they should meet in London if possible on the following Saturday. The next Saturday, turned out, in the event, not to be possible. Beresin had camp orderly officer to do for the week-end of his arrival. The following week they met.

Now the quickened pace, the uprooting process, the quickening of military duties, caused a change in Richard Beresin. He clung to his exquisite habits, burnished his contempt every day and held it coldly up to his fellows with politeness when he considered they had appeared mentally untidy before him. He said his daily prayers to his deities; but even a philosopher should be in some way efficacious. He was going very soon now back to War. How had he spent his spell of leisure? It was not enough of a figure that he had filled this space with to satisfy him. Not conscious of it, the animal things had their way. Why had he not Miss Brunker to his account? His apathy in Mars Villa, following on his emptyhandedness in the Hotel, what compensated for that blank canvas? He became more ostentatiously the jeune seigneur that all spirited youth should be : the natural man within swelled and concentrated itself, on the contrary, in equal measure.

The kettledrums and violins gulped and stuttered, "Come along with me, and have a Jubilee," in the restaurant in which they ate. The members of the orchestra whistled, gave cat-calls and in some instances sat on their instruments and yelled like drunken babies. The chef d'orchestre dominated this disorder with his sharp protruding stomach and nose that never allowed you to see both his small pink-brown eyes at once. After a lawless performance, repeated three times, the band retired to eat.

"Nice place, isn't it?" Beresin said, in the rather exhausted silence that followed.

"Yes," Tets said, "it was nice," her eyes directed at furs and queer female dresses.

He had to make her drink. He looked with leisurely satisfaction at her brown curls, brown eyes, brownish dress, white flower, white teeth, white gloves, and hard, bloodless face. Her beauty was as formal as a playing card, as neat and clean as a fish. Her red lips stuck out in a pulpy abstraction. She drew herself up from time to time free of her stays and sighed. They both guzzled. Bronx and Beaune, the war-wine that appears on tap, brought the right weighty cheer into their hearts.

Their kisses in the taxi on the way to the Alhambra partook of the disordinate character of the orchestra in its last bout. She arrived there in physical disarray, her eyebrows raised, eyes staring, lips in reminiscent uncontrol. She wept with laughter at the Bing Boys. Robey, with his primitive genius, flattered the mood of the evening. She did not deny the Bacchanalia its culmination. As they drove through the black streets afterwards they lay in each other's arms and sealed their unwisdom with the ultimate convulsions of love. The eating up of the pennies and the yards on the taximeter was an intense and palpable symbol of time.

The next morning Beresin found a warm mass beside him in bed, and realized, as he would have done at the presence of a pool of blood or a dead body, that the preceding evening had been marked by a human event. The mass stirred, and a cumbrous bestial scented arm passed round his body. In the middle of a thick primitive gush of hair, he found the lips with their thoughtful pathetic spasm. He looked with curiosity and uneasiness at what he found so near to him.

The corpses of the battlefield had perhaps cheapened flesh? Anyway, realities were infectious; and all women seemed to feel that they should have their luxurious battles, too; only they were playing at dying, and their war was fruitful.

"Willie, do you love me a little bit?"

What should he say? He loved her as much as he loved a luscious meadow full of sheep, or the side of a tall house illuminated by a sunset, or any pleasant sight or sound that he might meet. But that is not what women mean by "do you love me?" He understood that. They mean, "Do you think that perpetual intercourse with me for the rest of your life would be a nice thing?" That was hardly a question to put to a sentimental theorist of nobility, a dealer in hardness. Was the mink to inquire of the panther whether he would always kiss so nicely, while he was giving the mink a preliminary lick before devouring his prey?

However, he answered softly enough, for he was sentimental in more ways than one, although more dangerous in love than in theory!

A woman was for him a conventional figure, and an inferior, to be treated like all other inferiors. When the moment pointed to a display of chivalry she changed at once to a figure of romance, and she became your superior. But social standing again controlled the scope and likelihood of this vacillation. He remembered Nietzsche's useful dissection of "l'homme passionné" and what the world called "passionate"; and that he had said that a fine woman was undoubtedly finer than a fine man, but was *much rarer*! He had chuckled at this big-browed old German fox's finesse.

Had he been an artist, and Corot, he would have attached himself to a series of valleys, and a certain delicate-tinted tree. But his woman, deflected from abstraction by her human admixture, would not have been Corotesque. That is clear.

It will seem, nevertheless, that this young man could not afford, as a Corot could, to disregard the results of his love, and its animal raison d'être. Corot might feel that Corot could not be improved on and display a certain large indifference as to where he scattered his seed; seeing that, however great the care he took, he was a culmination, and not likely to produce another Corot; and equally unlikely to cause women to bring forth Daumiers or Daubignys! Had Beresin reasoned too much, he would probably have been an ardent theorist of a more sifted hygienic stock.

Back in Pitport, he forgot his week-end with Tets in exactly the same spirit that the majority of men forget their dreams. He was imbued with a sense of the speed of events. There was a whirl behind him and there was nowhere time to look steadily at anything. Time had become as material as a taxicab. The battlefield was his destination, wherever he was for the moment. Death was extremely busy and he was in the ten-league queue, pass or not pass. He shifted and shuffled nearer.

He wrote to Tets and arranged meetings. She wrote nice and quite literate letters, with a stereotyped nonchalance of tone.

Two weeks later he felt a desire to exhaust a little more his idyll with Tets. The rawness of his raptures jarred on his memory. He wished to continue if not complete their miniature love. Tets had to be seen.

She came up from Paynes obediently. Her retrospective ardour now appeared, flatteringly, to apply to *him*. He did not have any longer to imagine dying indigo queens. He found her above his expectations as he met her on the platform. He had not had a very distinct negative of her. He approved of his fellow animal, and rapt her into a hectic bluster of cheap music, excessive food, bad drink, purse-proud spectacles, dominated by some small ape, specializing in comic hysteria. With her, he deliberately chose the vulgarer sites and scenes contemptuously, to keep her in her place.

That she should in any way be appearing to share his finer life would have been inappropriate. He liked relegating her a little more than he would, in any event, unconsciously have done, to the places where coarse things prevailed.

For two days they wallowed breathlessly. She appeared perpetually in a sort of mesmerized inattentiveness. She hurried, excited and a little unhappy, along with him, her eyes staring away, clouding, crying, dark rings coming under them. His eye fixed on her person like a small blasting flame, and he did not leave her till the end of the second day, when that illumination had burnt itself down and grown normal. His train left before hers, and he left her crying, sitting like a child sideways on a seat, and shaking.

His equanimity gave way to discomfort as he watched this sight. Had he really been immersing in a harsh, seething brutality what was fundamentally a *child*? Objectively men are so small, and startle each other by pictures of weakness. This last picture, as he left the Tets show for good, remained an emotive key in his mind as regards this last sweetheart.

A fortnight later Beresin sailed for the East. He did not go into action for some time. He was lucky when he did. He was away for eighteen months. Letters from Egypt reached Tets, short notes describing odds and ends of life in war time. Her second letter announced a complication. Tets must expect a child. Slowly growing, henceforth, from a speck, until it became an appreciable human cloud of new being, Beresin was faced with a complex and weird monument to his parting licence. Something had been started that nothing could arrest, in Tets' case, and with him away so far. From what he knew of her, he accepted the girl's indication of him as father. He wrote her what he considered with reason a plain and friendly letter; he enclosed a cheque for ten pounds, which he recommended her to husband.

"I cannot marry you when I get back. But I will keep the child. Write me what money you need."

He saw the figure sitting sideways on the seat and crying. It was to this figure he wrote. That had been a sort of foreshadowing of the child. The moving adult mass in the bed, so much larger and more formidable, had cast up, as a parent does, the little dressed derelict crying on the platform, a temperate atom of everyday life. Tets was small and pathetic. He was patronizing with his larger manifestation (an equivalent of which Tets equally possessed) Tets' smaller physical manifestation.

Beresin derived acute satisfaction from the sight of this diminutive pathos: the small, in fact, in this case, almost synonymous with the Beautiful. So no virtue can be alleged on account of his pity. The letter brought not much consolation to Tets. She divined a very tough self-preservative instinct behind the promises, pity and ten-pound note. She shrank herself up into a child again and wept, although there was no one (except perhaps her more mature and formidable self) to see it. The burning-away process that Beresin had conceived as characteristic of Tets, now set in no longer as the visual preserve of the perspicacious. Everyone near Mars Villa could note her diminishing on the one hand, as she grew on the other. From two sides now, retrospectively and ultrospectively, she guttered away. She was sent to London for the most scandalous stage of her pregnancy.

In Africa Beresin found that he had more than singed himself in contact with the peculiar flame that gnawed away at Tets. In the form of Tets herself he began to be devoured by it in turn. The big white scented mass recollected, made a Thébaide of his dug-out. He was snug as a beetle in the midst of a trencher full of dough. His enthusiasm for particularity did not stand out against the eloquent attacks of his animal spirits. Extreme home-sickness, in the first place, was a thing he was as susceptible to as anyone could be to sea-sickness. The distance intervening between himself and his attachments made him giddy, as though the troop-ship had mounted to Egypt, instead of laterally progressing through the waves. Tets also dominated and engulfed the composite picture of his harem—of Caroline, Maisie, Maude and Billie. What a pass to have come to! He goes out on the female hunt; lodges in his trap, incidentally: now he is being slowly devoured by his prey. He finds himself toying absent-mindedly with—what is this? A marriage ring! He calls in Paris, with its painted sweetmeats, to his aid. Entire cafés full of boon-companions and of women are emptied into his dug-out. Then again he looks round at the Black and the Brown. They, as we all know, help you along with the White. But much more than that, this caviare of a dark and acrid skin is the test, surely, of whether your palate is a noble, an adventurous palate, or a plebeian one! This was perhaps the bitterest pill. Beresin could never bear to think of that failure! Without the presence of mind, ever, when in face of this discomfort, to reflect on the quality of the "mets" and therefore the extent of his disgrace, he was simply blackened in his own eyes for ever, ethiopianly blackened.

There was one, only one, thing he could remember with equanimity from this time : one little flash of the true stuff. It was when at the moment of perhaps his supreme discomfort—the second chronologically—he seized his cane and beat the vociferous young negress who was the cause of it.

"You nasty black baggage! Take that on your horrible hide! And that and that! I don't like you! You're all dressed up and nowhere to go! How dare you! Take *that*!"

Except for that masterly gesture, even at the moment when he was being ignominiously certified as possessed of bourgeois senses, and with grave disabilities for inclusion in the ranks of the elect, except for that it was a period of complete eclipse of his self-esteem. Then, he was at present associated with two or three genuine dooks, as an officer. One of these nobles did not like him, and abused him to the other younger nobles. What could it be? Beresin wondered. Was it a further judgment on him, like the discomfort of his senses at the hands, or lips, of the Negroid and the Nautch? Was it now the turn of Blue Blood itself, as it had been a moment before of Black, to turn him down; or for him to be unqualified to mix with? Beresin in the presence of the real thing was shy. The actual breathing, walking flower to which so many doctrines, Nietzsches and Gobineaus, reverently point : this magical, masterly thing? Could the flesh and blood of the disciple be expected to support that sight with equanimity? He was awed at the polish and purity of the vocables, of the exquisite vowels, when two of the nobles were talking together. Ah, but his middle-class enunciation——? Then the attitude of mind—so free, so cynical—how well calculated to allure the Philosopher, and make him place Truth somewhere where she could learn such beautiful manners! The short, scrubby physique, the thoroughly villainous stupidity of the noble, who was also his colonel, and enemy, appeared to him in the highest sense, peculiarly, attributes. The stupidity, which he also saw, was the divine stupidity of the Noble! The physical commonplace—which he noted—how characteristic, paradoxical, and in fact the "real thing"!

Here were fresh despondencies, then, that threw him back more yet upon the female presence which was the twin domination in his life. And these two masters that destiny had bestowed on him were at war. Or rather, was it not a Master and a Mistress? The Mistress did not also move in quite the same circles as the Master, the prancing noble; friction ensued, therefore, where possession of Richard was in question. Billie and Caroline had been other forms of Tets. But Tets was enthroned; for although one of several, she was softly sculpting a Totem, whereas others had not had that art—or craft.

He wrote her a sort of love-letter. It was a sort of one because it was wrung with repugnance as well as passion. Oh, why was not the Home-girl a Haristocrat? Then she would have been as likely, as well as vigorous, a nymph as could be found on the banks of an English stream. No, nothing but a *sort* of a love-letter could be written; a tentative, shame-faced, blowing hot and cold missive. It blew hot in parts, where the endearments came to be written. He told her what a romantic bore the Desert was; that Suez was a sink of ennui. He wished that she were there! He could do with—he divagated and dreamt almost obscenely. So much amassed idleness, heat, and the staring red inflammation of youth! He tied the letter up with the others and it went on its nebulous errand.

In return, he got a letter from Lutitia's parents informing him in injured and more or less injurious terms that their daughter was dead.

He received this bitter communication in his dug-out, on the North-west frontier, while he was engaged in censoring the men's letters. They could be summed up in the hackneyed type of man's letter, "Dear Ma, this war's a fair bugger," with the interminable, piteous "in the Pinks." The one he was actually looking through kept referring to Kate's apparently well-known penchant for soldiers. Kate was certainly the writer's sister and he seemed strongly to dislike the thought of her frequenting any man of the same calling as himself and friends. Beresin was wondering if Driver Lawrence had some past English guilt on his mind, or whether it was from sheer dislike of and a form of vengeance on his comrades. Ma, even, too, was addressed fiercely, and would seem to have been not quite free from similar tendencies.

Beresin's irony was chastened by the arrival of his own letter.

Now the ghost that his senses had brought all the way from England to vegetate in his dug-out or hut was dead. There was

106

an eerie feeling in it; he looked at the two photographs placed neatly on a shelf five feet above the ground. One still smiled, but he felt now that they were objects of ill-omen. They were shortly after put back in his kit-bag. He was sorry; but it did not make him reflect. That night, lying in his camp-bed, he remembered that the night before he had been luxuriating in the anticipation of sleeping with Tets again when the distant leave to England came; practically sleeping with her there, in fact, for a moment and to some extent, while all the time she was dead. The child received a little tentative thought. The parents shortly received a cheque from him for £40.

And the year passed, chiefly in Mesopotamia; when he came home he was much the worse for wear, after dysentery. At his request, Tets' mother brought her daughter's child up to London. He waited for her uneasily at his hotel. He occupied an unnecessarily handsome room, and stood in the full glory of impeccable mufti. At their last meeting he had settled up with Mrs. Stapledown for board and lodging.

The mother was surprisingly silent and looked at him in an uncertain way, several different interests and opposite emotions cancelling one another on her face.

"How do you do, Mrs. Stapledown? You don't know how upset I was. I was dreadfully upset. I loved your daughter. You don't believe me, I expect? No? I intended—— Ah! this is our baby? What a jolly little baby! I don't know what to say to you! I'm afraid you——"

He took the child in an embarrassed way. The feeling of this warmth, and the weight of the springy, limp object—warmth and weight *his*, like his own hands—pleased and embarrassed him still more.

"Yes; I do! I'm a mother. I loved my girl. You have done wrong, *very wrong*, Mr. Beresin."

She stood rather breathless, her eyes shining.

The clumsy way she was being held increased the baby's alarm at the stranger. The face puckered slowly, and sitting helplessly on his knee she began to howl. He recognized at once in the child the Tets touch. The little convulsive crab-like being sat there on his knee like a transfigured Tets.

He shyly and slowly pedalled it up and down on his knee.

107

There was a moment full of embarrassing innuendoes when he had to give it back to Mrs. Stapledown.

"Never mind, my precious, then!—there——!" The grandmother also appeared to be substituting Tets for the infant.

Beresin helped regularly with the rearing of the child, and saw it fairly often. For the first year and a half it was, with its reveries, its dead white face and beauty of minuteness, very affecting. It had the same unusual interest at that stage as Tets promised when he first saw her. The horrible gift of speech had not descended on it.

He got it called Veronica, for it to have a name similar to Lutitia's. But when Veronica grew big she lost her beauty. The pulpy and stormy little totem became a dull human being, with whom decay set in early. She was unnecessarily robust with a mania for exploiting the beauty of smallness! She would attempt to stimulate interest, cause pity, or induce amusement, by mincing or conducting herself in babyish style, to mesmerize you into seeing her "en petit."

From Beresin's point of view it was lamentable. It was as though she had divined, in the telepathy of her infant state, the cause of the father's infatuation, and his more distant emotion at her mother's helplessness, and attempted, with a coarseness not even elephantine, and a bitter lack of tact, to perpetuate it.

The whole of their future relations, beyond the first years of babyhood, were struck by what seemed like a blast of God's irony. Also she was the homeliest description of a woman. No aristocrat could have had a less appropriate child!

3

Junior

(Previously unpublished. Written 1950s)

The station was at rest, the main lines were quiescent, and the local train which stopped at Cruse could be seen, unambitious and seemingly unready to move, inert on its side-lines, almost out of the station. A sluggish gathering of people were standing beside it or in mild movement; and as he noted the identity of one of them, John Leslie hesitated for a moment. Then he proceeded along the platform, and was soon one of that particular gathering himself.

"Ah, Leslie, may I congratulate you?" came the expected voice.

"Thank you," Leslie answered. "How is your asthma?"

"Still gives me a good deal of trouble you know."

"What a bore, what a bore." And Leslie put a ratio of real sympathy into his voice, but he appeared anxious to secure a seat. "So long—I'm a bit late." He hurried on. He stepped briskly forward and was soon seated in an empty first-class compartment.

When the engine had snorted a little discontentedly, shaken the train up once or twice, and begun to draw the train out of the station, Leslie sighed and relaxed, lighted a cigarette, and returned to his main preoccupation. Could he not entirely blot himself out, like . . . oh, Maclean for a while?

He had had a son, and he was in flight from Man and Woman. A woman, Kate Gosport, had embarrassed him in a way he had not expected. She had done the equivalent of stripping the bedclothes off, where he lay with his wife, and then had done the equivalent of joining them, desirous that he should spare a seed or two for *her*, and that started off the disgust. Other women, afterwards, had seemed too fulsome, and an old friend

109

of theirs had kissed him. With her he was unexpectedly discouraging. His wife saw he was not well, and had hurried him away and told him to take an alka-seltzer. He felt humiliated. He could hear the women saying that often happened, that the male played his part in the excitement, and developed headache or stomach ache.—Then he heard a woman precipitately approaching. His first instinct was to hide behind the curtains. Instead, he flung himself down on a sofa, his face buried in his hands. At least she should not kiss him! She went away exclaiming and lamenting. After which his wife arrived. She attempted to put him to bed. He had a blood-curdling picture of himself, propped up in the middle of the bed, surrounded by commiserating women. He turned his wife out, gently but firmly, and made an uncompromising escape down the service stairs, secured his hat, and here he was! They possessed a cottage in the Gloucestershire wilds, not very far by train. That was his destination.

As he fled from the house, he reviewed his recent life. He was thirty-five, and three years earlier he had married Perdita Murdoch, an exceedingly attractive girl, simply in order to sleep with her. The last thing he ever thought of was breeding; he hankered after no little John Leslie. When, just now, the frightful little object for which Perdita had been responsible, was the centre of a cult, a dozen women vying with each other to do reverence to this little horror (which Perdita should have hidden, until the incubation was complete), he knew that this was a pretty faithful picture of himself, of Perdita, and of everybody present at that age. In his imagination, he reduced the entire company to creatures of this kind. A small dark wriggling monster. Then he knew that there was a piscine phase of the foetus—and he could visualize them all, at that stage of life; collected in a tank. As a little fish, he could see himself glassily eyeing Perdita. The sharp-sighted are apt to be granted this fundamental vision of the human, in the moments immediately succeeding procreation —the female adoration of the just-born abortion, striking a spark. So reflected the violently disturbed John Leslie.

Ugh! shuddered the philosophic male : since it is as natural to wish to copulate as it is to eat and to drink (the wren goes to it and so forth), should one form an obscure association with one, or with many women of an inferior class—was that the solution?

110

The *only* solution for a man averse from orgies of birth, from
the excruciating publicity? Should there be some socially submerged, or subterranean, Perdita? The rites of the Middle Class
were repellent!

He hurried on foot to the station, by a shabby route where
there would be little risk of being overtaken. He could telephone
from the country. John's father, Joseph Leslie, was the most
prominent and eminent architect in the Midlands. But the architect's was practically an extinct profession—all the architecture
anyone wanted could be supplied by the builder. But any job
that came the way of the architect was always a big job, and it
always went to the enemy. As a consequence, Joseph Leslie was
a very prominent citizen, whose income lagged far behind his
prominence.

John Leslie worked in his father's office (when there was any
work to do). This might have been quite uncomfortable, had it
not been for a small fortune possessed by John : so his life was an
easy one. He and his wife possessed one of the handsomest houses
in the old part of the city, a much finer one than the firm of
J. Leslie and Son had ever built, because, to be fair to them,
this was not a period that called for fine building. The young
Leslies' house was a centre for the younger set in Blundon. In
keeping with their economic state of modest eminence, John had
bought in Gloucestershire a labourer's cottage, and inexpensively
transformed it into a bright and well-planned little holiday
retreat. It was named "The Birdsnest." Greatly to the surprise of
the village, he arrived and without luggage. The population of
Cruse was reading in the Blundon newspapers about his wife
and himself; receiving up in their town residence the young
mothers of that important city, to introduce them to the recently-
born heir of the Leslies. There was a photograph of the young
Mayoress toying with the newborn; in the background was a
"brilliant" feminine throng. Yet here was young Mr. Leslie
alighting from the Blundon train, and, luggageless, entering the
empty Birdsnest (would he be followed, in the twinkling of an
eye, by the motherbird? and the nestling—why not?). Soon Mrs.
Bateson, the Leslies' char, arrived, and then she was hurrying
to the shops, or the shop and a half, to buy provisions. And then
the following telegram was brought into the post office by Mrs.

Bateson, and was read by everyone in the village before it was
sent off : "Come down to the Nest for a day or so. Love to babe
and to Mouseums." The village chuckled at "Mouseums," and of
course he knew it chuckled, for he was under no illusions regarding the privacy of their life at Cruse (he hated Mrs. Bateson).
But if he had not put "Mouseums" at the end of the telegram
Perdita would have been surprised—even shocked—and might
have arrived by the next train.

"Mouseums" was a bed-name. He seemed to carry his bed
about on his back! In the working-class he would not have
written "Mouseums." Perdita would have been all that was
necessary. But, as it was, Mouseums took the bed into the village
post office. As to Mouseums herself, now that she had presented
her visiting card, it was, he knew, the end of irresponsible lust.
There would be no more Mouseuming. No. He would always
recognize what a splendid *Esquire*-like "piece of goods" she was,
but a real live mouse had sprung out of the mousehole. And
when would Mouseums have another babe? He could not ever
see himself being carefree again. She had chalked herself up *ONE*
(in full working order, a fat hen in the form of Venus) with
uproarious publicity.

How could he explain to Mouseums that she was not quite
Mouseums any more?

The Birdsnest smelt too much of the mating season, and John
flew away from it, up to the crest of the hill, where there was a
rock containing a sunlit hollow of which he was fond. He crept
into it today in flight from The Birdsnest, with a sort of devotion.

The plain that lay at his feet was like the sea for him, only
much more interesting, with its hamlets, the waters of a river, a
watermill, two windmills, and a fine herd of cattle. In the
distance the horse—three of them—and, in this almost treeless
expanse, a Cross. He knew almost every object in the plain by
heart. This rigidity was, for his curious mind, peace. The introduction of a donkey—so little as a donkey—would have broken
the monotony—he would have begun to speculate regarding
the origin and purpose of this animal. But today it was otherwise.
He had not come here to be lulled by the familiarities of the
plain. He came there to think relentlessly about living.

All beings were walking factories for procreation, as seed

implanted in a flower. But what *we* see in the flower is the grace, the beauty. Only the bee sees the seed.

Now, the woman is like the bee—she has a practical eye. The man is like the artist, he is the valuer, the enjoyer. Having paid himself the compliment, he turned to more practical matters. He was as much a part of this factory, of the roof and crown of things, as is the female—I beg pardon, the beautiful girl, the Turkish Delight. They are both of them just as prosaic as a tintack factory, or one for the manufacture of mackintoshes. On the other hand, whatever it is invents all this appears to have recognized that people would not have found this a very pleasing task. Consequently, delight-producing machinery was installed in the very centre of the head, limb and bust factory. This little accessory, hugely delicious, produced *love*—nothing else in human life does.

That was that. His young wife had covertly observed him devouring the honey with which she was amply supplied, as if that was the aim and end of the proceedings. She must have known that he was not a man of the Factory. He was not the kind of man to examine her Hope Chest and make practical suggestions. Now her hour of Victory had come—her handiwork in the Factory was on public view—all the ladies sang its praises in full-throated chorus; and one, with more than her share of saliva, had inundated his cheek with sputum tinted red with lipstick, to show him that *he* was in it too.

He sprang out of his privacy at the sound of a deep voice. His long-legged muscular body was aggressively erect in an angry bound. The smiling face of an old countryman looked amused. He confronted the intruder. This man's gnarled and loam-grey countenance was so much implicated with the trees and the sheep, the cattle, the mill, that it was impossible to resent his smiling thoughts any more than he would care what a tree thought, or a sheep, or a thrush.

"All I wished to do, Master Leslie, was to wish 'ee good evening, and to offer my 'gratulation. The paper says he is full 18 inches long and weighs seven pounds."

"Now how in Hell!" was Leslie's first thought. His second was that he ought never to have come to Cruse. But this was a good sort of man, and he liked his kind, easy-going face. "Ah," he said, returning the amiability, "they're saying that, are they? They know more about me and my private affairs than I do myself!" They both laughed.

He was genial with the ancient intruder, and set off down the hill to roam about on the plain beneath and to tire himself. It was dark when he returned to the cottage. A telegram lay just inside the door. "Don't blame you. Wasn't it awful? Darling, wish I were with you. All love. Mouseums." This produced a very unwelcome sensation. His sex awoke, as it was intended to. He almost sped back to Blundon, to Mouseums. But, at the critical moment, he snarled, "Not while Junior is there."

"We are a beastly race," was John Leslie's remark (to himself), as he stepped down upon the platform at St. Giles next day. He had decided to fly from Cruse after receiving the telegram from Mouseums. He was much too near to that lady, and in a minute community, where all his business was known. Now he was switching to Devizes, and there he proposed to hide. On the way he had been reviewing darker and still darker theories of *la condition humaine*. He had ceased to confine himself to the horrors inseparable from the female state. He had left that rather obvious target, and considered the whole field of eyes and noses, of nails stuck along the tips of our extremities, of bad smells and nice smells, the clowning of the intellect, its somersaults into religion and into no-religion. Indeed, everything you could think of, male and female, mental and physical, to use the popular dichotomies.

In St. Giles he purchased a suit-case, several pounds of apples, to weigh it down, a change of underclothes, a cheap umbrella, and several other articles. He visited the St. Giles branch of his bank, which communicated with the Blundon office. At last someone unknown to him began to ask questions. One of the St. Giles clerks apologized, but said might he look just under his chin : that was where his famous mole was. The voice from Blundon asked him a few embarrassingly intimate questions, such as the name of his Tewkesbury uncle, where he lived, of what he could see from his drawing-room window in Blundon, what was the colour of his hair, and whether he had ever been in the hands of the police (if so, why). He was then put through to his branch bank-manager in his home city, and he said a few secret things to him, of the sort only known to bank-managers. The St. Giles people, convinced by this time that he was not an impostor, supplied him with all that would be necessary for two or three weeks. With the name of William Coverdale, properly furnished with luggage, he went to the station and bought a ticket for Devizes.[1]

The train journey to Devizes he shared, in an otherwise empty first-class compartment, with a young lady who, at other times, would have been uncomfortably attractive. Since his marriage he had had no adventures; Perdita had had quite a taste for the frivolous accessories of her business; in fact he got so much sport at home that he was not tempted to supplement that with what might offer abroad. Perdita was one of those women who was partial to her own man-bait.

So, his eye rested sternly upon the heavily-baited woman installed at the other side of the carriage, she with her back to the engine as he was facing it, with a professional ruthlessness. He was very well able to understand what lay at the top of the nylon; the warm and scented cave of the skirt had no mysteries for him. And from what he could gather by the behaviour of the heavily-eyelashed eyes, and from a sultry sigh which could only mean one thing, it must be that this young person, like Perdita, was prone to indulge herself, cheek to cheek and stomach to stomach, with her prey.

But Junior, the uncompromising figure speaking not of Love but of the toad-life at the bottom of the tank, rose before his eyes.

When he had reached this point in his domestic scrutiny his expression became so ferocious that the young lady was extremely alarmed. She considered the advisability of pulling the communication cord.

John was assailed with an idea which was remarkably unscientific. He wondered whether all women had not a little

---

[1] Additional material in the Cornell Lewis archive provides for an extra paragraph in the story at this point, describing Leslie's ruminations on the St. Giles scene, among other things. But the version of the story as a whole used in this book has a continuity which gives every basis for the editors concluding that it is the finished version as Lewis saw it.

monster like Junior, concealed somewhere among their intestines, all the time? When they got married, they . . . He examined the young lady, who offered herself for immediate reference. Yes;— she held herself forward, almost crouching, which would be the position in which it would be natural for a woman, under such circumstances, to hold herself. Hers was certainly a secretive look . . . as though she had concealed on her person a time-bomb. *Everything* bore out this absurdly unscientific theory of his. He felt like asking her *why she crouched in the way she did*. Was she the possessor of an infernal machine?

Luckily they stopped at a station, and this graceful young lady left the carriage—casting a sideways look of the most authentic terror at John, and John shrinking back from her. He saw her mount into the neighbouring carriage.

They were not far from Devizes. While he was up at Cambridge, John Leslie had come here to start on a hike, and so was familiar with it. That rare sight, an intact seventeenth-century street, had so attracted an American, that, at the end of it, he had erected a small but very select hotel with a few seventeenth-century features. It was rather expensive, but that was a reason why it might be possible to find a room there. As he entered the bogus Restoration portal the first thing he saw was his fellow-passenger, the young lady who had fled from him only a short while before. He started, and she turned to an elderly lady at her side, and it was obvious that she was narrating the fearful experience she had had, and the old lady directed a most startled glance towards him. The mother bird, no doubt.

After this he secured a room, washed and brushed himself, and went down to the panelled lounge. In the somewhat agreeable surroundings he had a little too much to drink; and when the young lady of the train passed him, he gave her an enigmatic smile. She hurried forward, unmistakably in flight from something. At which John Leslie burst out laughing.

As he was definitely now doing a disappearing act he began thinking of Burgess and Maclean. That was the obvious case to study. Were they disguised? Ought he to make some radical change in his appearance? He went to bed turning this over in his mind, after a dinner in which he had had more to drink than usual. (He felt quite sure that Burgess and Maclean would have oiled their flight, though, as seasoned diplomats, they would not have drunk so freely.)[2]

He had breakfast in bed the next morning; and had ordered several morning papers to be sent up to his room. The first thing he saw was his face looking at him out of the *Daily Despatch*. It was unmistakable. The haircut would betray him at once—that kind of pointed fringe with marked recesses at either side where the hair was thin. His moustache had a characteristic upward movement at the ends. Placing the newspaper upon the dressing-table, he brushed up his peaked fringe. He left a larger recession upon the left-hand side and covered up the right. Then he shaved off his moustache; and returning to the large mirror suspended over the dressing-table, he examined himself critically, glacing down at the photograph from time to time. The difference was mysterious—he had not believed it would be so easy to alter his appearance. DISAPPEARANCE OF YOUNG MARRIED MAN spread itself across the whole breadth of the *Daily Despatch*. Unless people read what was underneath—and often they do not —they would jump to the conclusion that this was a murderer, or, at the least, some very anti-social person.

He planned to have a stroll, to visit the local branch of his bank. He passed from his bedroom into the Without, determined to look and to *feel* somebody else. He imagined himself a young, or a not so young solicitor from Birmingham—but with not a trace of a Brummagem accent, Marlborough and King's, Cambridge. As he passed the desk of the hotel he thought the clerk looked at him as if to say "I haven't seen *him* before." But as he was emerging from the baroque entrance, he met—face to face—the Young Lady of the train. He saw her face sharply change into a look of almost radiant recognition. She told him by her smile that she knew who he was. He gave her a sudden beam in return. She held up the morning paper.

"You've cut off your moustache."

He stopped. "You are very observant," he remarked.

[2] An alternative 450-word version of this section of the story at Cornell extends the time element at this point from a single night to a week and gives a more elaborate version of Leslie's stay at the hotel and additional material about his state of mind. But again the version of the story used here maintains a continuity and a "tightness" which bespeaks a "finished" quality.

"Not really, Mr. Leslie. I should not have identified you if you had not made such horrible faces at me in the train. You frightened me out of my wits."

"I beg your pardon," he answered. "I did not mean to frighten you."

The young woman shook her head, laughing. "It was my fault for being so nervous. But if you want to remain incognito, don't make faces at people."

"I will try not to." John gave her a friendly nod, and pursued his way.

For his wife to notify the police of his semi-disappearance (for she knew that he was at Cruse) was bad enough; but to have his photograph plastered all over the newspapers, as if he were a murderer, or at least a suicide, that was another matter. Invoking the assistance of the public! That was just like the possessiveness of his wife—or, rather, impudence. Well! It would have been to her advantage to leave him alone. She had not the sense!

He rapidly came to a decision. He must return at once and confront her. By summoning him to her presence she was making a mistake, as she would discover! It would have been much wiser to let him play at Burgess and Maclean: he would soon have bored himself—just as the two fugitive F.O. clerks must long ago have done.—To be *in flight from Junior* was an emotional vanishment which deserved sympathy from her and ought to be respected.

He walked quicker and quicker: but at last he stopped. He stopped dead; lest this should attract attention, he began to gaze into the shop beside which he had halted. It was a shop displaying Ladies' Underwear. He examined, with dismay, brassières, roll-ons, nylon stockings, heavily laced nightgowns, a glass case filled with deodorants—bottles marked Dior or Hartnell, man-baits, lascivious perfumes destined for the masculine nose. John Leslie's nose gave an involuntary twitch, assailed by a "glamorous" sickly odour, worthy of a fifth-rate *harem*. He recognized it as Perdita's personal perfume.

Abruptly he began to retrace his steps to the hotel. He covered the ground quickly. The hotel porter informed him that a train for St. Giles was due in about one hour. The bill secured and settled, his belongings packed and brought down into the hall,

118

with great expedition, he set out for the railway station. He was on the station platform at least a half-hour before the departure of the train.

Tea had just been brought up, and Perdita, with two woman friends, prepared themselves for this ritual, when John marched, rather aggressively, into the room.

"John!" Perdita shrieked. "Darling! And without a moustache! Where on earth have you been?" She stamped him with a kiss in the centre of the mouth. Then she sat and gazed at him as though she did not quite believe that he was there.

John Leslie was alarmingly composed. He looked back at Perdita as if surprised, a little, at what he saw. "The man-hunt is over," he said abruptly. "Isn't it?"

"The man-hunt? What do you mean, John?" Perdita looked at once puzzled and alarmed, for his manner had shown a strange reserve since his arrival.

"I had a kind of sleepwalk," he said slowly.

"And it took you as far as Devizes," interjected, smilingly one of Perdita's two friends—a woman he had never liked.

"It is dangerous, so people say, don't they, to wake the sleep-walker?" John looked at his wife, ignoring the other woman.

But, still smiling, the officious friend answered immediately. "How long would you say, John, that the sleepwalker should be allowed to continue his wanderings?"

"As you insist on speaking for my wife, Agnes, the answer to your question is obvious : until he wakes up."

"But, darling, we could not ignore your disappearance, could we?" Perdita protested. "We did not know that you were sleep-walking, did we? You might have had an accident . . . you might be dead or anything!"

"My husband disappeared . . ." Agnes began.

"That does not surprise me at all," John interrupted her.

"John!" Perdita looked shocked. "You are behaving in an extraordinary way, aren't you!"

"I don't know what you mean, my dear." He looked towards Agnes. "I do not want to hear Agnes's life-story, do you?"

Agnes rose. "I think I had better go," she said. The other

119

woman followed suit. In spite of Perdita's protests both of them left. Perdita, very much ruffled, returned. Once more seated in front of him, she said to her husband. "Well!" She sat staring at him.

"I am glad those two women have gone. One of them, Agnes, is persuaded that *she* is more competent than you to handle Man. How beastly all that part of the Sex War is. The suggestion is that a man is a different sort of creature from woman: it is woman's fate that she must (in order that she should fulfil her function) mate herself with this more primitive type of animal. From these premises ensue the situations with which we are familiar, which are such a bore, don't you think?"

"Up to what is all this leading?" enquired Perdita.

"I have no idea. When I married you I did not realize I was marrying into a pack of females. Really, I was sleepwalking away from that, I suppose.—Turn it round the other way. If I were an ostrich, and you found yourself always in the presence of ostriches, would you not get extremely sick of ostriches after a time?"

"Ostriches! Are you quite well, John?"

Ignoring her remark, he continued: "You may say that the Clubs (men's clubs) are there to meet this ostrich difficulty. But it is the home being a woman's club that I object to."

Perdita did not know exactly what to do. Physical contact was indicated as soon as possible. But she could hardly place herself upon his lap at the moment, or attach herself to his neck. So she temporized.

"I see what you mean I think. There are far too many women around here I agree. You haven't got as many men friends as I have girl friends."

John laughed. "I am glad you see that. That is what I meant by asking you how you would like living among ostriches."

The telephone bell rang; Perdita rose and picked up the receiver. After her "Hullo" came a gruff muttering, and she answered, "Yes, my husband has returned. I should have informed you." There was a sound like the gargling of a rhinoceros. "My husband tells me that he was sleepwalking." There was some growling. "Well, he does not wish to say I suppose," said Perdita. Alternate gargling and growling could be heard.

120

"Well, Sergeant, I will ask my husband to telephone you in the morning . . . Yes. Very well, about ten o'clock."

Perdita returned from the telephone. "The police," she said, as she sat down.

The telephone rang again. The person at the other end was of a tenderer sort on this occasion. "Madge darling!" shrieked Perdita. "You are back—how wonderful! . . . I see, you've had a delicious holiday and now you are back in dull old Blundon . . . Yes, my darling John is safe and sound, but . . . do not be so horrid . . . Righty Ho . . . Bye-bye."

Perdita cried "Bother!" when the telephone bell rang again as she was on her way back to her seat. But picking up the receiver she hurled endearments at "Barbara": Yes, John *was* home at last . . . No, not yet, he had so *much* to say about himself . . . "Yes, Junior's tired of being a baby, it was all I could do to stop him from getting up today." (And the young mother threw such a roguish look at John) . . . "Righty Ho, I'd love to, my pet, bysie-bysie."

Gloria, the house-parlourmaid, entered with a telegram upon a salver, which she handed smiling to John. He tore it open and read: "Sweetybags, Johnnie's photograph in the *Western Telegraph* is terribly like. His hide and seek must be approaching an end. Charlot insists on returning. Longing to see the babe. Love. Joan."

He placed this on the tea-tray. There had been *no* interval this time: as soon as one telephone call had ended another began.

"Not if I know it!" Perdita was shouting. "I'm going to be the perfect wife . . . I don't think so . . ."

John could hear no more, for he had left the room.

It was seven days later, and breakfast was at an end. Neither John nor Perdita had spoken for about ten minutes. John was reading the letters in *The Times*, and seemed amused. From the other side of *The Times* Perdita's voice had a thrill in it. The smile fading, the face going cold all over, John slowly put the newspaper down on the table in front of him.

"John," was what she said, "for the time being I will stay with my mother. I have communicated this decision to Mother . . . I said I would be there for lunch."

John Leslie sat looking stolidly into his wife's face. "I can see that almost inevitably that had to come," his voice was unemotional. "That is the necessary consequence of what has occurred—or not occurred."

Perdita burst into tears. "Oh Johnny!" she wailed.

"You will take your baby, I suppose?" said John.

"Of course," she cried, looking up at him with her face flashing with hatred. "It is not your child, by the way. Dick is the father. You have not the guts to have a child."

John gave a half-laugh. "I thought there was something funny about the timing of our infant . . . or rather, Dick's. Also it is black-eyed, and we are both blue. Well, I am very glad. This may come in handy."

Perdita gazed at him, slowly registering all his outward and visible signs of the horridness within. Like a public man sitting for a caricaturist John sat with an amused smile.

"I wish I had brushed you off, when you first came crawling around."

"Now I would enthusiastically help you to do that," John answered languidly.

"I wish I had slapped your silly face . . ."

"I wish," he interrupted, "when I was silly enough to invite you to park your naked loveliness in my bedroom until death removed you, you had slapped me on the kisser."

Perdita began to lose her stormy poise: "I wish I had known a man was apt to be a *eunuch* as well as a *skunk*."

"I wish I had known your fat carcase, helped out with deodorants, contained a hideous little worm that fed in it— which all your friends would dandle when it issued forth, as it squinted and gurgled at them."

Perdita's breast was heaving. She sprang up. "You are mad," she panted; "an asylum . . . where you could chat with other lunatics . . ."

An excited clap of laughter from her husband stopped her.

"I shall inform the police that you are insane." She began rushing towards the door. "As you are insane," she spoke with her hand on the open door, "it is not safe to remain here." She watched his smiling face for a moment. "You unutterable beast," she added.

"I am sorry, Perdita, that you should have reached the point at which you call me a displeasing name. The best thing you can do is to hold a small piece of ice in your mouth for some time, at the same time rubbing some 'frozone' on your temples."

His wife slammed the door.

4

Pish-Tush

(First published *Encounter*, London, February, 1956)

Miss Jevons, like all women who live by themselves, dwelt in a stuffy aroma of platonic domesticity. She had long understood that she now would never be joined by a man, so had built up a neutral atmosphere which took the place of the male. She was coming to the end of the middle years, but psychologically she inhabited a private youth of her own, which her lonely condition almost imposed upon her. If she had worked in an office, or something of that kind, she would have conformed to the view of herself formed by her associates; but as it was she remained young, since there was none there to make her feel anything else. And this was in no way contradicted by the fact that as her hair lost its colour, she rather dreamily supplied a little artificial colour, which she bought in a bottle.

Physically she was tall and fairly slender, with a small head, by no means unattractive. She was a faded, sandy blonde, with a straight sensitive mouth, and inquisitive pale blue eyes.

As a woman with a small fortune, and a nature not too aggressive, she had a fair number of friends, mostly living in London, survivals from her youthful life. Only two of these lived in Chelsea, one of them richer, the other poorer, than herself.

On the other side of the road a large red house, with large flashing windows, was reflecting the sun into her sitting-room. She sat near the window, her long neck, thin, but not quite so gracefully thin as she imagined it, arched out; and her eyes were directed downwards, where, upon her lap, a handful of money was collected. Now pushing these coins about with her long thin fingers, she was searching for something which had disappeared. Suddenly a very pleasant, curiously unalarming voice reached her ears.

"The half-crown is lying an inch or two to the right of your left foot." There was a short silence, during which Miss Jevons sat looking at the floor. The missing half-crown was where the voice had said it was.

"I must apologize for addressing you, Miss Jevons. I am a very harmless *spook*, but I am quite aware that I am not supposed to speak. My position is rather like that of a mouse." Frances Jevons sat rigidly, without moving. She was frightened. Bending forward she picked up the half-crown; it was her instinct to remove without delay what had been an excuse for communication. The money had better be put away—another half-crown might fall to the floor. She scooped up the coins and poured them into her bag.

Speak she would not, whatever happened. This low, gentle voice had sounded just as though it came from somewhere or something just above the armchair; she only possessed one. It might, of course, have come from a dictaphone, though how such a device . . .

In about a quarter of an hour Barbara would be arriving. She wished she had been coming sooner. What had the voice said . . . it compared itself with a mouse; it said it was not supposed to speak. If she heard that voice again she would telephone to Mr. Letheridge and get him to come up . . . but now the silence began to frighten her, and she considered the advisability of leaving the room, and waiting for her friend in some other room, perhaps the kitchen. A shriek ready to shape itself in her throat, she forced herself to look at the stretch of wall just above the armchair. Nothing was there. Picking up a novel, she turned to the marked page and began reading : "Captain Storford's lithe figure could be seen moving in the stable, he could be heard tapping his riding-boot with his crop, and with the free hand he was twirling his moustache. Would he come out and confront Eric?" Even Captain Storford—about to horsewhip, as he was, his contemptible rival—even he was not able to draw her away into his fictional world. She sat reading the words over and over again. Finally she closed the book. Was the spook, or whatever it was, watching her? Or had this something, like the mouse, a nest beneath the floor-boards or in the wall? She sat bunched up; the clock ticked louder than usual. Suddenly there was a small sound which might have been caused by a piece of furniture, if it was not something less material. When she heard the front door-bell she sprang up and with as much noise as possible made her way to the door.

"My dear! You don't know how glad I am to see you! Something very odd has just been occurring." Frances Jevons's eyes protruded a shade more than usual, and she began speaking a little breathlessly. But Barbara answered that something far more extraordinary (she felt sure) had been happening to *her*. And, without waiting to enquire what her friend's sensation was, Barbara plunged immediately into an account of the startling event which she had been so sure would outclass her friend's sensational bagatelle. It interested Frances; she readily gave up her "spook." Twenty minutes before, she could not have believed with what ease that subject could be dropped. Barbara's piece of hot gossip occupied most of the conversation during a not very prolonged visit.

She had joined a new club; she wanted Frances to go to lunch there in a few days' time. Barbara had an old friend of theirs lunching with her, and Frances agreed to be there too. That settled, the visitor left. Frances went back to her room determined to be very firm about any further voice having no material identity.

The Voice had plenty of opportunities during the next few days of renewing its supernatural contact, but it was not until the fourth day that Frances Jevons again heard herself addressed from nowhere. It was about ten in the evening; she was sitting, her legs outstretched, on the sofa, and had just taken up a detective story, when, so softly that she could only just hear it, the voice began.

"I hope I am not intruding. Tell me if I am. It is so boring being a spook, though, I know that is no excuse. Because one is bored oneself that is no reason why one should bore other people."

That, thought Frances, was excellent reasoning. Her first instinct was to jump up and say to this immaterial intruder: "Yes, you are intruding, and I will put up with no more of it!" But Frances had to admit that she was inquisitive about this unseen being who spoke so gently and apologetically. The Voice was cultivated, perhaps Edwardian. It occurred to Frances that, should it be her lot to experience a survival of this embarrassing

126

kind, what she would find most boring would be the enforced silence.

"I shrink from gossip with another spook," the voice told her; "it is not a pleasant thought, but suppose you were in this position —of being a creepily surviving intelligence, allowed a voice but nothing else. I would like to bet that you would prefer silence to intercourse with another shadowy voice."

The living woman tried to imagine herself in that predicament. She said to herself that she knew what *she* would do. She would try and find some sympathetic male spook to swap impressions with.

The voice appeared to pause, so that she might have time to reflect.

"I *did*," the Unknown continued, "strike up an acquaintance with a gentleman in the same pass as myself—just a voice and nothing else."

"Can you read my thoughts?" Frances Jevons was shocked to hear herself asking. She bit her lip and did not know which way to look.

"No, not really," came the soft tones of the Voice, "only a kind of telepathy, you know."

Suddenly an unexplained noise occurred—there was a kind of crack, and several things fell to the floor from the somewhat overloaded table. Frances jumped violently.

"I am sorry," the Voice protested. "These things are really not my fault. I am obliged to adjust my nonentity in an aggressively overcrowded space. I am so sorry if I frightened you, Miss Jevons, I was trying to make my voice a little more resonant by throwing it into the bell-shaped hollow of the lampshade. I am so terribly sorry."

There was angry silence.

"I hope you will replace what you have knocked down," said Frances crossly.

"I will ask you to let me do that while you are out of the room. Such an operation is apt to be a little noisy."

There was a short pause, involving several sharp sounds.

"Go away, please," Frances said. "Do go away."

"Oh please don't send me away. I was about to tell you what occurred when I spoke to a man spook. It was typical. He was a

127

strong and silent man—especially silent. No one would know he was there, and he attached great importance to that. I was talking about Oxford in the old days; we had both been up there. I can't keep absolutely still. I waved a little as I spoke, and a vase crashed on the floor. He was furious. He attempted to make me leave the room, the only warm one in the house, and sent me to Coventry. The people we were with were quite amusing, and one day I gave an involuntary titter. When they left the room this stickler for silence rushed at me. 'We are not supposed to be here. Can you not realize that?' I told him I was as quiet as a mouse usually. But he would not be pacified."

"Is there anyone else here?" Frances asked.

"No, Miss Jevons. We are quite by ourselves."

"What a wretched life you live . . . if it is a life," said Frances.

"To exist, even like a fly on the wall, is life. To be able to *think*, a great deal. I used to fear extinction."

"You are easy to please."

"I did not say I was *pleased* with my lot. I hope you will not think me fresh, Miss Jevons, if I introduce myself. My name is Constance, Mrs. Constance Blakely. My husband was in the Foreign Service. In the F.O., you know. We had no children."

Constance exhaled a small sad sigh, and fell silent.

"Tell me how you became a spook, as you call it?" Frances asked.

"I gave up the ghost, as they say, in the course of a pneumonia epidemic. How does one die? One rather violently goes to sleep. But I happened to wake up. I quickly realized that I could see, could move myself anywhere I liked, just by willing; and I was aware that a diaphanous nonentity accompanied me. What this is I understand no more today than then. I am the energy that it takes to move a bird about. I am the centre of a will—a will to see, to move, to speak . . . and the will weighs something—depending on how much one is willing. This is as much as I am able to define. I am an ariel, only confined to houses. It seems natural to this queer mode of existence to be in a house. I should not be comfortable . . . oh, in the garden." She appeared to shiver a little, or at least she made a noise resembling that. Then she continued. "Have you not sometimes felt something less than material, detached from the temporal? Then you felt for a

128

moment what I feel all the time." Constance paused. Frances was not asleep, as the Voice had thought she might be. Then this strange monologue began again.

"I have been in this room for nearly two years."

Frances shuddered.

"There is nothing to be frightened about. My presence here is no more alarming than having a phonograph and a number of discs. It would be ridiculous no doubt to say that I am just the same as you, except that I cannot make love, eat or drink, write a letter to a friend, dance or ride—indeed, *do* anything. All I can do is to talk. And I cannot do that much either, because anyone I would care to talk to is terrified of me! How silly that is I have tried to show. The 'spook' is perfectly harmless—except for the poltergeist; we do not borrow money from you—as the living do; we do not infect you with disease, as the living do, nor do we do any of the other disagreeable things the living are apt to do."

There was a silence. Then Frances spoke.

"You *feel* as well as think. What are your feelings about the people you . . . live amongst?"

There was a faint laugh. "Are you fishing for a compliment? Anyhow, I can answer you easily. My usual reaction to people is what it used to be before I found myself in my present odd position. Usually, I find myself *bored*. Let me add, because I am moved to converse with you it is a proof that I am interested. For instance, I am much entertained by your way of handling that vulgar little creature who blew in the other morning."

"Who was that? Oh I know—old Brewster, was it?" Frances gave a short laugh. "You heard that, did you?"

"Yes, I had just come in. I had been downstairs."

There was a great coolness in Frances's voice as she enquired whether the Voice was welcomed by Mr. Letheridge in the downstairs flat. With mirthful intonations the Voice answered that it would not venture to speak within the earshot of Mr. Letheridge, who, if he heard the sound of a spook, especially a female spook, would have a fit.

"I assure you, Miss Jevons, that your co-operation would immediately be sought with a view to exterminating the supernatural nuisances . . . Mr. Letheridge is, of all the people I know, the one who inspires me with the deepest terror." Frances did not respond; but it was obvious that she was somehow relieved.

This was the introductory phase in Frances Jevons's association with Constance. Thenceforth she was accustomed to consult Constance on certain questions, and to share with her the day's absurdities. It did not take long for "Constance" to become the mode of address on one side, "Frances" on the other.

Thus it was that the first of a series of *contretemps* occurred, in about ten days' time.

The *Evening Standard* was handed in every day at about five-thirty by an oldish man, who would have something to say on the banner headlines, "He's hung for it, and time too!" or "Polar Star was the Queen's horse. That's 'er second this week." Frances always assumed a rather bluff and blustering voice as she gave him the penny ha'penny. By six o'clock she was usually judiciously ready to defend hotly her opinion on this or that. Late Night News and Constance were apt to be contradictory. This evening it was Homosexuality which was the big issue. Frances, for once, was on the Judge's side. She fired a broadside across the tea-table, in favour of heavy sentences for accosting. "I don't see why he should get away with it because he has a nice tenor voice. It's not such a good voice as all that, either!"

Outside the window was a verandah running the full breadth of the house. This was approached by a stone stairway leading up to the front door from the small square garden provided for by the flat underneath. The occupant of the ground-floor flat often mounted these steps, and, instead of knocking at the front door, would walk along her verandah and tap on the window to announce his presence; or sometimes, as now, he would call to her through the open window.

"Hear, hear, Miss Jevons," rang out the fine masculine voice of Lionel. "I'd give them the cat! A public beating—in a row! I would whip them till they bled!"

"How sadistic!" breathed Constance.

"I didn't hear you." Lionel coughed suspiciously under the window. "I beg your pardon for intruding. But it is rather important. Might I have a word with you?"

"Coming!" cried Frances, as she crashed around her bristling sofa. A minute later she was in her hall, facing the tall figure of her neighbour. These encounters always occurred in this way; he would not seek to enter, nor would she invite him to do so. He would knock on her door, to bring to her attention some outrage which he felt she should (1) know about, or (2) take some steps, with him, to put a stop to.

His face showed that, on this occasion, he was ruffled in some way, and he was holding something back. (He had heard the voice of Constance when she had observed how *sadistic* he sounded.) But he had a big outrageous blemish upon the peace and decency of their dual domicile to bring to her attention – for, after all, what happened to him happened in a sense also to her. An injury to one he was inclined to regard as one done to both; and now he had something very outrageous to impart to her.

"This is intolerable, a matter for the police!" he protested. "The abominable Bouncer (the next-door dog)—that filthy animal—how dare he behave as he does! He has left his visiting-card, if you please, in the centre of my doorstep!"

Frances looked scandalized. "Bouncer ought to be shot!" she exclaimed. "I would shoot him through the letter-box if he came near my doorstep!"

An enthusiastic growl came from Lionel; she had been particularly emphatic, and even picturesquely dynamic, in order to cover up the presence of a Voice, which Mr. Letheridge would suppose was a visitor. In a warmly apologetic tone, and glancing towards her sitting-room, he said : "I say, I hope you will forgive me for barging in on your conversation." But Frances Jevons told him it was nothing—that, as she was by herself, there was no intrusion.

(She pretended not to have heard the word "conversation.") Then, as a secondary matter, but one which it was impossible to ignore, had Miss Jevons noticed an invasion of barrows coming from the slums of Victoria—bringing with them house-to-house pests, knocking on doors and trying to sell one articles which are usually a side-line of the milkman, from bedding to petticoats, from razor blades to electric irons. Yes, of course she must have noticed an infesting of hawkers and street-traders, and of persons soliciting at doors, with bundles of feather-brooms. Phew! beastly

131

things—full of fleas; one had jumped on him from a lot of dirty feathers. And they filled the streets with incomprehensible cries! Sometimes they were accompanied by dogs. As he mentioned the fleas and the dogs Miss Jevons swelled with indignation and shook herself, scratching a little in the region of her ribs. She expressed herself rather forcibly, by word and by gesture, about Chelsea being used as a hunting-ground by such marauders from the neighbourhood of the Vauxhall Bridge Road or the disreputable markets nestling against Victoria where the Station premises looked round to the south. And, his eyes flashing almost as much as if he had been discussing the lawlessness of Bouncer, Lionel Letheridge said: "They should mobilize a body of Vigilantes, with truncheons and torches. I'd join them like a shot!"

Back in her sitting-room the two girls had a good laugh about Pish-Tush, as was Constance's name for the man downstairs.

But Pish-Tush paused at the top of the stairs, and the hoots of mirth and the disembodied merriment counterpointing the robust hysteria of Frances caused him to frown. "It is rather unnecessary for Miss Jevons to go back to her friend exploding with laughter!" he said to himself. "She has always taken a very serious view of the invasion of our territory by that arch canine pest, Bouncer. It has always seemed to me that we stood together regarding his flagrant trespasses and depredations, I almost think encouraged by Mr. Parkinson whose head I shall certainly punch one of these fine days. Of course, there was mirth in Miss Jevons's room as I arrived, but . . . well, I will put the best construction on it that I can."

And Mr. Pish-Tush made his way gravely down the steps, loudly clearing his throat.

In her sitting-room Frances Jevons, wiping her eyes after having let herself go on the subject of Pish-Tush, made the following remarks.

"This is not a maisonnette; these two flats are constructed in such a way, standing as they do apart from anything else, one on top of the other, that you find yourself perpetually involved with the neighbour upstairs, or downstairs, as the case may be. Since he lives downstairs, and as the garden falls to his lot, old Pish-Tush is in the nature of things a little in my pocket, not to say in my hair. His temperament keeps him boiling with rage from morning till night. I can hardly cold-shoulder him and object to holding a conference at least once a day—always on my doorstep, for he refuses to come inside, especially at the Christmas season, when mistletoe is apt to be hanging over every door, particularly in the flat of a single lady! . . . It is a most awkwardly built house for a single man. I try and convince him that nothing would induce me to get into bed with him. But Pish-Tush—I must call him that, I think!—remains sceptical. The fact that I am unmarried and he is unmarried . . ."

Constance, from her abstract electro-magnetic perch, gave forth wails of polite hysteria. "Frances, it is humiliating for you, but you must bow the head to the master sex. If I were in your position I would inform him I was a hermaphrodite, but it was best to call me *Miss*."

"*Then* I am quite sure that Pish-Tush would be so embarrassed that he would blush every time he saw me. I prefer to remain the single woman."

A little later that evening Frances was going out to dinner (having apologized to Constance for being so piggish, but she had to stoke up). As she was descending the steps, she became aware that Pish-Tush's door was open and he was obviously speaking on the telephone.

"Disgraceful!" . . . "Outrageous!" . . . "Scandalous!" he fired indignantly into the mouthpiece, obviously for Mr. Parkinson who must be at the other end (the owner of Bouncer living in the house next door). When she returned two hours later the excitable Lionel Letheridge was lying in wait for her just inside the gate. His face was full of indignation—the word "disgraceful" was waiting just inside his lips ready to rush out.

"I say, Miss Jevons, that fellow Parkinson has gone a step too far—I think you will agree with me when I have told you. He called me an ill-educated sausage-nose . . ."

"I say!" exclaimed Frances.

"But wait a minute! He said that because I could not afford a dog of my own I made the lives of other dog-owners a misery. To which I replied that the next time I saw him I would punch his sausage."

"I say! That was pretty straight from the shoulder! Besides, your nose is a very elegant sausage—in fact I have never seen a

133

man with a nose less like the article of food mentioned by
Mr. Parkinson. His nose is rather like the inflamed beak of a
buzzard!"

"I say, Miss Jevons, what a capital eye you have!"

"But you must not assail that inflamed beak. You are at least
twice his size. You must not kill Mr. Parkinson."

"That is all very well, Miss Jevons, but am I to be insulted
by the master on top of submitting to the maximum nastiness of
the dog?"

They growled together in the shadow of the hedge; and then
Frances, looking, with her unusual height and dramatically ragged
way of dressing, like a female Don Quixote, stalked up to her flat.

If Pish-Tush was going to "sock" the neighbour because he
was so small, what should her attitude be? Constance was still
there, and, after answering enquiries regarding her digestion,
Frances sought enlightenment of the ghostly oracle. The answer
was that Pish-Tush did not impress Constance physically, although
he was a big man, and if there was any chance of Mr. Parkinson
blacking his eye, then that would be great fun—especially if
Bouncer would join in and succeed in removing the seat of Pish-
Tush's trousers. Frances laughed a little hollowly; for the
thorough-going distaste felt by Constance for her neighbour did
not entirely please her. She felt that a certain restraint was
appropriate to those no longer of this life.

A few days later Frances Jevons had a shock. She half-rose
and reached across to a small bookshelf and placed her hand on
something like a piece of fish. But the dead fish was alive, for
the dead fish shuddered; and it was not solid, or rather it was
a slice of another dimension—for there was nothing there that
was visible. She snatched her hand away and sat with the hand,
which had had the disagreeable experience, nursed in the palm
of the other.

"That was me," the apologetic voice of the invisible Constance
was heard. "I am so sorry. It was like putting your hand down
on to the fishmonger's chilly wares."

"Yes, a little bit," Frances agreed.

The voice of the unseen was so civilized—what was said so
acceptable to human senses: but something reminiscent of this

was a familiar experience—for instance, when some coal-black or yellow-Asian face speaks with the cultivated voice of some Oxford or Cambridge undergraduate. But a cold slice of fish was a disagreeable novelty. That would take some getting used to.

"Constance, I *hear* you, and I feel perfectly at home: if I could *see* you what should I feel like?"

"Well, in the first place you could not see me. I have been left my Voice, but nothing to go round it—not above it—nor underneath it."

"What are your powers of movement? Can you move through walls?"

"Oh no, Frances, nothing miraculous like that. We can get under a door, provided it is not fitted with those india-rubber things to exclude draughts. Think of a very light substance, whose shape and, in a way, whose destiny we control. Our *centre* has no visible shape. Where we go this evanescent substance goes, I do not quite know why, but we cannot dispense with it. It is the shadowy equivalent of a body. We can let it float like a cloud, or we can fill it up or concentrate it into a substance we are able to pull through a keyhole—provided no key is there. I cannot explain this voice or brain or will of mine."

"Is there no use you can make of this volatile aura?"

"Oh well, yes—if you can call it a *use*. We could deliver a slap, for instance; we can weave it into a *rope*, with which we can attach ourselves to a jet aeroplane. We could tie up a bunch of flowers or act as a plume for a knight in armour at a carnival."

"I should have thought you would be too unsubstantial for that."

"We can do quite a lot with our wispiness if we will it to be so."

The friendship between the two women grew, until the personality of Constance acquired something almost like a plastic reality for Frances. Frances shared with her shadowy friend the interest in the males who came her way, possibly (with luck) developing a flirtatious coloration; or, in one or two other cases, figures from her not too remote past put in an appearance.

In the case of the latter, having their roots in the younger years—this big, vibrant, tossing body, still in life, unlike her friend

—there were amorous entanglements, yes, orgasms which tended to make the presence of Constance embarrassing.

When it was all over, however, frank conversations ensued, not without boastfulness on the part of Frances Jevons. Constance's tact was admirable, bowing with delicate humility, as the woman of the past should, who hated the live organism, with the flattery of one who could no longer be *corps à corps* with the male. She saw Frances vaunt her fascinations – this in spite of the fact that she was now almost a sexagenarian, and reveal her five-foot-ten of not so enticing *décolletage* to the femininity sharing her intimacies. Frances would coyly whisper, "Jack is coming this evening – mustn't look." And the other would answer, "I promise." Though secretly the once elegant Constance regarded her friend's "harem," as she thought of it, as a very moth-eaten lot.

But Mr. Lionel Letheridge, when he would stump up and station himself outside his neighbour's window, seething with indignation, would find, as often as not, that Miss Jevons was in entertaining conversation with some woman, where formerly she would be by herself. As the days and weeks passed Pish-Tush grew more and more aggrieved. He developed a deep and aggressive jealousy for this female, whom he regarded as an unknown interloper, very seriously interfering with his daily dramatics with his woman neighbour.

"Miss Jevons, have you seen the news?"

Squawking, "I will come to the door," Frances stalked out of the room, after a wink for Constance. As she flung the front door open, Pish-Tush crashed out : "Awfully sorry. Hope I am not interrupting anything. There is great news—I thought you would like to hear it."

"I am devoured with curiosity." Frances produced an inquisitive grimace.

"Well, that unspeakable cad Parkinson has been fined heavily by the West London magistrate—an unusually big fine. Bouncer paid a visit to the charming front garden of a noble lord—you know, that Georgian house in Mayhew Street. He was caught in the act by the butler."

"What fun !" Frances said.

"Yes. The magistrate deplored that no restraint was imposed upon so incontinent a dog. He described Mr. Parkinson as one

136

of those pests whose imagination was defective, and who should not be allowed to possess a domestic animal."

On another occasion he asked Frances if she had anyone living with her. And then, at last, mounting as usual, and placing himself rather quietly outside her window, he overheard a female voice saying: "I should tell old Pish-Tush, if I were you, not to appeal to you about everything—but only when it is something of interest to you."

"Oh, it doesn't matter," he heard the voice of Miss Jevons. "It probably is a good thing, a watch-dog."

He moved softly over to the front door and knocked. When she came he said: "You have no one with you?" and when she answered, "No," he said: "Would you mind if I stepped into your sitting-room for a moment. There is an echo . . ."

She went back into her room and he followed, speaking as he advanced. He looked round the room. "It is strange . . . I could have sworn . . ."

"Nosey Parker! Busybody!" Constance spoke quite distinctly.

"So there is someone here who is invisible . . . and not remarkable for her politeness." Flushing scarlet, he retired from the room, flashing angry questions at Frances as he went.

"There was someone in the room, as you see . . ." she replied.

"No, I *saw* nothing," Pish-Tush broke in.

"Ah, she was hiding."

"Very successfully!" Her neighbour stepped out of the house with that parting shot.

It was some days before Frances saw her neighbour again. She was just about to open the gate when she saw him on the other side of it, raising his hat and stepping aside to allow her to come through.

Moving forward, she thanked him. "I'm just on my way to *Sugar and Spice*, not too late I hope for my daily *Procea*."

Mr. Letheridge told her he had just come from that enterprising shop. "They seemed to have plenty still of everything."

She observed that it was in danger of becoming too popular; and they chatted a little in a very genial mood. This urbane conversation she lived to regret. Two days later the disarming softening up of the *Sugar and Spice* talk was still effective. She was

137

without any real resistance at the moment her neighbour sprang his great surprise.

It was at eleven in the morning that the test came. She was engaged, as was so often the case, in heated discussion with the domestic spook, the subject usually originating in rapes, murders, escapes from Broadmoor, divorces, scandals in Court circles, from reports in the morning newspapers. Frances was very shrill: an imperious knocking at the front door drew her, shrieking comic protests, across the room and out into the hall. When she threw the door open she found the invariable Pish-Tush, his face full of enterprise and of pleasurable expectation. He was nursing some contraption in both hands, held up against his stomach.

"I want you to allow me to spray several of your rooms with this. It is a substance which is perfectly harmless . . . to *us*; but its properties have a most salutary effect where" (he coughed) "certain undesirable guests are concerned."

And as he spoke he advanced into the house, looking to left and right, and then, talking all the time, he quickly stepped into the sitting-room, Frances, wide-eyed and vaguely alarmed, retreating as he advanced.

"I would much prefer it if we fixed a day. You can't possibly go in *there* . . ."

"Oh just a little gentle spraying." But he was already inside and spraying away for all he was worth. "It is by no means disagreeable," he was saying.

". . . On the contrary—on the contrary, it is vile! Come out at once, Mr. Letheridge! Do you *hear*?—at once!" she stamped her foot.

"Rubbish—rubbish!" Squirt—squirt, he went, rapidly moving around the room.

"It's D.D.T., that's what it is!" cried Frances, waving a handkerchief in front of her face. "Mr. Letheridge! Please leave my house at once. This is perfectly disgraceful. How dare you come in here, spraying that disgusting stuff . . ."

"Nonsense, nonsense, Miss Jevons!" he boomed, as he pushed his way out into the hall. "It's just what you want. One has to get used to it—but it's jolly good stuff! Jolly—good—stuff!" he shouted, as he charged on into the dining-room, on the other side of the front door."

Frances remained in the hall, exploding with more and more determined protests. Something brushed past her head.

"Goodbye, dear, goodbye." Constance's voice sounded hoarse —it was almost breaking. Flushed and excited, the red countenance of Pish-Tush burst out into the hall. "Ah, I see something!" he exclaimed, his spray pointing up into the air.

Frances struck at his sprayer, almost knocking it out of his hand.

"I say!" barked Pish-Tush.

"I will send for the police, Mr. Letheridge! I shall sue you for this! I am serious."

Spraying as he went, triumphant, regardless of feminine threats, he reached the back door, which led into the lane at the rear, an iron staircase leading up to the tradesmen's entrance. But as he reached the end of the passage there was an agonized scream, and he jumped away from something. He stood looking down at his foot, exclaiming: "Well, I'm damned! You heard that?"

He turned quickly towards Frances, his face radiant but perspiring.

"How about that, Miss Jevons? That was escaping under the door." He came towards her. "Can you say now, Miss Jevons, that this purification was not necessary? It is the one thing vermin abominate. You should thank me, shouldn't you? You don't aprove, do you, of phantoms—all that supernatural vermin, larking around dwellings—making their home among us? . . . I shouldn't be surprised if that was the voice which called me *Busybody*."

"That is precisely what you are, you interfering idiot! Go! Get out of my house! And never come near it again!"

"You will thank me for this. It is thoroughly insanitary. Association with those surviving from another time is unwholesome—very unwholesome. They feed upon the vitality of those who tolerate them. They are parasites. The whole question ought to receive the attention of Parliament."

Lionel Letheridge looked more owlish than ever. His eyes and mouth conspired to hypnotize with owlish authority.

"Why don't you learn not to meddle with other people's lives? You private policeman—you unpaid detective! Don't come to

139

me any more with your idiotic stories! I will make you pay for this invasion of my premises. Now, will you go out of that door ... or must I summon the police?"

Surprised and crestfallen, without a Pish or a Tush left in him, Frances Jevons's neighbour left, a misunderstood man, a public-spirited hero whose unselfish deeds were strangely misinterpreted.

"She'll get over it," he told himself, "and I shall no longer hear her confabulating with some most undesirable spirit."

Things began arriving the following day for Frances's neighbour. There was a parcel from Harrods, there was a parcel from Sketchley's, and a registered letter. Frances refused to take anything in for Mr. Letheridge, as formerly she had been ready to do.

She sat miserably in her ill-smelling sitting-room, feeling incredibly lonely. At length she decided to have a change of scene. She telephoned to the Rev. Joynson, who occupied a pleasant little vicarage not far from Ware, and arranged to pay him a visit beginning on that very day. This was an elderly cousin with whom, along with Sadie Joynson, she and her sister would sometimes visit the seaside, especially a place near Aldeburgh, where another cousin lived.

She remained in the country for about a week, at the end of which time the effects of the piratic behaviour of Pish-Tush were beginning to be forgotten. The appalling stink left behind by that aggressive busybody, that too, she felt, must have lost its pungency, only the fact that he had driven out the sympathetic Constance would remain to distress and anger her.

So she decided to go back to Chelsea, determined to keep Lionel Letheridge in his place, and severely to discourage his trespassing in future. Accordingly, she said farewell to her cousin on the following morning, and by about five o'clock that evening was once more in her now dismal flat. About five-thirty her telephone rang. It was an unfamiliar voice; and then she learnt that it was a Detective Inspector, who asked if he might come round and see her at once. He declined to reveal what his business was, and she awaited his arrival with sinister foreboding—about something quite shapeless—for she could not imagine what his errand could be. When the man arrived he informed her that a week ago her neighbour, Mr. Lionel Letheridge, had been found dead under mysterious circumstances. They had forced an entrance into her flat the day before, as a result of what a certain General Goffer-Smith had said.

The Detective Inspector, whose name was Manners, at once enquired if she could throw any light upon what had happened. It was evident that her departure had seemed to them a curious circumstance, occurring as it did at precisely that time.

Frances Jevons was anything but deficient in the comic sense; but she also realized that she was a serious suspect. She saw that if she gave an exact account of what had happened, prior to her departure for the country, that might be regarded as material to build up a case. Nevertheless as she had nothing to hide she considered it best to relate (more or less exactly) what had passed. She began by giving an outline of her relations with Pish-Tush, and then (without, of course, mentioning anything in connection with the invisible Constance) described how Mr. Letheridge had, with his usual schoolboyish abandon, persuaded her to allow him to spray her rooms with some concoction he had been recommended by his friend General Goffer-Smith. The smell was decidedly disagreeable; on an impulse, to get a little fresh air into her lungs, she had gone to the Vicarage of a relative in Hertfordshire.

The Detective Inspector explained how they found Mr. Letheridge. He was in bed, in his night clothes, and a deep dark incision stretched all around his neck. This had been the cause of death. There was no indication whatever of how this came about. The flat had not been broken into, and no trace of any kind remained as to what implement was used to effect the strangulation, nor had they any other clue so far : although they had made all those enquiries which, up to the present, had suggested themselves. Frances shuddered—watched by the Detective with stolid alertness.

"You shudder, Miss Jevons," he remarked dryly.

"Yes," said Frances. "Didn't you, when first you saw this rather gruesome sight?"

Detective Inspector Manners had attained to his relatively

envied position in his branch of the Police Service by tenacious industry, and he had his likes and dislikes. Of cleverness he did not approve. He looked sharply at Frances Jevons. But, try as he would in the ensuing weeks, he could not add Miss Jevons's name to the list of British murderesses. Badger and ferret, badger and ferret as he would, he was unable to unearth a single fact incriminating her.

As she lay in bed, that first night, Frances shuddered again. She was convinced that she could tell the Police how that foolish man received that deep incision all around the neck—done, they believed, with some malleable metal cord : Constance had described how she could, if she wished, make out of her aura a cord. And the back door of her neighbour's flat had a limited amount of space between itself and the floor level. She knew how Constance had made her exit from her flat, and there was every reason to believe she could make her way into *his* in a similar fashion. She could imagine her lying in wait under his bed. How she would introduce the silken cord around his neck Frances did not venture to surmise.

Perhaps the encirclement might begin with a gentle and immaterial gliding around that part of the neck where it was possible to effect a junction; gradually take on substance, until it became a most deadly instrument of destruction, pulled tighter and tighter by that mysterious indomitable will of which Constance had spoken as the essence of her being. It was easy to imagine the wretched Lionel Letheridge struggling wildly upon the bed with this invisible enemy. She shuddered again. Oh dear! She reflected that not until she had left this neighbourhood, yes, and had a long holiday too (perhaps she would go to Africa)— not until then, if ever, would she be herself again.

SECTION IV

Play-Shapes

Sectional Introduction

All but one of the stories in this section happen to have been written during a brief but blissful respite from the hardships and uncertainties Lewis endured as part of his North American exile, 1939–45. John Slocum, an American expert on James Joyce, helped Lewis considerably during the writer's initial period in America. He loaned Lewis a house in Sag Harbor, Long Island, N.Y. As Lewis put it in August, 1940: "A large house has been put at our disposal and we have been leading a fairly idyllic life for some time with thank goodness no rent to pay."[1] By early October, however, this happy period was coming to an end, though not before Lewis had made maximum use of it for his creative purposes. He finished *The Vulgar Streak* at Sag Harbor as well as writing the stories in this section and another tale, "Children of the Great." As it happens, two of the stories in this "Play-Shapes" segment are set along the kind of delectable shoreline which Lewis obviously found so congenial at Sag Harbor.

None of the Sag Harbor stories has been previously published. The three texts in this section come from copies in the Cornell archive. "The Weeping Man" is based on a typescript carbon copy as is "The Yachting Cap." Both can be read against a backdrop of Lewis's own North American origins and interests. The marine element in the two stories is the creation of an artist who—himself born on a yacht off the eastern Canadian coast—returned repeatedly to shoreline themes in his painting. "The Weeping Man" reflects the Anglo-American Lewis's lifelong infatuation with North American language. The story's dialogue is a crackling exercise in the conversational pyrotechnics of American speech, just as much of *The Apes of God* studiously reproduced the inane parlour patter of London's Mayfair. "The Man who was Unlucky with Women," on the other hand, is set

[1] *Letters*, p. 273.

144

in a wholly different locale, typical of the urban English scene which Lewis many times interpreted in his fiction as dully serene on the surface but not exempt from cave-man eruptions of violence from time to time. The monstrous fighting dances performed by two of the characters in this story—with the text again originating at Cornell—invites comparison with the lethal shuffle of René Harding's attacker in the memorable Beverage Room scene of *Self Condemned.* There is a grotesque touch of canine savagery too, similar to the serio-comic intrusion of the murderous Jacko in "The Bishop's Fool" (1951) or to Charlie Chaplin's cinematic use of a dog as the uproarious arbiter of a boxing battle in one of his early film classics. The story dates from the 1950s and, again, the text here is based on a carbon typescript.

I

The Yachting Cap

(Previously unpublished. Written 1940)

The beach extended to left and right. There was nothing there but the man and the ocean. The ocean's name was "Atlantic." The man's name was "Kipe."

Atlantic rolled in, cold and kingly. Kipe crouched in front of it, twelve feet from the big revolving blades of its green waves.

The *man* was that by courtesy only. In the dictionary he would be so described. His was the same anatomy as that of Napoleon. His teeth found in a cave would be classed by the anthropologist as belonging to the contemporary species. Buttoned and pinned into a cocoon of rags, there was something inside, the skin of which a woodtick or a mosquito would not mistake for a dog or a dromedary.

The most human thing upon this beach was a great white yachting cap, crowning the animated scarecrow that grovelled in the dusty sand. The gilt of its crest glittered. It was emblazoned with a flowery monogram. It was fresh as paint. It gave back a spotless glare as the sun struck it. It bespoke the summer-decks of a sumptuous houseboat.—It was the headpiece of a tycoon.

The previous night it had been lifted by the wind—as he sped along on his roadster—off the head of a yachting millionaire. It had sailed down a dusky gully, coming to rest beneath a shrub. Kipe had witnessed its descent, at first with alarm. Almost it had alighted upon his head. He scuttled away. Later he came back. As luck would have it, the cap was just his size. It fitted Kipe as if it had been made for him.

The wild hair beneath the peak of the splendid yachting cap grew up to the two shifting points of light, which were the eyes of an animal. Nothing that ever trod the decks of a yacht, to take

147

or to give orders, ever had eyes that hid under a peak so craftily, nor observed the ocean with so much fear.

But Kipe unwound his puttees, impregnated with the dust of a continent, as a mummy might gingerly unwrap itself if it wakened and felt constricted, and thought it would ease itself of its desiccated bands.

The legs that thus had been embalmed were shrivelled and yellow. The cord that fastened the boots had a knot his nails scratched at for some minutes before they loosened it. At last they gaped, a brittle foot-armour. A more painful disinterment came next. But at length two tiny feet, with beautiful insteps, cautiously wriggled out into the ocean wind. They received the baptism of the drifting spray. They curled and shrank back at the kiss of ocean.

To unpin, to unbutton, to untie what had for so long been collected upon the trunk and limbs, was a work that demanded —in the tramp-tempo that scorned the clock—some considerable measure of time.

Forgotten garments came to light. Inner swaddlings that he had not set eyes on for a decade were disclosed. He stopped to stare at these in dull surprise. The final act was when, handling it as the collector does an exquisite antique, he arrived at the oldest of his possessions—the nearest to his body. It was peeled off bit by bit, with precautionary stops, lest it should disintegrate. This was the pride of his wardrobe. A once azure polo-shirt.

Still wearing his yachting cap—surely appropriate for the element beside which he found himself, and which he was about to invade—Kipe rose. He slunk forward, his eyes shining, towards the softly crashing waves.

The shore was narrow, not much above fifty feet back from the water to a shallow bluff. It was so narrow that the waves seemed too large for it. It was rather a sandy shelf than a beach. No one ever came to it because it was too real. You could not play with the ocean, at this particular part of the coastline. It was on top of you, it was too near to you. It was too big : it was too "rough."

Kipe crouched before the big revolving blades of polished water in the attitude of a boxer set to cover up, faced by an antagonist at whose battle-habits he could only guess. He eyed it fixedly, seeking to discover an opening. He saw none. He continued to eye it askance. But he was stripped to meet it, he could not retire now—not with this cap on his head! Was he not a smart bum, trained to fool nature, and a worse thing than nature, man?

His two small hands went up and screwed down the splendid yachting cap upon his head. It was his talisman. It gave him a sort of right to be where he was. It was like being an official of the ocean.

He knew what he was about to do, as he had made his way seaward. He would remove his clothes—a physical revolution comparable to the removal of a gland. A fleeting *will-to-play* of sorts had got the better of his judgement, debauched by the nautical finery of the irresponsible man of affairs. It all came out of the cap. A strange conceit, a bravado had possessed him.

He twitched and stared and bristled, studying the tough slick waters before him, rolling according to some law of malice. He scratched. The salt air was biting him all over like black flies in the Canadian bush. How did one get into all that anyway? The bird-eye ambushed in his whiskered head seemed cocked to enquire. Lots of guys did make it. It was a trick—like getting your leg across a mustang. He had seen cowhands getting their legs across mustangs out west. He had never seen them dealing with rows of shiny waves, one behind the other. That was a new one on him.

Its voice—its great spellbinding roar, cowed him, as if it had been the voice of the Law. As each wave spoke its great reverberating line and passed, he scowled. That cap of fine linen, of gold braid, of blazoned letters, did not belong where it sat at present, upon what looked more like a birdsnest than a human head. Nature was always wise to things like that!

With a frantic movement Kipe stepped towards the oncoming wave. It was voluntary. Until the water was dashing about his ankles, he was unaware of what he had done. He could suport the stinging of his skin no longer. To bury his body in the waters was his overmastering desire.

He took a second step. The water sported for a moment beneath his belly. He quivered with pleasure. The ebb of the wave disturbing his foothold, Kipe tottered, then twisted round. Presenting his back, he arched himself for the delicious torrent.

Though the next wave tried to drag him back by the heels, he held his ground, and shuffled sternfirst down to meet the next, to obtain a fuller purging of the spinal tract.

But as he now reversed, to face the ocean, he swelled with confidence. He even gave a frosty hiss, which was no laugh, but had one of the main components of mirth—the same thing that causes the cock to crow. He swaggered a little, in his splendid headdress, and clapped his arms together as the next wave hit him, and nearly knocked him over.

Intoxicated with this new variety of conquest over nature, he stumbled jauntily along the beach for some yards. He was living up to the dignity of his yachtsman's cap. He encouraged a wave to throw him down, swarming nimbly up the sagging shelf of stones. Then out of the rolling backgrounds of the ocean, a *larger* wave than any yet loomed up, foaming and rearing to strike.

Kipe, as he saw it, gave it a terrified look, amazed at its size. He sprang to escape but stumbled. The next thing he knew was that it had fallen upon him, like a liquid hill. Its chill volume blotted him away inside it—his eyes *shut off*, his nose and mouth bursting with sea-water, his limbs pinned down. It ground him under it as if it had been a millstone : it sucked him back as if a magnet were fixed at the bottom of this pebbly ramp to draw down unwary bums.

But Kipe was smart. It would take a pretty smart wave to put him out. And Kipe was tough. To be rolled down into green chasms from which he would never come up alive was the big idea, he knew that well enough. With toes digging into the sliding hill of shingle, he fought his way up against the weight of the receding wave. He drove his claws into the steep ramp of stones. He forced up his head through the water, and drew in a draught of salty oxygen, before a new mass of water almost washed him back.

With his last ounce of smartness Kipe dragged himself out of reach of ocean. But he knew he had almost croaked all the same. He flung himself back on the sand, thinking of that, as he wheezed and spat. Thinking of that—that Kipe had almost been wiped out !

A half-hour later Kipe rose from where his clothes had been.

All had now been returned to his person, upon which they were again buttoned, pinned, and tied—in the same order of seniority, the polo-shirt in the place of honour, next the skin.

Certainly Kipe had a slightly wolfish look about the gills, where the damp hair clung to the pinched contour of his chin. His eyes were sunken and bloodshot. His hands still shook. His whole body slightly shook. Otherwise there was no change.

He stood and stared, with expressionless fixity, at the ocean, his lips moving but his eyes still. The great revolving shafts of its waves rolled majestically in, cold and kindly, some yards ahead of him. He turned slowly away at last and began to ascend the powdery sand.

Scarcely had he got in motion when a thought struck him. A very strange thought indeed. He stopped. With an eye suddenly flashing with indignant understanding, he snatched from his head the still impressive yachting cap. He held it for a moment in his hand, gazing at the glittering accessories of sportive rank. Then with a snarl, turning again towards ocean, he hurled the splendid headpiece at a gracefully impending, beautifully foaming wave.

He watched the wave seize it, and rush down with it into the depths below. He watched for a moment with a puzzled intentness. It did not reappear. Perhaps, after all, it was only the *cap* the waves were after!

2

The Weeping Man

(Previously unpublished. Written 1940)

"I believe this is the silliest story I've ever read!" said Mrs. Allen Crumms with genuine exasperation.

"I was just thinking the same about this," said Mrs. Shirley, putting down her book.

"Every year these mystery stories get stupider and stupider. A clew as big as a house has been staring this detective in the face for a hundred pages now and *can* he see it?"

"Perhaps it's one of those books where the detective is meant to be an imbecile?"

Mrs. Allen Crumms shook her head.

"No. It's one of those books where the writer is an imbecile." Mrs. Shirley laughed and held up the book she had laid down.

"No one can say that Morgan Blaine is an imbecile."

"Is that by him? He's a highbrow. Just as bad. But it must be pretty awful, Janet, for *you* to find it silly."

"It is awful. Perfectly awful. His hero is the most foolish young man I've ever run across in or out of fiction."

"Perhaps it's . . . what do you call it? *Satire*. Is it satire do you think? Usually what those people write is that."

"Oh yes, it's that undoubtedly. But there are certain decent limits even for satire. At this point for instance the young man is throwing a fit and crying his eyes out . . ."

"Crying his eyes out! Is he a man?"

"Apparently. Quite masculine in fact. It's because his pal has accepted a post as instructor in the Chilean navy."

"What!"

"He has a great objection to the navy."

"What a revoltingly stupid story. I should stop reading it."

"I can't Cynthia. It's so silly it fascinates me."

The two ladies—in order of seniority, Cynthia Allen Crumms and Janet Shirley—were sitting on the Allen Crumms private beach, at the mouth of a small cave. The sound of masculine voices came growling and rumbling from inside the cave, while the ocean did a bit of growling too on the opposite side of them, for the wind had risen slightly. There were occasional bursts of laughter. One of the voices within, when it laughed, laughed too much, with a juicy abandon. So it was still laughing usually when the others had stopped.

"I woudn't read a story about a man who was always crying!" Cynthia Allen Crumms told her friend. "You highbrows!"

"I'm only a middlebrow : lower middlebrow."

"Why don't you read a good honest detective story for a change Janet?"

"About sleuths! . . . But you've just said yourself Cynthia . . . !"

"I know but anyway my detectives don't *burst into tears* upon the slightest provocation."

Three sunbathing men in beach drawers now appeared in the mouth of the cave. As a group, it was all very neolithic, except for the deckchairs and the elder woman's sun-bonnet. The bodies of all three males were burnt brown or dark yellow. Two were hairy, the darkest had no hair—which was humiliating. This one's voice was apologetically low, but not for that reason. In reality an absence of dollars—he was a college professor—was more decisive in regulating the volume of sound he produced than his absence of hair.

"Who is that, Cynthia, who *bursts into tears*? You've been crying over your book Janet?"

"Bob" Allen Crumms was a ponderous sixfooter, who had put on weight where there had been weight already. He looked down at the woman, as he spoke, with a big tolerant blue eye.

"No Bob," Janet smiled at all the hairy middleaged brawn with the kind blue eyes, "It wasn't me. There's a man in this book who's always crying."

Bob rumbled indulgently.

"A cissy huh? What's the book?" He picked the book off her lap. "Morgan Blaine. He's the guy who writes about bullfights. I read a swell story of his about a bullfight in Sonora."

Janet nodded.

153

"It's an amateur boxer he's . . . er, depicting here. But he's always got his handkerchief out. As a woman, I resent it. That's *my* stuff."

"Look Ralph . . . You can tell us. Do men cry?" Cynthia Allen Crumms enquired of the college professor, whose voice was less toughly resonant than his companion's.

"That depends," Ralph answered.

"That depends!" echoed Bob. "How does that *depend*?"

"You cry much, Ralph?" asked the third man, Steve Shirley, with a savage laugh, and Bob joined in, with the roar of a lazy old lion.

"No Steve," Ralph answered. "I'm kind of *dry*. I'm the dry-eyed variety. But it *is* done quite a lot."

"What! Men cry a lot?" clamoured Janet argumentatively from her chair. "Since when?"

"Since when? Since the Depression," Ralph said.

They all laughed guardedly.

"But they always have," Ralph added.

"You cry, Bob?" Janet asked.

"No old Bob doesn't cry," Steve declared, his hairy chest well forward, a hairy hand upon his wife's neck.

"No I guess I'm one of the drys. And I *know* Steve is. We're all drys here."

"So it is rubbish! I thought it was," said Cynthia.

Bob scratched his head. He wore his hair *en brosse* and he looked like an enormous greyheaded schoolboy.

"I do remember though that I saw the Navy cry on one occasion."

"The Navy, Bob?" Janet expostulated.

"Yes when I was at Princeton."

"How was that Bob?" said Steve.

"At a boatrace, as a matter of fact. They were certain of winning. A destroyer had been moored in the river so that cadets could watch the victory. When the Navy lost . . . towards the end they suddenly went to pieces . . . when they lost, the cadets watching from the decks of the destroyer (I remember noticing that) were *crying*."

"They cried!" Cynthia exclaimed.

"Yes. Certainly," Bob said. "They were *very* disappointed."

154

"Well!" said Janet.

"Pugilists cry of course," Bob added. "Sprinters cry when they lose. But *not* milers."

"They're too all-in to be able to I suppose!" Steve laughed scornfully.

"Soldiers too," Ralph ventured to remind them. "All the Civil War generals were great cryers."

"Now Ralph, stop! Not the generals!" Cynthia, who was a Southerner, looked stern.

"Oh yes. Not the rank and file. It's always general officers who dissolve in tears."

"I'm glad whole armies don't!" Janet said.

"Ralph's kidding you!" Steve laughed, stamping about, his chest stuck out, a hirsute propagandist for the masculine ideal.

"No I'm not Steve. Have you never read any history? The 'Iron Duke'—The British general you know who won the Battle of Waterloo."

"I've heard of *him*," said Cynthia.

"Well, he shut himself up after Waterloo and had a good cry."

"No!" Bob boomed.

"Why?" asked Janet.

"Lots of his pals were killed and it kind of upset him," said Ralph mildly.

"The British seem to be that way a little," Steve was prepared to allow Ralph the British as cryers. "Did you read, Bob, about the British Prime Minister last week . . . ?"

"Churchill? Yes, he was in tears in the House of Commons the other day," Ralph said. "That's nothing unusual. Lord Baldwin used to cry! And his friend Sir Samuel Hoare, when he and Laval were found out."

"Yes, but *they* are a lot of old women!" Janet exclaimed impatiently. "They don't count."

"But all European politicians cry. Hitler *always* cries," said Ralph.

"Well well well—shall I be left any illusions!" Cynthia sighed. "I haven't cried for . . . how long is it Bob?"

"I forget my love. Quite a while."

155

"He couldn't cry if he tried!" she said, pointing at her husband. "He has a heart of stone although he looks so kind."

Steve bent down and fondled Janet for a moment, to show sex was still knocking around whatever might be happening to men otherwise. He whispered in her ear and she shook her head. He stood up and looked tough by way of general comment on the conversation.

"Come along Cynthia," he said. "Let's leave Janet with her weeping men. Let's have a swim before it gets too rough."

Cynthia sprang up.

"C'mon Bob!" she cried. "Swim!"

"I guess I'll go up to the house," Bob said. "I have a call to put through to Boston. Be seeing you later," he said to the others as he turned away.

"I'll come along Bob too. I have some mail to attend to."

As they walked up the hill Ralph said, "It's funny how stereotyped our minds are. Especially as regards men and women."

"They are rather," Bob agreed.

"One cries, we say. The other doesn't. Both have tear-ducts however."

Bob laughed.

"I don't know what's happened to mine. I have *tried*—in confidence. Nothing doing. I once would have given a lot to have the use of them for a while. Ever so small a duct!"

"What was that for, Bob?"

The big schoolboy face looked ashamed. He puffed a little; partly the steep incline and partly embarrassment.

"When Cynthia was young she was very beautiful Ralph."

"She is still that."

"I know. Well I fell for her very heavily indeed. It was a bad case of downright idolatry. Even to this day I've never looked at another woman. You're younger than I am Ralph. You don't know what I mean."

"I guess I know Bob. I've known you and Cynthia for some time."

"Well. I was not the *only* suitor."

"Uh-huh."

"I was not the only pebble on the beach. There was another.

156

And once for the best part of a week I thought I had lost her. I nearly did . . . even now I hate to think about it."

"I see Bob. That was when you . . . ?"

"Yes that was when. But I was as dry-eyed and self-possessed as if nothing was happening at all. I reproached myself. I *could* not be feeling what I thought I was feeling, I told myself. A drop or two would have made all the difference."

"Puritan training," declared Ralph. "I'm the same. Not that I've ever wanted to that much."

They went into the house.

"How about a snort?" suggested Bob, with his finger on the bell-push. Somehow talking of the past had made him want to prolong this moment for a little while before attending to the business call. A highball would crystallize the old images that had been disturbed and begun drifting about in sentimental herds. But Ralph Denning was also glad to continue in contact—in propitious, sentimental contact—with his influential host a little longer. There was something that had a bearing upon his academic career he was anxious to broach.

Some half-hour later they were still talking—or Ralph was talking, and Bob was listening, kind but bored—when there were rushing footsteps : that rushed and stopped.

Both men looked up in astonishment, Ralph a little peevishly. Janet Shirley, the water still beading her panting body, stood in the doorway. Her face was livid under three weeks golden tan.

Bob stood up, and Ralph followed suit.

"What is it Janet? Anything wrong?" Bob asked.

Janet nodded, then burst into tears.

"Whatever can be the matter Janet! Is anyone hurt?"

She shook her head violently.

"Have a highball Janet," Ralph suggested.

"Bob!" she cried, taking a step towards him. "It's Cynthia!"

"Cynthia?" Bob frowned. "Is she ill?"

"No Bob. She's . . . she's . . . she went way out—too far as she always does. She got cramp . . . Oh Bob! Cynthia is . . . *drowned.*

There was a silence. Ralph broke it.

"Are you sure Janet . . . ?"

"It was impossible Bob to save her. Steve did his damndest.

He nearly drowned himself. He was splendid. But it was no good at all."

Bob stood staring at her, his big schoolboy face, under the grey hair, *en brosse*, expressing, at first, stolid incredulity. Then his mouth went slowly down at the corners, like a baby's about to cry. His eyes opened wider and wider; he saw not Janet Shirley upon whom they were fixed, but a row of U.S.A. naval cadets in their pretty uniforms, all dissolved in tears.

Ralph, who had been looking at the floor, jumped as Bob burst into a great roar of laughter. He looked at him in consternation. Bob was holding his sides, where he was a little over fleshly, as if in sudden pain. He stamped up and down upon his bare feet. But still he laughed. He laughed until at last the tears came into his eyes.

3

The Man Who Was Unlucky
With Women

(Previously unpublished. Written 1950s)

I

Richard Dean, or more familiarly, Dicky Dean, looked down on the world around him from a height of about six foot two inches. He was not height proud, but he was satisfied at being such a big chap. Then Dicky Dean possessed a small fortune, he could live fairly comfortably without exerting himself more than a tree, or a cloud. The consciousness of this fact influenced him to behave differently from how he would if he had had nothing. When he come down from Oxford, as everyone knew that he had enough money to live on, he was offered several jobs; he accepted a literary editorship. This gave to his life a gentle movement like the oscillation of a hammock, and it augmented his small fortune appreciably.

On a mild June afternoon Richard Deane entered a lift in the Nuffield Wing of Guys Hospital, and as he stepped out of it at the appointed floor, he did so with his large clam eye resting upon a door. The door was opening, and out of it stepped a man, who closed it behind him, and passed Dean as he made his way towards the lift. Dean noticed very red lips, dark hair, and a movement of the striped trousers suggestive of an expensive tailor.

He reopened the door through which this man had just passed and entered the room saying "Who was that?"

"Who?" answered a girl who was facing the door as she lay in bed propped on a steep wedge of pillows. "That was Antony Hope-Carew."

159

"An American?"

"No. Does he look as if he were a Yankee?" she asked.

"Could be," Dean said. "His clothes had an American look." The patient shook her head. "No," she said. "The Honourable Antony Hope-Carew is his full designation, so that disposes of the question of his nationality."

Dean had, on entering, occupied his customary chair; and now he sat staring at her. There were two girls (1) Madie or Madeleine Daintwich and (2) Madeleine Daintwich. The second of these two girls had just come into existence. The number one girl he had known for about three months before she fell ill, and was transferred to this hospital. The second one looked exactly the same, but he recognized nevertheless that this outward similarity was deceptive.

Yet she was absurdly like the girl he had set out to visit less than an hour ago. He stared stupidly, his broad clear slab of forehead marked by a single light furrow, the rest of his massive face having become blank. The expression it had worn as he came up in the lift had been wiped off. He repeated in the back of his head "Hope K'roo"—giving it the deep roo sound employed by Madeleine. The bright red of the lips of Mister Hope-Carew was probably due to their recent sweet collision with the big powerful red lips decorating the face in front of him. Because this woman had been visited by another man, this puritanic giant was instinctively repelled by the lush red sex-fruit.

He rose to his feet and moved towards the door.

"Dicky, where are you going?" he heard Madeleine enquiring, before he had gone more than a step or two.

"Well, it's not much use my stopping now," he said in answer.

"I don't understand," she said. "You're behaving very oddly, Dicky."

"I forgot," he told her. "I am taking a girl out to lunch. I shall be late."

"A girl? Is she attractive?" she asked.

"Not bad," he said, and left the room.

Dean returned to his flat. In his books of references he had no difficulty in identifying Antony Hope-Carew. He was the son of a peer. As to his occupation, he was in the F.O.; his club, Travellers, his residence, the Albany.

Dean sat down and reviewed his recent schoolboyish behaviour. He had been very fond of Madie.

He had imagined that this was reciprocated. His good opinion of himself was at least as if he were seven or eight feet above the world instead of merely six foot two; and, correspondingly, his small fortune operated as if it had been a million dollars. It was very difficult for him to imagine a woman to whom he had given himself up continuing a relationship with any other man. So now what had he done? Nothing irreparable. He would convey to Madeleine the enormity of her offence as best he could. But he would telephone to her at the hospital asking her if any of her male following were in her neighbourhood, that day; if there were no Hope-Carews that day he would pay her a call. That would be the best thing to do. He would do that the next morning.

But before he could do all that he received a letter from the hospital by the first post. It told him that she, Madeleine, had been feeling unwell ever since he had left her so brutally. She then assured him that what, apparently, he suspected was idiotic. She had no love but Dickie Dean. And more of the same, which he thrust into his pocket with a contented smile.

II

About five years later Richard Dean was up in London for the day. He had proposed to catch a train back to Exeter about eleven the following morning. He had completed what had made the journey necessary much sooner than he had expected, and he went back by an afternoon train the same day.

It was about half past seven when he reached his home, a small bungalow-like building, which he and his wife had rented for the summer at Willington—a strip of houses fronting a narrow beach, but with a good hotel, which had justified a railway station. He found the front door locked. He walked round to the tradesman's door, but that was locked too. A small side-window was not latched, he found, and so he pushed it up and climbed in, throwing his suitcase in first.

He was about to move around to the living-room which occupied most of the ground-floor, when a door opened upstairs and there was a heavy tread. He stopped, suitcase in hand, and looked up the staircase. Someone was looking down at him. It was Alec Bannerman, in his shirtsleeves. Richard Dean's heart began beating excitedly.

"Why are the front and back doors locked? And what on earth are you doing up there?" he called up the stairs. "Are you there alone for some reason? Where is Madie?"

Alec Bannerman received these foolish questions with a strange smile.

"Your wife's in bed," he said. "She has a kind of cold. I am in attendance, getting her some bovril."

Dean had stood looking up, his face growing pale. When the other had stopped speaking, he stood for about a minute, trembling a little. Then he dropped the suitcase, and ascended the stairs, two at a time. Brushing past Bannerman violently, he entered his wife's room, and slammed the door behind him.

Madeleine's face lay on the pillow beneath him as it had five years earlier, with much the same expression. He pushed back the clothes, in spite of her protests. He stepped back from the bed.

"So that is how you spend your time if I turn my back for a few hours!"

"You horrible beast!" was her only rejoinder.

"I don't expect Alec Bannerman is the first one. But he will have to do as co-respondent . . . I notice his garments here; I will ask him to fetch them."

He left the bedroom with the same violence that he had displayed in bursting in a few minutes before. He banged the door behind him.

"Been listening, you cur?" he shouted. "Collect your clothes in the bedroom. I shall be waiting for you downstairs."

He noisily descended the stairs, turned the key in the front door, went into the living-room, and sat down facing the wall. He had the sensation of being a schoolboy in the middle of something at which schoolboys usually cried, but no tears came to his eyes to relieve him. He had been treated very badly; here he sat downstairs, while they were laughing at him upstairs, while Alec put his pullover and jacket on, and tied the laces of his shoes. *He* had taken his place, he had become the husband. But he didn't pay the rent of the house—he didn't pay anything. He had no money, so he couldn't pay anything. But he would smash his ugly face for him. He would hammer his face as if he was knocking nails into some pieces of furniture. The next moment the intruder was coming down the stairs, and a moment later he saw him. He sprang at him as he was entering the door, he launched a blow in the middle of his face and cracked his head against the jamb of the door. The blow echoed sinisterly through the house; his wife heard it. For one satisfying moment he experienced the joy he had been savouring in imagination. The next few instants—a chain of events were a bitter awakening. Alec Bannerman, in no way daunted by the sledge-hammer blow he had received, shed his jacket and threw it on the ground. After this he began jumping about, and, before Dean knew quite what was happening, he received a torrent of blows in the face. He attempted to send his great arms windmilling down upon his attacker, but appeared unable to reach anything, except for a blow upon the other's shoulder. Dean was driven back into the room by a series of well-directed blows which he was unable to ward off.

Alec Bannerman was a medium-sized young Australian, who seemed almost small compared to Dean's height and over-all heaviness. But this well-knit, belted figure began springing to left and right like a mechanical toy, and his fists landed upon Dean's face as if to order—bang bang, bang bang, and so on. The giant's obvious intention to land a blow like his attack in the doorway utterly failed, his fists seemed to spend their force in the air, or to land nowhere in particular.

A compact, seemingly heavily-loaded machine, was battering away at him, and, before he realized what was happening, he was at the other side of the room. This experienced fighter had, in the course of this pulverizing advance, as Dean would discover later, blacked his eye, knocked one of his teeth out, and demoralized him from head to foot.

They had reversed, and he was falling back towards the door. Then a fine blow caught him on a part of the chin where, delivered with sufficient force, a man is violently converted from the erect position to the abjectly horizontal. Richard Dean crashed to the floor, the back of his head, hitting the bare boards near the door. There he lay for some minutes : when he recovered his senses, he became aware of his wife standing in the doorway; she was saying, "Have you gentlemen finished?"

"I don't think your husband has ever learnt how to fight," said Alec Bannerman. "Yet he began a fight just now. If he agrees we will call this little business at an end."

The victor was moving the length of the recumbent body towards Richard's head.

The stricken husband rose slowly to his feet. Balancing himself by placing a flattened hand upon the table, he said to the young Australian, who stood with his hands clasped in front of him, "Will you leave us as soon as it is convenient for you to do so?"

Alec Bannerman picked up his jacket and slipped himself into it, and then, looking back he said, "Well, good night."

To this, Madeleine answered, "Good night, Alec."

As soon as they were alone, Dean mixed himself a whisky and soda, and stretched himself out in the largest chair in the room. He slowly drank the whisky; the big healthy body did not take long to recover from the beating it had received. At last he turned round towards his wife. "Having received a beating from your lover, I have to sit here for a moment. After that, I will pack and drive away. I naturally want to get out of this place as soon as I can. I shall of course attempt to sublet it at once. You will have to give up your keys to the house agent. Tomorrow morning I will discover who is the best agent round about here. Please give me the latchkey of my flat. I will collect all your belongings and send them wherever you say."

"You realize that you have no evidence for divorce," Madeleine said.

"We'll see about that," he answered.

"It is a pity you're so rigid, Dicky. Why aren't you a man of the world?" asked Madeleine suddenly.

"If I had been, I should never have married you. What did you marry for? When you marry there is such a thing as friendship, but your technique involves betrayal from the start. I suppose you began fooling me well before the episode of the Honourable Antony. And now you ask me to share my bed with a dirty little Aussie like Alec."

164

"A snob, aren't you? You don't take anyone seriously unless they have been at Oxford or Cambridge."

"Snob!" roared Dean. "You're the dirtiest little snob who ever went marketing her sex, where the coronets are thickest!"

"You use the language of the cad you are!" she said.

He sprang up and spat in her face. She rose from her chair, wiping her face with her handkerchief, exclaiming, "You filthy coward!"

He swung his boot up against her bottom, which shrank away from the ultimate offence.

"You wouldn't have dared to do that when Alec was here, you cur," Madeleine told him.

"Ah, he would stand guard over your niceties would he? Well," he barked finally, "be off with you now that I have saluted your over-large backside. My lawyer will communicate with you."

Madeleine left the room, and ascended the stairs expeditiously. She evidently wished for no further farewells. A few minutes later Richard heard her descending the stairs.

"I must go out and get some dinner," said Madeleine, before she left the house.

Dean went upstairs and had a wash. In the mirror he saw that his eye was blackening. As quickly as possible he packed away his clothes and papers, and in about twenty minutes left. That night he slept at the hotel; and next morning, he took the train to London. But while he ate his dinner in his room at the hotel, he reviewed the background of the five years which stood behind that evening's events.

Two years after their marriage he had returned home unexpectedly one afternoon, about five, and entering their flat, was surprised to find a man asleep upon the sofa, a handkerchief over his face. Upon hearing the sound of a heavy tread, the man had removed the handkerchief and revealed the face of the Honourable Antony Hope-Carew. He sprang up and cordially greeted Dean, apologizing for his situation, alone in their flat. He was waiting for Madeleine's return, he said. She had had to go somewhere. They were going to the theatre; he wondered if he, Richard Dean, would join them. It would be great fun if

165

he would. In fact Richard had agreed to do so, and taken this surprising introduction in the best part.

At the theatre they had been introduced to the Lord Roxbridge. In the course of the evening he had heard the young lord indulging in what was apparently a facetious remark directed at himself, but he had overlooked this, and indeed, the whole affair. He thought it best to warn his wife severely against entertaining gentlemen in his absence in their flat. He believed nothing of that kind had occurred since. But that, of course, was idiotic. At the time of the disagreeable surprise in Guy's Hospital, when he had seriously to face the question of the risk of marrying a woman apt to have too great a liking for men in general, he had come to a fatal decision. He had decided to risk it, and to marry. He now saw how foolish this had been.

III

Dicky Dean did not marry again. But there was one curious result of the ignominious battle at Willington that he took very seriously. The humiliation so easily imposed on him by the young Australian had left an ineffaceable impression on his mind. Up till that time he had been so large and athletically built that no one had been inclined to insult him. He had strode about so menacingly, not a man to quarrel with, that he had been quite satisfied to leave it at that, and not to make himself a really formidable figure, like so many other Englishmen.

He proceeded at once to go to a gymnasium where a tough little ex-fighter taught people the simple rules of self-defence. There he practised boxing with men of all sizes; and at the end of a couple of years of hard training, became a most efficient boxer.

What had impressed him in an indelible way about the success of Alec was the manner in which, with great unexpectedness, he began to spring about. Probably it was not natural for so large a man to imitate this particular feature of the pugilist's technique. But he had been so deeply responsive to the image of this jumping figure, that he, in his turn, as a pupil in the art of self-defence, acquired it. It surprised the ex-boxer very much to see this large man jumping up in the air as if he were a kangaroo. But, after laughing at him a little, he abandoned that critical

166

attitude, for he found that the combination of size and unusual agility was quite effective. In order to keep his hand in Dean would pick a fight whenever there was an opportunity, and knock down a variety of people in all parts of London. He avoided conversation, he did not reproach his victim first, but just weighed in with his spectacular agility.

Although he did not marry, he admitted to the status of wife one or two women, and at last one of them, like Madeleine, invited a man to spend a few days with her, at the flat where she lived with Dean, during the latter's absence. But Dean unexpectedly returned, and found a large, not very nice man enjoying a glass of whisky with the unfaithful woman. The fellow got to his feet, and Dean said at once, "Will you please come outside with me?"

"Don't you go outside with him, Bob! He will kill you!" the woman squeaked.

But this did not stop Bob from going outside, and in a very short time he regretted his impudence in taking his ease in another man's flat. This was a fight which Dean undertook with far greater relish than the usual scraps that he found for himself here and there. The large grey form sprang about with a furious agility, the great arms and legs, in his hairy grey tweeds, in constant movement, as he delivered blow after blow upon the large fresh face of the man he had found in his room, while the fists of this interloper never succeeded in contacting the jumping man before him.

It was evening, and a handful of people watched this encounter. But also a very large wolf-hound in a garden about fifty yards away watched it, with a growing feeling that this grey, hairy figure, filling his horizon with wild movements of a kind he had never seen before, was in some way a challenge to a wolf-hound. After a certain amount of gruff menaces, this animal, his master being temporarily absent, moved barking through an open gate, and, feeling more and more anger at this war-like exhibitionism going on in his own street, approached the combatants. Instinctively feeling, perhaps, that he had not so much time as all that to settle the hash of this unlovely person, Dean discharged a whirling fist at the other man, and laid him out upon his back —a knockout, as it happened.

167

But the tall grey jumping figure now stood alone, facing the enraged animal, who sprang up at him and fastened his teeth in Dean's neck. At the same time the force of the wolf-hound's spring swept him over on to his back too, where he lay struggling with the animal, attempting to remove the jaws tearing at his neck, but without success. Some of the spectators attempted to distract the ravening animal, but that only seemed to stimulate his ferocity still more. From a ghastly cavity in Dean's neck the blood poured out, and before very long it was apparent that he was not able to defend himself against this new type of aggression. About ten minutes had elapsed before the dog's master became aware of what was happening, and with shouts and gesticulations he came running up, so that eventually, and with dignified protests, the dog retired, and his master adjusted the lead, and got him off the scene as quickly as possible, evidently anxious to be spared the sequel to this attack.

But the young lady with whom Dean had been passing his life of late appeared on the scene, and [by] her and the other people who had gathered as interested observers, Dean's lack of animation was noted with surprise and alarm. One of the men went up to where he was lying, and put his hand down in the neighbourhood of Dean's wrist. He rose, and went into a house a few doors away. In a few minutes he returned and told the others that he had summoned an ambulance and asked for a doctor. The ambulance appeared in a surprisingly short time, and Richard Dean and the young woman with whom he lived were carried off by it to the casualty ward of the hospital.

It was found, on arrival at the hospital, that Richard Dean was dead. Whether he had bled to death, or had died of a syncope, was not stated in the brief account of this tragic occurrence in several newspapers. His death, too, was attributed to the dog, and it was generally felt that the possession of these large dogs should be very severely limited to well-known people whose responsibility could be relied upon. Reports, however, of this wild fighter, and his objectionable behaviour in different parts of London, appeared in the press, and seemed, somehow, to excuse the dog.

SECTION V

Impostors

Sectional Introduction

"The Two Captains," the title story of the projected 1950s book which in the end never appeared, dates from the period after Lewis began to lose his sight. This would place it at about 1953. As was his practice during the blindness which afflicted him from 1951 to his death in 1957, Lewis attempted a hand-written draft of his work. His words were then read back to him by Mrs. Lewis, a tireless source of help and encouragement and he instructed corrections to be written in on the draft he himself had written. From this combination of versions, a typescript finally was made, a carbon copy of which provided a basis for the version of "The Two Captains" printed here. As noted earlier in this volume, the handwritten draft helped with minor corrections to errors which occurred in the typescript. On initial examination, the story seemed to date in fact from the late 1940s. But from the nature of Lewis's handwriting and for other reasons, the date of composition ultimately appeared to be considerably later.

The drafts of "The Two Captains" were made available by the Cornell Library, as was "Children of the Great," one of the stories dating from the months of 1940 spent by the Lewises at Sag Harbor, Long Island. The idea for "Children of the Great" apparently originated with Lewis's impressions of the son of an artist associate in Britain, even though the story's setting is American. Here again the editors have worked with a typed carbon copy of the story from Cornell.

With "Doppelgänger," on the other hand, the printed version from *Encounter* has obviously sufficed, as with "Pish-Tush." The real-life origins of "Doppelgänger" should be obvious from even a cursory analysis of the character of Thaddeus Trunk and the fictionalized details of his writing career. "Doppelgänger" was the first Lewis story published in *Encounter*.

170

The Two Captains

(Previously unpublished. Written mid-1950s)

I

Mr. Murray Mason had one of those ill-built but strenuous faces suggestive of thwarted power which are usually deceptive. The man possessing such a face, and there are numbers of them, is neither a Bradlaugh nor a Godwin, neither capable of defying God and Mr. Speaker at the same time, nor of providing a Bible for Anarchists. The thwarted look signifies, perhaps, storms locked up within, but not necessarily great equinoctial storms, passions maybe of the commoner kind. In Murray Mason's case (for the John in his name was silent) whatever the activities beneath the surface might be, an arresting face resulted, one which would warn you to keep awake in his neighbourhood. A War-Captain in a crack regiment, he had forced his way up very much from the ranks, from the mud of the Trenches. Though he had been out of the Army for three years, the "storm of steel" of what had been for him a very active war still sang and roared, at times, in the background of his mind.

It was about seven o'clock. Murray Mason put down the *Evening Standard* for a moment to rest his eyes. He did not care whether the Electricians got an extra two shillings and six-pence an hour or not. It was scarcely human to expect that his pulse should beat any quicker at the news : that a man capable of fixing his electric light would soon be receiving more money than he did. In Great Missenden, this suburb of his upon the leafy fringes of Greater London, every evening about seven, the electric light became so dim he was obliged to rest his eyes now and then. No fault of the little guys who scraped a living assisting our bulbs to blaze, but of politicians incapable of cleaning up the messes they had engineered.

171

This ex-War-Captain was a commercial artist. He wished he was either more *artist* or more *commercial*.

Picking up the *Evening Standard*, he turned to the crime. The Tillingtons were in the news again. A third member of this gifted family had had an unexpected meeting with a Police Constable. Both he and the Constable approached this meeting from an equally idealistic standpoint.

Asked by the Magistrate how it was that, for the third time in succession, he had been found in the same position—namely, with the upper half of his person inside the window of a shop, and his nether members outside, and why one of his pockets swelled with the burden of thirty-nine more fountain-pens than the average man would carry around with him, Tillington elevated his shoulders, conveying that he gave the whole business up as a bad job.

"Since the war, there hasn't been any police snooping around the streets at night. But this one 'ere was on his way home from a binge. Now, was it like a gentleman for the Officer to seize me by the seat of the trousers and to pull me outer of that shop like that?"

The Magistrate said, "I don't know whether Sir Walter Raleigh would have handled that part of your person with so little ceremony, or what the constable's claims are to a fastidious gentility, I am sure, but I think he acted very properly under the circumstances."

"Yes sir, very properly sir, very. But if Your Honour would allow, I will disagree."

The Constable intervened, saying that Tillington was proposing to vault into the shop, and escape. To which the indignant Tillington retorted, "It shows the kind of person yew're used to associatin' with!"

When asked why he had his bottom protruding from a shop in that way he answered indignantly, "Where would *yours* be, Mr. Rockaly (the Magistrate's name) if you saw a suspicious character lurking near a shop window full of Parker Pens as I did. Wouldn't you, sir, go after those pens and put them away in a safe place ... in your pocket sir, as I did?"

"First removing the window-pane with the aid of a stolen diamond?" enquired the Magistrate.

Tillington was offended. "There ain't nothing stolen about *me*. I'm in the black books of the cops. My poor old mother and dad are in a position where this behaviour of the Police hits them right where they stand. My poor old dad's hair has gone the colour of a sea-gull." (Laughter in court.) "There is some people so ignorant they wouldn't know which side of their shirt was last week's and which this." (Renewed laughter.)

"It was your young brother was it not (a promising young criminal) who shot two mounted policemen from the bedroom of your residence, killing one; what did he get for that Tillington? Twenty years wasn't it?"

Tillington's manner changed. After the pattern of Sarah Gamp,[1] on a legendary occasion, it was an unwritten rule that young Arthur should not be mentioned. He drew himself up.

"Twenty bloody years . . . yes, Mister Rockaly, you're bloody well right. Twenty years . . . for a kid what's too young to swing! That was a *crime* that was . . ."

"Which, Tillington, killing a policeman?"

"Killin' a cop?! . . . no sir, a crime against my kid brother to put him away for half a life-time."

"If the law were written by me," said the Magistrate, "for killing a policeman a boy of even ten would hang." (Murmuring in court.) "And what did your elder brother receive for beating that old woman within an inch of her life? Only twelve years, was it not? You are a terrible family."

The father of this brood was a clerk in British Railways. His old face, with hair the colour of a very dirty sea-gull, might be seen any day of the week at the ticket-office-opening at one of the smallest stations in the periphery of Greater London. His view of the feats of his notorious family was similar to that of the prisoner at present facing Mr. Magistrate Rockaly. He was a much-photographed man, and if he caught your eye as you were buying a ticket, he grinned in acceptance of your assumed sympathy—and admiration for such a paterfamilias.

The Commercial Artist read with satisfaction of the "attempted suicide" of Tillington—a trickle of blood at the wrists. A noble family disgraced, by being pulled by the seat of the trousers out

[1] A character in *Martin Chuzzlewit* by Charles Dickens.

173

of the shop-window, must demonstrate against the harshness of the Police. Noblesse Oblige.

By birth Murray Mason belonged to the same class as the Tillington family, and the attitude of that class to the "Copper" is not affectionate, as is that of the middle class to the "Bobby." So in reading in the Press of the treatment by the Police of "plucky kids" he would mutter "swines," automatically and reminiscently without really feeling anything.

With contempt penetrating the sympathy he felt for the sorrows of the Tillington family, he lay back in his chair resting his eyes, when there was a timid knock or two at his door. Murray twisted his head towards the knock and barked a military "Come in." The door opened slowly, a girl lifted herself up the necessary five inches on to the floor of the studio. This was nineteen forty-eight. The food was inadequate, and five inches made a call upon a girl's muscles which they would not have done before the War. Swaying a little, with a tired dancing gait she moved self-consciously across the floor, smiling at Murray. It reminded the veteran-of-thirty of a camel parade.

As he had no sister, he did not visualize the existence of the female with all the problems of the mating season, perhaps having to fight her way to the mirror, and how, at last, the poor family sent out its shop-counter princess, undulating along the slum. Cicely was, for him, an individual, and he was taken in a little more by the cheaply-scented feminine masquerade, than he would have been had he grown up in quarters not much ampler than the Eskimo, Max Factor overlapping his masculine fraction of the available space and imparting a glow to his trousers.

Murray rose, and wound his long arms around the little underfed slum Princess. The pathetic little face poked itself up towards his, appreciating the warmth of the "boy's" flesh as it came in contact with hers. Her heels beat a quick tattoo as she clung to him, pretending to dance, and swaying about a little. They had never been out to a dance—perhaps this was a hint.

"No darling," she whispered. Murray desisted and drew back, wiping the Max Factor lipstick from his face.

"It's a good thing I'm not a married man!" was his stock comment.

174

"If you was, I shouldn't be letting you kiss me," said Cicely.

"So *you* say, Sissy."

"And so I mean," she retorted, bracing herself defiantly, against an imaginary married man!

"Sissy."

"Yes."

"How do you feel this evening, girlo? Could you take the Sports Girl pose. About a half-hour or three-quarters would do it."

"I feel fine. Do you want me to dress, Murray?" She enjoyed wearing the "tennis girl's" outfit.

"Yes please, Sissy. You'll find them in the usual place."

Murray had fixed up "Miss 1948" where he usually had it.

Soon Cicely came out from behind the model's screen with a supposed Wimbledon swagger, striking, with the tennis racket, at imaginary balls, as if the air had been full of them.

The average female of the working class at this period could support very little fatigue, so it was not easy to get a really good model. Murray had soon discovered that evacuees become women were defective in stamina. Having worked until his sitter gave every sign of imminent collapse, he told her to rest.

It was about twenty minutes before she recovered enough to be sociable. She was now in her own clothes again. She shared Murray's frugal supper, with a glass of beer to wash it down.

"You *are* thin, Sissy. Here, let me feel that little arm of yours." He leaned forward and squeezed her pathetic little bicep. "Now one of those emaciated leggies." The mention of her leggies sent her into an explosion of squeaks and giggles. He placed his hand on her small thigh just above the knee. Sissy protested, "You tick-erl!"

"You're a skinny little creature, my girlo. While you were down at Mrs. Sespan's did you have anything to eat, or did the old hag pocket the evacuee money and starve you?"

Sissy gave a quick giggle. "We had a lot of soup. We ate all the gooseberries in her garden . . . ooh you should have seen her chasing young Bert!"

, "I bet you didn't get your little teeth into any meat, did you? I would summon all those lousy people who lined their pockets that way during the War."

Sissy appeared to take incredibly little interest in how much

175

or how little she ate during the war. She was only amused at remembering some of the misadventures of their hosts, and the odd bomb which had dropped now and then within a mile or so of their refuge. She was not prepared to direct her attention to anything except the ridiculous and laughable, whatever revealed her as a little laugher.

"Roy is as fat as you are thin, isn't he? I wonder where he ran into all those rump steaks and suet puddings?"

"Roy, you know, lived at headquarters, he fed pretty well there I think. Mum told us that he was getting the size of an elephant."

They both laughed. "I haven't seen old Roy for some time. Let's see, will you ask him to come round and see me tomorrow, Sissy? When he leaves work."

"Okay. He was speaking about you only last night."

"Oh, what did he say?"

"He said he wished he had your job." Sissy giggled.

Murray Mason watched her. "Is he fed up?"

"Oh I don't know. He was going off the deep end last night. Mr. Ross had blamed him for something."

Murray Mason stood up and stretched and yawned. "Well, I must get on with that Tennis Girl."

Cicely stood up, rather disappointed.

"Well," he said, "say to Roy if he has nothing better to do. He may be meeting his girl."

"He hasn't got a girl." Cicely laughed. "He had one, but that's all over long ago."

"He's a cautious old bird, Roy. He's five years younger than I am; what he'll be like when he's my age I don't know." They were now walking towards the door. "Five bob, Sissy. Come in on Thursday if you're free. You are free? Good."

They embraced, and he thought how thin her face was too—altogether she was like one of those skinny little chickens. He slapped one of her little buttocks. He crowed at her—she giggled at him. She waved her hand, and before he closed the door again he adjusted the latch to *shut*.

Cicely disappeared down the lane, swaying her little body, imagining herself a tennis girl, a wow at Wimbledon. Whereas he returned to his work, thinking deeply about Roy.

II

Roy bore very little resemblance to his sister. He had been in the Army for nearly six years and the Government had fed him up and exercised him, as if he were a horse. He had been burned by stronger suns than could be found in Great Missenden, in the last year or so of the War. It is extraordinary how long those burns will last in the young.

When he left the little insignificant Branch Bank, in which he worked with a man not much older than himself, called the Manager, he asked himself what old Murray Mason wanted. He did not find out until nearly two hours later. As they sat in Murray Mason's Studio, drinking beer, the Artist said, "Roy, why don't we rob your Bank? It asks to be robbed every time I go there. It is a little box of a place, containing all the loose cash in Great Missenden. It does seem a pity, if it could be done without danger, not to transfer the cash from the Bank into my pocket and your pocket."

"All day long I'm sort of half thinking about *other people* sticking us up, Mr. Ross and me, but I never thought about doing it myself."

Murray laughed boisterously. Whenever he entered the dolls-house size Branch Bank, he eyed the naked wealth revealed in the course of every transaction over the counter, however insignificant, with an eye which had become wolfish in the Army. But the Wolf was out of the picture now; he was just the good fellow, freakishly suggesting an exploit which was purely in the realm of Joke.

"I expect that people who work in such places soon get to feel a tabu belonging to the Money-shops?" Murray was watching his friend, but no expression of any kind was visible on Roy's wooden face, who answered at once without emotion.

"Yes, we do get to feel, I suppose, a sort of superstition about money. It isn't the metal and paper, of course, representing pounds and fivers. It's the thought of what it can do. When I was up at our Head Office where there was millions and millions, one felt a bit funny at first. But down here, you know, there isn't practically anything."

177

"How much *is* there in that little box of a place? Ten thousand?"

"Good lord, no," Roy replied in big-eyed surprise. "Ten thousand!" He laughed. "There isn't as many hundred. Ours is just a convenience for the local tradesmen."

"Yours is hardly a Bank at all. I always think of it as a dolls-house—I suppose that is why I thought it would be such fun to rob it—it would never enter my head to rob an ordinary life-size Bank."

They both laughed.

"Then I think it must be because I am *restless*. Mr. Underwood, the fellow I work for, isn't paying me as much as he should, and I think I shall switch over to another line of work."

There was a shade of disappointment in Roy's face. "You won't be leaving here, will you Murray? Or will you be able to carry on in this Studio? You don't mean you will be giving up Poster work?"

The commercial artist looked at him quickly. Roy was not indifferent to him, that was obvious. He now looked a little worried, and said, "That I really can't say for the moment. I should hate to leave Great Missenden; but that will depend . . ."

They now talked a little about life in London; in Hampstead or Hammersmith, or perhaps in the neighbourhood of Victoria Station. Roy's family had lived there before the War, he was born in the Vauxhall Bridge Road. Murray decided that Great Missenden, for him, was just as good as Mayfair. Roy was not so sure, he liked the big Cinemas. At last there was a silence. It was Roy who returned to the subject of his Bank.

"There is one bad thing about the place where I work; it is not centrally heated, and since I left the army I feel the cold twice as much as I did before."

"Go on. I never seem to feel the cold, at least not in England."

"You ought to spend a good cold December day on your feet for seven hours, in our little bank."

Murray laughed. "Well, we ought to burgle it, and then perhaps they would build a bigger Bank!"

Roy smiled. "That would not be easy. Because it's small, you underestimate its strength."

"I should have thought it would be dead easy. Who would

stop you . . . after midnight? The Police don't patrol at night, as they used to." (He was instinctively repeating the remark made by Tillington to the Magistrate.) "It is isolated. When there is so little money as you say they have there, they don't take a lot of trouble about its safe keeping . . . Someone inside would have to be in on it. If I wanted to rob that little Bank, I should go in with you . . . or with the Manager!"

This seemed to tickle Roy a great deal. "You wouldn't find it easy, not with Mr. Ross!"

Murray picked up the heavy bottle of beer, and was about to pour out another glass for his friend, when Roy sprang up exclaiming, "No, old man," and placing a hand on Murray's wrist. "I didn't know how late it was. I must be toddling along."

Murray saw him off, and on the way out they cracked a few jokes about cracking cribs and Bill Sykes and that sort of thing.

"A spot of beer makes the time melt away, doesn't it?" Roy said.

"Being in good company has the same effect on me," Murray replied, with a flattery undisguised, and only not nauseating because the "like yours" was omitted.

III

Nine months later Murray and Roy met in the Kitchener Arms and walked round to Murray's place—in Roy's case to delay going to bed, as in Great Missenden there was no alternative.

Roy wandered around and gazed inquisitively at a drawing for a Cinema poster.

"What girl is that?" he asked, pointing at one of the figures.

"She is a mixture. The face from a photograph. I'm afraid she doesn't look as luscious as I intended. But I am so damned sick of cooking up girls who will make some little rat's mouth water! What a trade!"

"Many would like to be able to do what you can do, Murray." Roy looked up to Murray, for whose life-like images he felt a primitive awe. Even more, the photograph of the young War-Captain standing up with an almost German stiffness in the little silver frame on one of the shelves, with, among the decorations, a Military Cross and a D.S.C., impressed him very much, filling him with awe of another kind.

"For the benefit of the ladies," Murray would say, when he found some male looking at it. But it caused Roy's spirit to stiffen with respect—the first time, even, his hands stole out of his trouser-pockets as he stood looking at it. Murray noticed this with contemptuous satisfaction. "For two pins he'd jump to attention!" he sardonically reflected.

"You are a very clever fellow, Murray, and you don't know it old man!"

Murray laughed condescendingly. Roy had not been there five minutes before he said, "Well, Murray, do you still itch to rob my Bank?" To which Murray replied, with an answering smile, "Every time I come in to cash a silly little cheque, I feel the same about those little wads of brand-new notes, smelling of the factory where they forge them all."

"Forgers? Hang it all, we're not that!"

"No, but the Government is," Murray told him, and took a good blood-shot gulp of beer.

Roy's slow-moving mind was twisted into a knot by the impact of an idea that the Government could do wrong. When he regained his equilibrium, he did not think he liked the last remark of Murray's. The London and Great Eastern Bank was by no means sacrosanct for Roy, but the Government was a very different matter. He cast on old Murray a rather questioning eye. Seeing this, the ex-Captain thought it would be best to deal with that error of judgement.

"All I meant by that rather horrifying remark was . . . well, the Party. The Party in Power at the moment can do what it likes with our currency, can't it? So when I used the word government just now I meant the fellow who is living in Downing Street at the moment. Mister Attlee is no forger, as we know, but can we say as much for all past M.P.s;" (he dropped his voice dramatically) "for instance, the *last* Government? Could you trust them not to . . . oh to do anything with the currency? I couldn't." Murray swigged down a red-hot shot of badly debased beer.

"I am afraid I am a Conservative," Roy said quietly.

This was a big smack for Murray. He was even silent for

about three seconds, then he said, in a rather "religious" voice, "I say, old man, I hope I haven't hurt your feelings. I had no idea you were a Tory. I must say it surprised me, you are such a liberal, progressive sort of fellow."

"I have been told that before, that I was not a typical Tory. But I have always voted Conservative, without caring much who won. Habit, that's all."

"I'm not much of a Labourite either, I must admit. So we shan't fight over *that*. When we're cleaning out the Kitty in the London and Great Eastern it will be the Labourite money anyway, won't it?"

"I suppose it will," Roy agreed, with a rather slow sheepish laugh.

"I shan't feel happy about it you know, old man, while all that money is reposing there in your coffers. My Army training won't leave me in peace—that little centre has to be cleaned up. Haven't you a feeling of that kind, Roy? It's really not a great deal to do with the *money*. It's just an Op, there's something there which oughtn't to be there!" Murray rolled about with light-hearted laughter; and Roy laughed a little too.

When Murray had an extra drink or two he always gave expression to his canard, as he called it ("I expect old Murray speaks a bit of *parlez-vous*," Roy would tell himself). He literally would wail about "This cock-eyed life in Great Pissington—I would rather be a lavatory-attendant in the West End! Alamein was not much of a place, but we were fighting for Egypt. It wasn't really anything but it sounded like something! What the hell am I in Great Missenden for?" He swept his arms around the studio—where his posters stood out frivolously in the gloom. "All that is bullshit Roy," he whispered hoarsely. "I should like to get away, to South America or Australia."

"I feel restless sometimes," Roy admitted. "But I would like to go to sea."

Murray looked at him, and broke into a short laugh. For in Roy's eyes of distinctly nautical blue a dreamy wife-in-every-port look had appeared.

"The sea is not your cup of tea?" Roy asked, slightly offended.

"No, old man, *my* cup of tea has no salt tang. The Channel Crossing is as much of the sea as I can take."

It was the *mot* of a cynical young man he had greatly admired. It had debunked the sea for him. It did not do this for Roy though it was another proof for him of the superior worldliness of Murray. As they were saying goodnight, Roy said to his friend, "You're a wild lad aren't you? You sleep with my sister, and now you have almost talked me into burgling my Bank!" And as he walked home he passed the comic little Branch Bank where he worked every day and he laughed to himself as he pictured himself and Murray breaking in—a couple of stealthy little figures. "Operation Bank" it would be, and he laughed again.

IV

A year had passed. Whether under the name of dinner or supper it was over and past for all the good people of Great Missenden, and for the bad people likewise. A modest-sized, not swift-moving figure, began to enter the glare, though at a considerable distance, shed by the enormous window of Murray Mason's Studio— from which a blast of light reached so far as to bathe this distant pedestrian, the only moving thing within a considerable radius.

Murray Mason heard the step outside, and, charcoal in hand, he stopped to listen. The bell rang, he rose and flung open the door. There stood his cold-eyed visitor, Roy Stubbs. Roy looked at him without speaking, coldly, steadily.

"Oh, it's you, Roy, came back at last."

"Yes, Murray, it's me," was the reply, and Roy, without waiting to be invited, entered, and strolled over to that part of the room where its occupant usually relaxed. Murray closed the door, and followed him, depositing the piece of charcoal on the way.

"Beer?" said Murray.

"I don't think so Murray. I have something very serious to talk to you about."

"Far more serious matters," Murray laughed, "than any you can wish to discuss have been helped along by a good glass of beer."

Roy Stubbs fixed a dull and resentful eye upon the other, and said in a new angry voice, "My business may seem very unimportant to you, but to brush aside what it does not suit your book to take any notice of . . ."

"Now, now, now, Roy, don't begin quarrelling with me. People who have been engaged together in certain enterprises . . ."

"Why not say *crimes* Murray, why not say crimes?"

Murray leaned towards him in an almost menacing way.

"For me crime is an abusive word, it is invented by those who hold the power in order to describe any action taken against themselves. You should not use the language of the bigwigs who pay you the wages of a skivvy to take care of all those bundles of paper they print, and the debased metal they coin. In a spirited action you took from them a small fraction of their pelf. Was that a crime—do you want to call it that now?"

"If that was not a crime, it *is* a crime, a dirty crime to rob one's comrade."

There was an angry flash in Murray's fine dark eyes.

"I understand your feelings, old man, but I cannot allow you to be abusive about me. As the Clerk, who was naturally the first on the lists of suspects, it would have been impossible for you to take care of the money we together so criminally took from the Bank, would it not? So I stepped in, you passed the money over to me and I took it up to London, where I put it in a safe and secret place."

"Thank you Mr. Murray Mason for putting our booty away out of reach of detection."

"Then a disaster occurred, which might have happened with anyone, Roy. I borrowed (and I know I was wrong in doing that) most of your share of the booty. To place on a horse which everyone pointed to as a snip. The name was 'Badahos'—you remember it don't you? It came in tenth. I have never been so near to putting a bullet in my head as I was then, Roy."

"I daresay. But if you spend other people's money you ought to pay it back, oughtn't you? Not hand me twenty-five pounds, and say 'I've lost the rest of it.' It is the One hundred and fifty pounds that is owing to me now old man. You know you couldn't have got a cent without me. If I hadn't provided the safe combination . . ."

"Rot! We could have broken it open. There were other ways . . ."

"No there weren't Murray and you know it. Mr. Ross still suspects me . . ."

"That will not affect your chance of promotion?"

"Of course it is liable to do that."

Murray screwed his eyes up to focus his visitor, as if examining a microbe.

"You," he said with cutting emphasis, "you won't get any more money out of me. There is nothing you can do about it. I wouldn't give you any even if I had it—and I have not."

Roy brought his fist down on the table and the glasses rose in the air and tried to break one another. "You have a sneer on your face, Mr. Mason. But you don't impress me by your sneers. I'll smash your face for you if I can do nothing else, Mr. Captain . . . but there is something much better than that I can do. You wait. There is a card I can play, my smart ex-Officer, of which you know nothing. My advice to you is to cough that money up at once, or you will sneer on the other side of your face."

Murray had been a silent escort for the enraged bank-clerk throwing off dark threats which he knew had no substance. As they approached the door he stepped forward and grasped the handle. Looking back into Roy's face, before he opened the door to let him out, he spoke harshly, and ended with a laugh.

"When you get home," he said, "put your head in a bucket of cold water. That is the best thing you can do." He opened the door with a laugh whose ring insisted that it must be a final laugh.

V

The only two places where Murray Mason was apt to meet Roy was at the Kitchener Arms, and at the Bank; but his visits to the Inn were infrequent, and when he was cashing a cheque Roy would hand him the money without looking at him. Two or three months passed without any further move on the part of Roy, and Murray concluded that he had finally got away with his high-handed theft. Then one evening he went round to the Arms. There was Roy Stubbs sitting at a table with a man he believed he had met somewhere, but he could not remember where. It was only as a soldier that he had ever met anyone who looked like that—all the signs which it was impossible to counterfeit of belonging to the highest class in the land—outwardly more or less like anybody else (that the shoes and shirts were made for them was only revealed to the observant) who were just Mr. This or Mr. That, whose rank was subtilized in the anonymity of the twentieth century. Murray sat on a stool at the Bar, revisiting in memory scene after scene to try and identify this stranger—while the particular cigar-scent which emanated from such divinities played round his nostrils to assist him in his search. Over and over again he thought he had got his finger on the name. On each occasion it was the right *class*, but not the right *man*.

Lazily wondering by what means Roy had come to know a man of that quality, he was rather startled by the familiar tones of a voice last heard in anger. Roy was at his side, he was being invited to come over and have a drink: "A very nice chap," Roy was telling him. "Captain Henry Kavanagh. He's out of the top drawer Murray, come and have a chin with him about old times."

He went over with Roy to the table, carrying his drink with him, and he felt the sensation, which always possessed him in the company of one of these people, a sense of being far nearer the gutter than he was. And he was conscious of the other man's expecting this and acting accordingly. He felt, too, that Roy felt, for the first time, that he was an under-dog like himself.

The last thing that Kavanagh talked about was the War. The nearest he got to it was in speaking of the "deplorable state of London" (he had been up to the West End the day before); he mentioned that he had been in the Cavalry Club and there saw Lord Montgomery. "Of all the British Generals I have the lowest opinion of Montie. He is like a Hockey Club Tout." When Alexander was praised by Murray, Kavanagh said, "Ah, he is a pukka General." The way the ex-soldier was in the habit of plunging into reminiscences (assisted by dirty old French maps) was what Kavanagh declined to do. Murray recalled another man of the same class, a Major Villiers-Brown, who was just the same. The "comradeship of Fighting Men" was something of which he was totally, and very firmly, unconscious. Sport was discussable, cricket much preferred to football, and Kavanagh appeared surprised when Murray referred to tennis; he seemed to assume that neither of the two men with whom he was drinking knew anything about tennis.

When Murray got up to go and said "Good night, Captain Kavanagh, I was very glad to know you," the other said, "Good night, Mr. Mason," and the ex-War-Captain strode away in a blue rage against Roy. He reflected, "As Roy didn't tell him anything about me he probably took me for some local garage hand or the man who keeps the grass cut at the golf club." He marched back to his studio cursing not Captain Kavanagh but Roy.

So as he was devouring the banana which concluded his evening meal he was amazed, on going to the door to answer a knock, to find Captain Henry Kavanagh outside, to breathe in that aroma of the Caribbean which no other type of man has access to.

"Don't be surprised," said the smiling figure. "Roy told me more about you when you had gone. I was interested to learn that you were an artist." He had entered without more invitation than the unmistakable delight in Murray's face and the gentle backward movement of his body and, talking as he went, was now passing the place where the photograph of the War-Captain stood. He waved his hand towards it. "And also that you had a most distinguished career in the Army." (He approached the photograph.) "The Rifles, a splendid regiment, and an M.C. with palms—with star—which means a splendid record of gallantry—you should be very proud of yourself, Murray Mason, you know." (He turned with a great natural smiling grace towards Murray.) "So I thought I would be extremely fresh, and pay you a visit on the spot—rather than go to bed—not to invite myself to swallow all your store of alcohol, but" (and putting his hands in his pocket he produced a large flask of whisky) "to play my part, and bring my drink with me. You are not offended I hope?"

He placed the bottle on the table. "May I sit down?"

"Please, please!"

But he jumped up again immediately to inspect the posters pinned up on the wall. "I know a man who collects posters. These are all cinema posters, aren't they?"

"Please don't look at those."

"Oh, but why? You pin them up on the walls, don't you?"

"Not to be admired, I assure you."

Kavanagh told him he was too modest. "For instance, that gel up there is just like a gel I know."

Murray Mason had sometime attempted to pronounce the word "girl" in that way, but had failed completely; it was as difficult as some words in French. It was people of a different race who made that sound when they were referring to a woman of the youngest variety. When a little later his visitor replied that something was not "in his line of country," the fact was confirmed that for the first time since his army days, he was in social contact with that unapproachable class who ruled England from their country palaces and famous clubs. He had one of these arrogant, matchlessly exclusive creatures in his studio, his captaincy in a crack regiment, being mentioned in dispatches, had made a snob of him; and to have this Hussar Captain drinking with him in his workshop was one of the rewards of valour. If you are brave *enough* . . .

And then they began "sloshing" out Kavanagh's whisky. The more the Hussar Captain drank, the more his *difference* developed. The opposite difference, in the case of Murray—past existence in the working class—was roughly elicited by the alcohol : he was obliged to check his inelegant exuberances. So, in sum, Murray did the checking, but Kavanagh continued to live among "lines of country" traced by flying foxes and did not damp down the aroma of the Caribbean leaf.

Kavanagh poured the last shot out of the whisky bottle. With a complimentary formality he began : "Captain Murray Mason, now that I know you, I regard you as a perfectly splendid fellow. I am a soldier, and your great record in action tells me about you all I want to know. I would put my hand in the fire for you, even if someone told me, and supplied me with irrefutable evidence, that you had robbed a bank."

Murray had been leaning forward to extract a cigarette from the packet between them on the table. He stopped dead, his hand immobilized a few inches from the cigarette packet. Then he sat bolt upright, glaring at Kavanagh. But his visitor was in no way moved by the sudden glare of the eyes before him, and went on equably with his exordium.

187

"I would say, all right, what of that. If a man who has stopped, almost single-handed, an entire brigade of the enemy— a V.C. show—may he not lift a few hundreds from a suburban bank? I would like to know why he should be treated as if he had spent the war years as a shepherd in the Highlands of Scotland. Is this man to be encouraged to act in the more lawless fashion for years on end, and then abruptly to be ordered to conform to the laws of the stay-at-home? Would it not be better to lock up for, say, five years this man who has lived outside the law for so long, and especially distinguished himself in acts of unlimited barbary? No; I should say to the censorious, it is quite natural that this heroic soldier should rob a bank. It would be surprising if he did not."

Murray Mason sat staring at him, as if mesmerized, without speaking, but as if he were on the point of bursting out of the spell.

Kavanagh said to himself "Is he going to kill me?" but after half a minute of silence, he decided *not*. He leaned forward and placed his hand on Murray's, and gave it a fraternal squeeze. This pleased Murray a great deal, inside whose mind a revolution was being swiftly enacted. He returned the squeeze, only fervently as well as warmly.

"Kavanagh, old man," he said emotionally, "I don't know what possessed me to do that!"

"Nonsense, old fellow," Kavanagh replied, "you are a man of action. That is just the sort of thing you would do if you felt the itch to *act*. There were many other things you could have done, such as card-sharping, persuading old ladies to part with money, false pretences, you know all that is contemptible, well dirty tricks in fact, would repel you. I know that anything of that kind would be impossible for you."

His head held high, the mask of the "White Man" sternly set, he looked over towards Murray Mason as one brave man to another, for whom a mean action of whatever sort would be unthinkable.

"Now," he said, "it did amaze me to hear that you had been capable of something, of something which, in another nature than yours, would be understandable enough. You, Murray Mason, are a *Sahib*, a gentleman. Excuse me for saying this, old

188

man, but how *could* you have behaved as you did towards that nice little chap, Roy Stubbs."

There were tears in Murray Mason's eyes. "Old man, you have made me see what an unspeakable cad I have been." Murray shouted, "What a dirty thieving little soldier. I wish to hell I had done anything but that . . . anything, anything. It is a stain, a filthy stain, on the whole of my military life."

He put his face in his hands and sobbed.

"You mustn't take it that way, old chap," softly urged the kindly visitor. "I know a man, a Wing Commander, who was with the troops who entered Germany at the end of the war. He stole from a poor old lady a magnificent old clock, an heirloom. When I was with him, a year or two ago, he became so miserable about it I thought he was going to smash it up. After calling himself the most abject things, he fetched some brown paper, wrapped it up—quite a packing job, for it was an extremely large clock—and addressed it to the old lady."

"I say, that was jolly decent wasn't it? That was sooper wasn't it?"

Murray sprang up, and began striding about.

"What a rotter I have been! What a dirty cad! And it was old Roy who did the whole thing really. I've never said that, even to myself . . . but it's the truth."

Kavanagh rose, and approached Murray. "I tell you what, old chap," he said. "I tell you what. It isn't much, is it? . . . Let's see, a hundred and fifty quid, isn't it? Why don't you sit down and make out a cheque without further ado, to little Roy Stubbs, put it in safe keeping with me, and I will hand it to him tonight if possible—do you know his address? He will be so overjoyed . . . and I shall get the credit! But I will tell him it was nothing to do with me. I will explain how you pulled a cheque book out of a drawer, sat down, dated it, signed it, and filled it in, and throwing it down on the table said, 'Here, hand this to old Roy!' "

Almost somnambulistically Murray went to a drawer, drew out a cheque book, sat down at the table at which they had been drinking, and filled out a cheque. Almost idiotically obeying Kavanagh's directions, he threw the cheque across the table to Kavanagh, who had resumed his place.

"Here, old man, give this to Roy!"

"Right!" Kavanagh looked very happy, for his little friend Roy Stubbs. "Do you mind giving me the address at which Roy sleeps—his home, perhaps."

Murray wrote out the address, and, when he had received it, Kavanagh placed it in his breast pocket silently.

Rising, Kavanagh said, "He may still be at the Arms. If not I'll take this to his private address." He picked up the cheque from the table and dropped it into the same pocket as the address.

The two men walked silently towards the door. When he had lifted his hat from where he had placed it, Kavanagh turned very quickly towards Murray, seized his hand, and pressed it. "Old man, you're one of the whitest men I know—you are one in a million, Captain Murray Mason. By the way, let us meet sometime in a more civilized place—the Cavalry Club will always find me."

Murray stood in the doorway, cooling himself a little in the chill atmosphere. The scent of Captain Kavanagh's cigar drifted back, it was like the aura of that noble spirit, whose warmth was fading into the damp night. Murray turned back into the studio and closed the door. Already the place looked entirely different. Was that where he had sat? Had Kavanagh been sitting over there, or had the whole scene been a product of the brain? At least the cheque book of his London bank was not imaginary. It was there upon the table.

VI

A week later, at his request, Roy Stubbs, when his day's work was over, had come to see Murray, and they sat there opposite one another, and he looked at the man he was visiting rather blankly.

"How have you been getting on, Roy, since we last met?"

"Oh, I don't know. As usual."

"Did Captain Kavanagh find you?"

"Find me?" Roy looked astonished. "I don't know what you mean old man. But Kavanagh is *not* a Captain. I discovered that yesterday."

Murray did not speak. In silence he slid a cigarette packet

out of his pocket, lighted one of his cigarettes and dropped the
packet back again.

"Roy, how many people have you taken into your confidence
about that little exploit of ours . . . at the bank . . . where you
work."

Roy flushed a deep pink. When he began to speak he did so
in a stutter. "Wer—wer—what d-d-d-do you mean? . . . I
s-s-swear Murray . . . n-n-n-no-one knows."

"Not Kavanagh?"

Roy remained silent, becoming a deeper shade of pink, beneath
the fringe of tan.

"Captain Kavanagh . . ."

"Kavanagh is not a captain," Roy interrupted.

"Not . . ."

"Not . . . No. This is what I discovered—yesterday. Kavanagh
is a phoney officer—never been in the army it seems. You know
how they took steps to preserve the aristocracy in this war . . .
they didn't want a shambles as they had in the first."

"I never heard of that," Murray protested.

"Well, they did. Old Kavanagh, I hear, is the nephew of the
Earl of Bristol. And he is the heir. That is why *he* was kept out
of it."

"I see," said Murray very coldly. "I see. Have you heard from
him . . . have you received any communication?"

"No. Why? I was in the Arms last night, but they told me
he had gone away . . . oh, upwards of a week ago."

Murray suddenly sprang up. His eyes were protruding, the
muscles had tightened around his jaw, he looked the War-
Captain . . . Very much the War-Captain on the Eve of the
Attack. "The dirty swine!" He exclaimed hysterically. Then he
suddenly appeared to remember something, and sat slowly down.

"What is it, Murray?" Roy asked gently.

Murray looked at him dully and angrily for a moment. "What
is it? Only that I gave that bastard a cheque for you, a week
ago, for one hundred and fifty pounds."

Roy gaped, and then he scratched his head. Then a smile stole
into his face. "Why, Murray, did you do that?"

"Why? Because I wanted to pay you your money. Does that
surprise you so much?"

191

"Well . . . why did you not give it to me? What made you give it to him? To Kavanagh, of all people."

"To Kavanagh of all people," Murray cried angrily. "What do you mean, of all people? Isn't Kavanagh a trustworthy enough kind of man?"

"Because he is the heir to an Earldom? Well, I shouldn't say that that made him more trustworthy, old man. The real gentleman thinks about things very differently from us—doesn't he? We are rather a sentimental lot. That class of man is not at all sentimental . . . not at all . . . One is supposed to get to know about people, you know, in a bank. We wouldn't trust anybody of *his* class—we should know we should be jolly sorry for it if we did. No, old man, I am on my guard at once when his sort enters the branch. Never trust a *real* gentleman . . . As a matter of fact Kavanagh's made a vain attempt to get me to lend him a couple of quid . . . me . . . that was typical!"

Murray stood up. "I wish to be alone," he said. He pointed towards the door. "Apologies and so on, but please go now."

Roy stood up, hesitated a moment, and then walked towards the door. When he had reached it he turned back, and spoke in a loudish voice : "That money is still owing, old man."

2

Children of the Great

(Previously unpublished. Written 1940)

The children of famous men are invariably stupid. Derek Gilchrist was no exception to this rule. But he carried things a stage further by *looking* stupid—so incredibly stupid that with him nature obviously had contemplated a test case. To have a sort of showdown with mankind; make them do something about it.

For why should this libel upon the great be perpetuated? Nature seemed to ask. Why allow these morons to bear the name their fathers made illustrious? Inherited money is unimportant, one may suppose, in nature's eyes. For there is nothing innate about money. But if a man causes a name to become so famous as that of the great historian, Patrick Gilchrist, the name, at his decease, should be abolished or made ineligible for common use. Certainly his foolish offspring should be compelled to drop it, and adopt some other patronymic.

Now Derek seemed aware somehow of all this. It was indeed the only trace of intelligence betrayed by that personage. His face was that of a sheep. But it *had* a glimmer in it somewhere: a light of sullen understanding.

It seemed as if he knew people would say—"Oh Derek Gilchrist will be there tonight. He is the son of Patrick Gilchrist you know" (as of course they always did remark)—and how those prepared in this way would thereupon picture to themselves something a bit out of the ordinary: somebody possessed of *some* of the insight and learning, the fearless wit, of the great Irish-American historian. And this edifying experience, his sleepily watchful eye announced, he was resolved to sabotage.

All that was left to him, perhaps that was the way he looked at it, was to be *a great disillusion*. And he was determined to take the fullest advantage of his only asset. He seemed to give some thought to the niceties of disillusion. Even down to the selection of his suits of nondescript tweed, unimaginative hair-cut, the dispirited slouch with which he shuffled into a room, he betrayed a consciousness of being Disappointment that it would be hard to match. No fraction of his personality remained, he saw to that, to which hero worship could attach itself.

Yet, there was in Derek a sardonic spark of the great scornful mind of his parent. He would rub their noses in it—those who to "see Shelley plain" would cross the ocean. Or that was the most charitable view to take of this almost obscenely dull fellow —left drifting about the world by the improvident Irish seer who begat him, forty years before.

Maud Jaffe was more fashionably dressed than usual (she knew how the scholar appreciated *lume*) as she set out to meet the son of the great Patrick Gilchrist. Having herself at college shone very brightly in the historical field, Gibbon, to her way of think-ing, sat upon a throne beside the Caesars. And Patrick Gilchrist was his peer. If the Roman Empire belonged to Gibbon, did not the backwoods of the United States before the age of steam belong to Gilchrist their preeminent historian?

Maud did not have to prepare little speeches to impress, as she moved placidly along in the car behind her father's chauffeur. She knew her stuff so well, she was aware that all she had to do was to make a few historical allusions as the opportunity offered, and it would be plain she was a master of her subject. But she had no desire to talk shop. It was, in the main, the social thrill of encountering the flesh and blood of one of her girlhood gods. It was that that had decided her to cancel a party engagement elsewhere: for in all other respects *this* party was the less attrac-tive of the two.

There were upwards of twenty people in the massive, rather shabby room, in the downtown apartment, when she arrived. Her practised eye, speeding from face to face, settled upon a handsome bearded young figure, the centre of an admiring group. He had unmistakably the Gilchrist eye. Oh yes—and the *beard*. He was truly complete. Patrick must have been just like that at —what? oh 'round five and thirty, she should say at a guess.

Her eyes feasted upon the massive profile—the curling chest-

ıut beard : the commanding eye. The eye of a man accustomed
o follow great rivers to their sources, in the footsteps of intrepid
rappers : or to be present at the most secret confidences of snuff-
:aking colonial statesmen, bewigged and full of resonant words.
Perhaps, like his father, he had acquired that look of high
command by the pursuit of the same momentous things? Perhaps not. Perhaps it was just an air you inherited, if born in the
purple (in the purple patches of Gilchristian prose!)

But her hostess was bearing down upon her.

"Maud, you great beautiful lamb!"

"Ty—You great tempting flower among women!"

"Darling! I am so glad you could come. I want you to meet at
once without more parley Mr. Derek Gilchrist. Follow me. Don't
trample on the guests in your eagerness!"

But Derek was preparing for his greatest triumph. That evening
he was shabbier even than was his custom. A pronounced spell
of indigestion had routed such few social energies as he possessed.
They were all busy coping with the acidity within.

This solitary offspring of the great Gilchrist, when Maud and
Ty approached, was sprawled out in a corner beside another girl,
whom he had reduced to silence by the simple method of leaving
her questions unanswered, and gazing, from beneath his untidy
pale red eyebrows, at the floor.

When Derek's eyes fell upon Maud Jaffe, a dull spark was
kindled in his eye. He understood at once what was expected
of him. The enthusiastic young face that was gazing at him—
already with that incipient disillusion, in this case amounting
almost to horror to which he was so accustomed—indicated that
this would be no ordinary occasion.

Sluggishly he heaved himself up, and stood with a sheepish
grin, his arms hanging helplessly at his sides. The displeasure at
being disturbed was diminished by the keen satisfaction of dashing hopes and disappointing expectations.

"A great admirer of your father's, Derek!" his hostess informed
him, a little severely. For everyone who knew Derek had reason
to complain of his backwardness in playing the lion's offspring.
Such few little advantages as he had in life derived from his
sonship, after all : yet he would never bestir himself a foot to
help his friends put him across.

195

He grinned again, more sheepishly than ever before, and emitted a sort of guttural *baa*, which was his laugh.

Maud Jaffe was a loyal romantic girl: she reproached herself with her mistake with regard to the heroically bearded young impostor, at whom she cast, over her shoulder, an indignant glance. No son of Gilchrist at all: some pretentious nobody, she was sure! *This* was the real heir of the body, the genuine historic piece. And she bent her brows upon Derek—settling into position again, slumped but still grinning—in painful concentration. She sought to discover points of similarity between this fresh complexioned nonentity, and the bearded giant of historical research.

"It's quite warm this evening," said Derek entrenched behind a matter of fact Dublin brogue. This he always employed when desiring to serve up his stupidity in all its native rawness. "Quite hot indeed," he added, looking at her blankly and pointedly. He had a great belief in the sardonic resources of the Irish manner and the Irish voice, used very formally, to convey a sort of brisk imbecility.

"It is warm!" she assented enthusiastically, lighting up her eyes, with a hero-worshipping glow, which brought the grin back to his countenance. There was a haunting goat-like introspection as he stared into the fire that wasn't there. (He was really more like a silly goat than he was like a sharp sheep.)

"Be hotter than this yet," he advanced the opinion. "We're only just at the start of it."

"I'm afraid so," she sighed. "I am afraid we are."

"Oh yes, it will be very hot. Quite oppressive. New York is no place for a human being in summer."

The other girl, who had been listening to this flow of words with a certain annoyance—for he had not given *her* the benefit of his views about the weather—now remarked, "That's what *I* said a moment ago, Mr. Gilchrist!"

He raised his pale red and slightly eave-like eyebrows.

"Did you now! That is remarkable. I did not hear you say it."

"No? Well I did. I thought you hadn't heard."

"Dear me—I must have done so," Derek observed. "If that was what you said," he added with an undertone of scepticism.

"I'm quite sure it was!" the girl cried. "I remember thinking

196

hat your father had described somewhere how the first Dutch
settlers in New York wondered at the damp heat."

Maud Jaffe nodded in grave confirmation.

"Even the Indians didn't like it. They were glad as a matter
of fact to leave Manhattan."

"Is that so?" Derek answered, with polite boredom. "Were
there Indians here?"

Both girls were silent. Both looked down, the original girl with
a slight smile.

"I should have said that the Indians with their copper skins
would be indifferent to the heat," Derek objected.

"Apparently not," Maud said.

Into Derek's eyes of cheap china blue—but faded, as everything else about him, by long years of ill paid librarianship—a
light of satisfaction crept. He looked almost animated.

"But how do you *know* that Miss Jaffe?" he enquired, with
his most forensically dogmatic Dublin delivery.

It was the other girl who answered.

"Because your father said so!" she smiled.

"Ah! My father. Of course. He wrote that did he?"

Reference had been made to the Great. The ice had not been
broken. The ice as a matter of fact was thicker than ever. But
the king card had been placed face up upon the table, curled
beard and all. And he had affected to disregard it, as if it were
not *his* trump, but theirs. Out of the corner of his eye, he watched
the scandalized expressions of the two women. It was a situation
after his own heart.

He was especially delighted with the effect produced upon
Maud. He did not take much interest in the other woman. But
the moment he had set eyes on Maud Jaffe he had experienced
an unwonted stirring in his phlegmatic depths. Really something
that he could never remember experiencing before.

It was so unusual for anything whatever to happen in this
morose interior—which exactly matched the deadly dullness of
the external man—that he was extremely astonished. He rubbed
his eyes—a frequent gesture with him, as if to keep himself
awake. This time however it was as though to make quite sure
that he was not dreaming.

A kind of reluctant animation showed itself. His gestures

197

became almost forcible once or twice. Instead of sitting slumped in a dreary apathy, which was his favourite position, he propped himself up upon an elbow, like an invalid who was just beginning to sit up and take notice. And unquestionably it was Maud Jaffe who was responsible for this change.

Of course this did not mean that he now wished to shine, or to impress, or anything of that sort. That was not the form his resurrection took. He merely wished to appear *so* dull, so unutterably stupid that his dullness might strike this lovely but learned blonde as *phoney*.

Yes, for the first time in his life he would have liked to have appeared interesting to a woman. And his instinct told him that his only possible chance of achieving this end would be so to excel himself in portentous commonplace that no one, meeting him for the first time, would believe that a person *could* be so stupid as he appeared. They would say: "No: a person cannot be so stupid as all *that*! He must be shamming. Probably he is hiding great powers of intellect beneath this mask."

Now, for whatever cause, these stirrings of a magnetic nature, in the dim innards of Derek, found a response in the secret places of the much more lively nervous system of Maud. Her eyes grew kind and soft—after the first few moments of horrified disillusion.

She was quite a bright girl, was Miss Jaffe; and she was capable of realizing that three and three need not always make up to six, but might quite well at times, and in certain cases, add up to *zero*. She was also capable of understanding that there were zeros and zeros.

A really adequate beautiful bearded replica of Patrick Gilchrist would have aroused in her nothing but awe. Any attraction other than an intellectual one would have been out of the question. But here it was a different matter—where the great original was seen so much through a glass darkly, and so shorn of all impressiveness—so pathetically degraded.

So, as she became reconciled to her cruel disappointment, and acclimatized to the unfortunate Derek, she began to discern all sorts of little touches—even traces in his features, and his way of rubbing at his eyes or hunching himself up—deriving she felt sure from the great man from whom he stemmed.

Was not this just such a son, when you came to think of it,
s Patrick Gilchrist would produce? As he would *wish* to pro-
.uce, and, being a man of iron purpose, consequently *would*
•roduce?

All his accumulated pessimism, was it not strikingly expressed
1 the person of Derek? That apathy of the latter, that nirvana,
,vas symbolically *just right*.

All of Patrick Gilchrist's teaching was beautifully explicit in
his huddled simpleton: or no, not simpleton—for she would
1ot admit that Derek was a simpleton. That was a mask only.
Jo—in this—how should she put it?—this *conscientious objector*
•f the "struggle for survival?" This man who did not seem to
nind whether he survived or not! Or rather (she told herself,
.s her eyes grew still kinder) this mind that was too fastidious, too
ensitive, to lift a finger to perpetuate something that was not
vorth going on with.

But Derek notwithstanding *did* perpetuate himself. Without
truggling at all—without lifting a finger (more than it took to
>rop himself up just a little on his elbow, and put just a fraction
nore animation into his conversational exchanges) he defeated
he ends of his scornful parent, that great pessimist, and even
·aised up offspring to carry on his name.

Even while Maud Jaffe was saying to herself how splendid it
vas for this great sceptic to have decreed extinction, in bearing
1 son who was an advertisement for stagnation, and a message
:o those about him (signed *Gilchrist*) that life was not worth while,
and should be allowed to die of inanition—even in the act of
:eaching herself to admire this wonderful nonentity, she was
paving the way for its repudiation.

For *pity* almost immediately set in. She began to pity this
lifeless shell, implacably labelled with the world-famous patronymic. And of course pity by imperceptible degrees, took on the
attributes of *love*. Love had already germinated before she rose
from the chair upon which she had sat down—a little hurriedly,
a little dazed—upon being introduced.

They met again, needless to say, and after many meetings,
when they had got to know each other well, they knew that they
would marry. Or, rather, at last *Derek* knew that he at last would

wed. He conveyed to Maud, with a moroseness that beggars description, his awareness of this fact.

But a spark of exultant egotism played somewhere in the depths of his flinty eyes, as he interrogated the beautiful creature in front of him (who had been thrown in his way through the agency of his dead father—an irony which the latter would have been the first to appreciate) and learnt that she shared his designs. That she loved him, as he gloomily desired her.

Thus the spell was broken—the dismal spell beneath which he had wilted and vegetated. The spell of the seer who had denied life and whose dead hand had weighed so heavily upon the corpse-like Derek, had been broken by the intervention of this big learned beauty, with all the stately grace of her Vassar dreamings—under the spell, she too, of Patrick Gilchrist.

These two so differently spellbound people, as a result of their encounter, set Derek free. He could not be made intelligent—it was too late for that, but the animal impulse forced its way to the front. Thereby all was changed.

"Darling Derek, you are so sweet!" Maud told him as she kissed his sceptically blinking eyes. "What did your father write? 'Men's shadows take all sorts of shapes: but none belong to them like that little shadow that is the size of a child, which occurs when the sun is almost perpendicularly impending.'"

"Did he write that, Maud? What in heck did he mean?"

Maud was delighted, and kissed the flesh and blood of her august master with great bluestocking gusto. With all the bottled up sensuality of the library and the study, her thirsty arms enclosed him in a passionate bluestocking hug. The numbed but tingling Derek, whose eyes shone with a dull triumph, was pleasurably placid, as his hand crept as stealthy as an indian along the silken trail of her amazonian limbs.

"You have never read a *word* he ever wrote, you great dunce!"

"Haven't I?"

"I shall have to take you in hand."

"You have already!"

"Yes I know, but I shall have to teach you about the past as well as about the present."

"Why?"

"Because your ignorance is such as to abash and to appal."

"Is it now!" he protested. "It often surprises *me* how *much* I know, on the contrary."

"You know nothing. It's obstinacy. You are as obstinate as a mule. And what's more you pride yourself on it."

"Not at all!" he retorted hotly. "I am not proud. But I don't see what use there is in knowing all about Choktaws."

"All right!" she cried, stroking his rather scanty hair with enthusiasm. "You shall retain your virgin ignorance."

"That would be best," he said. "Spare me all the evil knowledge that is yours."

"We won't tamper with your ignorance—it shall be respected, you sweet sheep!"

They had first met at the beginning of the Depression—even in that there was a symbolic propriety. In the late spring of 1940 they sat out on the loggia of their beautiful Long Island home, with two of their three children sitting with them.

Patrick O'Connell Gilchrist, their eldest, and ten years old, was reading a book. Already his finely sculptured head was of a severe and meditative cast. The book dealt with the early migrations of the Celts. The second child was leaning on the back of a chair, and staring at two birds stalking in stiff jerks upon the park-like tree-shaded lawns.

Ornithology had marked him down for its future devotee. As to Derek, he was now, when he could summon the energy, a sort of yachtsman : he stared at the waters of Long Island Sound upon which the sail glittered.

Since Maud was a rich girl, his life had greatly changed. Derek had become a partner in a well-known publishing house in New York. It was rather bright at times, before he entered it. But since that date its yearly book list had grown duller and duller, and more and more unenterprising, until at present, from having been only a moderately successful firm, it was now one of the most prosperous in America. Upon any tendency to imagination on the part of the other partners, Derek acted as an infallible brake. They had begun to defer to his judgement on all matters for they had come to look on it with awe. No good book ever got past him.

Patrick looked up, and said to his mother, "As we are Celts,

201

mummy, I suppose we *ought* to feel some . . . well, *family* interes
shouldn't we in these rather tiresome people (tapping the book)
Oughtn't we?"

"Why?" asked his father, grinning sheepishly. He still had
his oily Dublin brogue.

"Not necessarily, darling," his mother answered. "Race is no
really important."

A puzzled look appeared upon the intelligent face of the young
historian, who obviously would be the image of his famous
grandfather, minus perhaps that gentleman's sardonic characteristics.

"But is not family important, mother?" he enquired, after a
moment.

"No!" uninvited his father supplied the answer, with a still
heavier grin of lazy mischief.

"Yes darling, *family* is," his mother said (disregarding Derek's
contribution to the discussion) as she knitted placidly at a big
brown something. "That is another matter entirely. That is of
great importance."

3

Doppelgänger

(First published in *Encounter* magazine, London, January, 1954)

"It is a capital debunking. In your best vein," said the Editor, a young man, all deep-pink skull and twinkling eyes, an Oxford accent fruity and faultless in the midst of the pink expanse; a Scottish pink only acquired after generations of exposure to the keen moisture of the Highlands and Islands. His tweeds were so expensive as to belong rather with the Oxford accent than with the Gaelic pink. "I did not know he was so *perfect* a phoney."

"A phoney?" I echoed. "Has my Trunk the look of a trunk with a false bottom?"

"Not that," he answered, "it looks as if the entire trunk was false. He has a great reputation, but why I can never understand. Trunk is a disagreeable smart-alec."

"He thoroughly deserves his great reputation *and* is a smart-alec." I paused a moment, to give him time to admire the paradox. "That, of course, is the difficulty. My story is about that conjunction."

"Ah no, sir, I cannot allow you to separate those two things in that manner. It is the *smartness* which is responsible for the reputation." The smiling composure of this undergraduate-debater warned me not to continue. He would expect me to admire *his* smartness. "Or perhaps that is what you meant. You meant that he has a great reputation *and* is very smart—that follows. The *difficulty* is that this should so often be the case."

I laughed politely. "No, they are quite distinct," I insisted. "What is extraordinary is that so often a great reputation (very well merited) should be associated with something ridiculous and contemptible."

"How do you mean?" he said cautiously.

"Well, to begin with, is it not amazing how foolish almost any man may be made to look, in historical perspective, as Lytton Strachey proved in his *Eminent Victorians*?"

"But did Strachey prove it?" aggressively pounced the Editor. "We recognize now that Strachey is historically good fun, but nothing more.

"It is not every *we* who recognizes that," I told him. "Strachey, without being conscious of it, was innovating. He thought he was guying the beliefs of the Victorian age, but his techniques were less exclusive than that. Take, for instance, General Gordon, the hero of Khartoum. His Bible Religion was fertile in satiric material. His utterances were so nonsensical, in the days before his death, that gales of laughter may be made to blow eternally around his name. But the tender passion is another source of uproarious amusement : and Gordon might have been made to oblige in that direction as well. He was a homosexual, we now know. Could Strachey have discovered a snapshot of Gordon in a playful moment with a negro boy that also might have been found distinctly comic. I remember how a certain novelist of my acquaintance had gone to visit Strachey in the country. Our satirist was seated on the lawn, surrounded by large books. But they had apparently remained unread because some under-graduates from the neighbouring University had put in an appearance. The hysterical shrieks of laughter of the Old Maid, not less funny because of the long and postiche-looking beard, the come-away-nearer girlish gesticulations of this extremely tall perverse amorist, were reported disgustedly by the visiting novelist —who seemed to think that a man of Strachey's intelligence should not publicly indulge in the tender passion, whether perverse or otherwise.

"Then liberalism would, I feel quite sure, provide for a Strachey of the future quite as much entertainment as Victorians ever did. The follies of the Victorians derive mainly from misunderstood religion : the follies of libertarianism, in the 20th century, derive chiefly from sentimental politics—in their turn deriving from sentimentalized religion."

The Editor had been attempting, all the way along, to plunge in with some debating point, and hold up what I had to say.

During my references to sexual perversion I experienced the utmost difficulty in restraining him from gleefully intruding. Now he was feeling that he had lost all his opportunities; nevertheless, as I firmly drew to a close, and sat back in my chair, he lost no time in taking my place.

He was twinkling at me in a superior way when he began, "I notice, sir, that you regard sexual perversity as *funny.*"

But I broke in at once. "The transports of the pervert, as those of normal lovers, are ridiculous—neither *more* nor *less*, ridiculous because (must I say?) the reproductive act, the swallowing and evacuating processes (self-preservation) are degrading, we look fools when we are at it."

"Oh, this is a hypothesis," he clamoured.

"If you like," I said. "But let us avoid anything that could be described as hypothesis and climb towards truth, in another way."

"I am ready to climb with you anywhere you like—I am awfully fond of climbing." (I could see that he was increasingly annoyed at my giving him so little opportunity to express himself.) "But I must first ask you to clear up for me a statement you made——"

I held up my hand. "Let us return to that when we have finished climbing. You wished to dispute the humorousness of the indecorous—that man at his most functional is man as he would not wish to be seen. All this talk of ours is about a public man, is it not? Well, when a man or woman becomes very prominent, he or she is transformed into a kind of public statue, in a certain sense and to some degree."

"Oh I say," the Editor burst out.

"When, sir, just now you spoke of debunking, did you mean simply a taking off the pedestal, so to speak; or—to speak symbolically, as I have been doing—to reduce poor old Trunk from the Greek statue that he has become, back into flesh and blood again?"

"I really don't know what you are talking about, sir," said the Editor angrily.

"Let me explain a little, then. This is what I mean by the Greek statue aspect of a great man."

"There is no such aspect," objected the Editor. "An Eminent Victorian may have enjoyed such a deification in his lifetime;

but the eminent of today are content to be men and women."

"It is not the eminent," I objected, "but it is the Public who do the deifying. However much a 'great' this or 'great' that may resist deification, the superstition of the majority operates as it did in the days of the 'Victorian Giants.' "

"To some extent," the Editor began.

"Well, let us accept the fact that the average of mankind looks upon the famous, especially if they are highbrow or intellectual, as dehumanized as a statue on a pedestal in a public park. They still can be startled by any biographer who tells them how a novelist, like Dickens, was attracted by an actress, just as ordinary men are."

"But what are we talking about?" said the Editor irritably.

"I can see that you had something more in mind by *debunk* than merely denying poor old Thaddeus Trunk a place in a public park or even a *plaque* after death." I stood up. "You meant that Trunk tries to occupy his monument. If all he did was to work upon his *legend*, to improve his publicity face, to write his *own* obituary notice more and more heroically, that would be tiresome, but it would not matter quite so much as what he actually does. He wishes to *live* his publicity figure. There it is inside his house—in his bedroom, in his bed, a publicity-figure, not a real man. So when is he ever the poet? He should drive out this publicity interloper and if he does not, someone else should. No poet as fine as he is should maintain so compromising a parasite. For a man's publicity is a caricature of himself; it is really how the public sees 'greatness.' Now it was this heroic publicity scarecrow which you had in mind when you spoke of *debunking*, was it not?"

The Editor had risen too, smiling broadly. He did not speak until I had concluded. Then he said, "You know what I meant so well that I will leave the whole question in your hands and say no more about it. However, it *is*, my dear chap, a tremendous *debunk*, and I congratulate you."

I took possession of my manuscript, which he was tapping forcibly with the tips of his fingers where it lay upon his desk. "There is something I should add to this," I observed. "You shall have it back in a day or two."

As I was walking away from the Editor's little office, I was saying to myself that I did not know whether my story could be thought of in the way indicated during my talk with the Editor, for it describes something which actually occurred.

When I got home I typed at the end of the story I had taken away with me the following addendum :

"The shallow or the inexperienced might absolutely misunderstand this story. Let me add, therefore, that Trunk is a very majestic Word-Man, a great poet, he has been a verbal craftsman of the highest order, he may be compared to Catullus (allowing for the different time and place). He must be saluted as though he were a great interpretative musician, a pianist of enormous resource. And he is a man who has so perfect a devotion to literature, that you will never hear from him a valuation which is tainted with the personal. His creative work, and how superb it is I do not have to say, benefits by the same natural detachment. Any mistakes of judgement he may have made derive merely from the occasional frailty of his reason."

THE STORY

Thaddeus Trunk, known to his friends as Uncle Thad, is passing into the seventies, without any particular change from his grizzly entrance into the sixties. As to Uncle Thad : he has always (defensively, I think) presented himself as an Uncle. He would say, humorously, "Your old Uncle Thad sez" this or that : or "Your old Papa Thad." He had always the itch to offer advice, to tell others what to do with their lives, to teach them how to Write, to teach them how to Read. He realized that this could not be done, unless it were done comically. And so, puffing a little through his moustache, and frowning portentously, he would say, "Listen to what your old bourgeois Papa tells yew!" or something of that kind. With a lot of cracks and quips, and mouthings and rumblings (about "Yew young avant-guardistas") and so forth, he would deliver what he wished to deliver. He would be the pedagogue or the soothsayer. Even at thirty years old, dear old Uncle Thad was paternal or avuncular. As a fact, some of his contemporaries were much more *avant-garde* than he was, since he was in love with the Past, being an American and so in any case he would be inclined to apologize for himself as a laggard in the March of Progress, and a snuffly old *passéiste* digging about among musty old manuscripts.

For ten years now he has lived in a high valley of the mountains of Vermont, U.S. For ten years he has been dying. Fur-capped, with leather leggings, and inflated to an impressive bulk in a short overcoat, lamb-skin-lined, collared and lapelled with cloth as stiff and thick as the bark of a plane tree, photographs of him sitting and milking his favourite goat Gianetta, spitting blood of course (glaring down toughly at the sight of the manly colour of his bloodstream), though it is asserted by those who have stopped up at the Camp Trunk with the Master that he has not had a haemorrhage for years—these photographs circulate in literary circles, from Montparnasse to Mexico City. And his reputation grows year by year, as he dies and dies, and spits and spits. He is photographed among icy peaks, alpenstock in hand, the white beard frostily bristling, as high above other men as it is romantically possible to get in the U.S. : that is the star photograph.

Stella, his wife, is an Englishwoman, possessed of considerable wealth. As he has no money himself this was for him a fortunate circumstance. The Camp Trunk used to be the Camp Baxter. Baxter was a tycoon who built and planned this property for himself but did not enjoy its amenities for more than a half-dozen years, when his firm became bankrupt. The Trunks, though it was rather larger than they actually needed, secured it for a relatively modest sum.

It is a sprawling, flat, wooden palace, with log walls of a dark brown, so that it has the effect of a dozen log-cabins welded together. As it is only of one storey, and as some of the rooms are very spacious, it spreads out over a considerable area. From the door leading down into the furnace-room at the rear of the house, to the extremity of the dining-room protruding at the front, it must measure over a hundred yards. A natural waterfall a short distance away provides the electricity required; a brick house by the side of the fall contains the plant. In the rear of the main building is a square courtyard, paved with bricks; beyond it stands the garage, a large incinerator, for rubbish, and a short distance away what Uncle Thad refers to as "Mr. Hazeldon's harem." That is the engineer, who lives in a spacious wooden building with his wife and sister. But once as many as three sisters of his wife were to be found there, girls in their late teens or early twenties. This seemed to Uncle Thad an unnecessary number of young women to be domiciled under one roof with one man.

Would Trunk die if he stepped down off this lofty mountain site? Probably. But meanwhile, according to report, he is in the best of health. The Camp Trunk provided a cheap holiday for a number of people (for all that is over now, and the past tense must be used about many of these details, where one is speaking of the inmates). Trunk himself preferred to invite *les jeunes*— "discipular" youths (a favourite adjective of his), usually from one of the colleges, and usually versifying. The dogs barked, the horses neighed, the cocks crowed stridently, when the station-wagon arrived in the thrilling air, catching the breath of *les jeunes* as they jumped from the door, with sparkling eyes receiving the tough, half-jeering welcome of their Uncle Thad, their luggage seized by their brother-in-verse, the rawboned if sweet-tongued Cobe, the house-boy. Should they arrive in a blizzard, it was Cobe's task to keep open a path for them between the station-wagon and the door of the kitchen.

Coburn, known as Cobe, is a young poet who imitates the Master's verses with great skill: though if Trunk's are often empty enough of meaning, Cobe's are often completely devoid of sense. When the elements are particularly beastly, the sight of Cobe, a gaunt snowman, whirling his shovel as if to cut paths through the air, is very impressive; and the monstrous figure of the befurred and bewhiskered invalid, looking immensely tough, as though he were charging through a storm of steel instead of merely whizzing snowflakes the size of a gooseberry, advances menacingly towards them, a figure of myth. In fact, an arrival in winter, the dying poet battling with the elements, was apt to be a "great experience" for the more impressionable. It bore out the most tragic accounts of the life of the "Great Invalid." If it is below zero the visitor is hurried into the kitchen where Cobe's wife and several other domestics pluck their coats from their shoulders and wipe the snow off their clothes. Then they traverse the middle regions of the house, and emerge in the very large living-room, looking on to an ice-caked lake. The house temperature is kept at eighty degrees. As they are taken to their rooms, they may pass Trunk's study, from which forever is heard the rattling of a most dynamic typewriter. It is dynamic because, all day long, it is attacked by a muscular young woman. For hours Trunk is dictating; he strides up and down, his heavy load of grey hair avalanching down upon his frowning forehead, tossed back, massive and leonine; as he shouts and spits his dictation, the eyes are long black slits behind their glasses, and the jaw muscles are always mobilized near the ear. He is a near-six-footer, and he feels the very picture of a "fighter," as he attempts to "tower above" the half-dead woman, endlessly hitting the keys, as he strikes out in words at a hundred institutions and a thousand "ticks" infesting the underworld of Letters.

The postman who, everyday about noon, empties the U.S. mail from the box nailed to a tree, seldom bears away fewer than seventy or eighty letters or cards. What this mountain post-man collects from Camp Trunk are notes to young poets in Pakistan, Bolivia, the Gold Coast, Malaya, New York, Teheran, San Francisco, Wigan, Guatemala, Borneo, Wyoming, Winnipeg, and anywhere else in the world where a little verse is written and the Venerable Trunk, milking his goat, and spitting blood, has caught the eye of the little verse-maker. The moment he sees a verse, in no matter what language (which he can understand or not), Trunk writes an encouraging note. They are sometimes incomprehensible, they usually splutter with expletives against the blockheads who mistaught the budding song-bird, or the general conspiracy to put a stop to Song. When the little song-bird's notes are choked with catarrh, or croak like those of a scabby little crow, the good Uncle Thad will observe that his correspondent should rest up a little, or try and shake the grit out of his iambics.

Was not this a little maniacal? For had not Trunk advertised his contempt for the Majority in all its forms, had he not sneered at those who would waste their time in blowing upon a tiny little spark glimmering in the recesses of Mediocrity? The horde of warblers he woos and wows must poison him with their dullness, and he must know that this is happening, and yet one side of his study is a mass of letters from all quarters of the globe. What idiot conceit causes him to play the Dispenser of Culture to what he regards as benighted Mankind?

Here we have a habit, like the extraordinary grimaces some men affect, until, two-thirds of the way through life, the face integrally includes the grimace. Or one may think of it as a nervous tic. Such a publicity complaint could exist nowhere except in the United States. And if you allow Publicity to master you in this way, it becomes a whole-time job, and at last you live for Publicity.

It is in solitude, it should be recalled, that major works of creative art are produced. Trunk lives in the solitude of high mountains. How appropriate, people thought; that is the place for the true creator. But the fact was that he lived up to his neck in human society. He was almost submerged, spiritually, by a horde of anonymous beings. Yes, through his childish mania for publicity, poor Trunk brought a multitude up into the mountains, polluting the air; and he may be regarded as a victim of the Public. Those who, like myself, know what he can do away from men, where he can be a great poet, and hold up his head among the Gods, have lamented at what we saw.

One day in September of last year the Trunk station-wagon met the New York train. The chauffeur had been asked to identify a small red-faced young man with a large pipe, which he did. As the identification was in progress, the chauffeur found that a tall man was standing there, apparently waiting to address him. In answer to an enquiring glance the tall man explained that he was a near relative of Mr. Trunk's, and had come to see him. So, when the station-wagon arrived at the camp, two people stepped out instead of one.

Uncle Thad arrived almost immediately, greeting the little fat nobody with a tough growl of welcome, handing to Cobe, who had followed him, a battered little grip and the little Minstrel's overcoat. Then he turned to the stranger.

"My name is—oh the same as that of your mother. I come from the town in which you were born. We are fairly closely related; that is not my only excuse for turning up here, but . . ."

The stranger was well dressed, his blue eyes sure, smiling and frank, his luggage inspired confidence, and whether for these reasons or one less easily explained, Trunk narrowed his eyes to welcoming slits, thrust out his hand in good western fashion, and said, "Cousin, come right in. Glad to see anyone from the old nest, spesh'lly a rel'tive. Here let me give your suitcase to the house-boy."

He took the handsome case and handed it to Cobe. "Put this in room nine."

Thus simply, and without more ado, the stranger became a guest. That was almost the last time that Trunk and the Stranger spoke to one another without friction. Trunk led the way through the labyrinth of the house until they reached the living-room, where Stella was sitting before a large tray and pouring tea. Trunk dropped himself in a low chair—he always dropped himself like an inanimate object, he never *sat*. He then rolled his head in the direction of the Stranger, who had sat down and was lighting a cigarette. "Meet Cousin . . . d'know his name. Comes from the capital village of Slabash County. He doan look so benighted as he oughter look. But I gave him a bed, and we shall see."

Mrs. Stella Trunk nodded a smile of bright intelligence at the tall stranger, whose appearance she liked at once. His grey hair was thick, but brushed over stiffly to the left. His features were handsome, and from the grey-blue eyes to the jutting chin there was, she thought, a strong family resemblance to Thaddeus . . . though he was clean as a new pin, and nicely dressed, and put his cousin to shame. However, it did enable her to see how Thad, it he shaved and brushed himself up, might be quite a presentable man after all.

Counting the new arrival with the red face, there were now five young men, all visiting poets. Sitting beyond the Mystery Man, who separated them from Trunk, for a short while they sat and looked at him, this cousin of Uncle Thad's. Then the red-face and the pipe made acquaintance with the other poets, and soon a brisk talk about a new book on Rilke was in progress, and this was followed by one of the young men moving quickly to the Columbia radiogram, and inserting a record of a Marienlied by a young American composer.

Stella had given the Stranger his cup of tea and conversation between them had ensued, on Stella's side enthusiasm regarding the beauty of Slabash County, on the Stranger's qualified agreement, and (with a shy smile) something to the effect that he much preferred Wiltshire. This aroused the rugged nationalism of Trunk, who was at once at his most belligerent. He began showing off for the benefit of his young guests.

"You should be ashamed of yourself, Cousin, preferring a pitcher-postcard of Ye Olde Thatched Cottage to the grand places we get born in over here, and should know better than to prefer the picayune . . ."

"I am sorry, Mr. Trunk," the Stranger energetically interposed. "I have no jingo reputation to keep up, so I can say what I think of Slabash County, and I prefer the English downs to the tick-infested bush clothing the jagged hills of my native valleys."

Stella laughed pleasantly. "Bravo!" she said brightly. "Thaddeus has all the nationalism that it would be bearable for one family to contain. Personally, a down bores me to tears. I think there is nothing in England that is a patch on the valley of the Hudson River."

There was loud applause from the chorus of young poets.

The Stranger's retort changed Trunk's neutrality to a watchful hostility. He did not answer the jingo taunt: he sat with a deeply abstracted air, showing that he was no longer interested in what the Stranger might say. When, however, this disturber of the peace joined in the conversation of the young poets, and expressed opinions with regard to the *literary* character of the poetry of Rilke, Trunk pricked his ears up, slowly turned his head, and stared at this bold guest. It was time that this person was stamped out, and he began discharging sarcasms at anything he said, turning towards *les jeunes* to mobilize them against this cousin—if it was a cousin.

"If you *must* inspire yourself from the pages of *Poetry for Everyman*, Mister Whateveritis, you might try to understand what is being written."

Poetry for Everyman was one of the popularizing handbooks written by Trunk fairly recently.

With a taunting smile the Stranger said, "Do you think that *you* understand it?"

There was a buzz of excited resentment at this from *les jeunes*, who all looked at the Master, expecting a pulverizing retort. But all he did was slowly to turn his head once more, and to gaze

213

curiously at his relative. One of the young men then took up the argument with the Stranger in support of Trunk's interpretation of his own book; but without hesitation the Stranger put him right, going into technical details which very soon silenced the young man, but, curiously enough, drew no correcting broadside from Trunk. The red-faced and pipe-smoking newcomer had something to say : but with a few observations from the Stranger, showing a thorough mastery of the subject, the conversation was allowed to languish.

Thaddeus Trunk knew that there was some mystery about this man who had come uninvited, and who immediately gave evidence of anything but respect for his great reputation. He decided to make no attempt to penetrate this mystery, but to wait for the Stranger to declare himself, in his own good time. It would not be long, he felt sure, before the cat was out of the bag. At dinner that night Stella, whose interest in the Stranger seemed continually to increase, placed him at her right, and talked almost exclusively with him. Only trivial matters were discussed, such as the hotel accommodation in Slabash County, and how amazing it was to an Englishwoman to find the immense distances people would travel—and after all Washington was five hundred miles away, wasn't it?—to spend a week or so with a friend. He, for instance, had he come two or three thousand miles to visit his relative, as she daresaid he had . . . ? Oh no, was his answer to that; he came from one of the great Eastern universities, that was all. They were sort of neighbours, really—Ah, that was *very* nice, and she did hope that he would make a habit of coming up there when he could spare the time (for she assumed, as he had come right now from that university, that he taught there).

The Stranger took part in the general conversation too. By the time he had drawn on the table-cloth a number of Chinese characters, had quoted intact a number of poems by Catullus, Ovid, etc., had corrected the Greek of one of the older young men, and had settled an argument about the pronunciation of Persian, it became obvious to everybody that this must be a high-ranking professor whom it was necessary to treat rather carefully, and to speak [to] rather carefully oneself. This cast a certain restraint over the party, seeing that Uncle Thad would never take very seriously any young poet who did not know a little Arabic,

214

Tamil, Phoenician, and Early German, and could not join in any Greek or Latin expedition which Uncle Thad thought it was safe to make.

The next morning, after breakfast, Trunk noted that his wife and the Stranger disappeared in the direction of the waterfall; and it was more than three hours later that he suddenly found them entering the kitchen door, poor Stella looking a little fatigued, but the Stranger being as quietly brisk as ever. There was no question of this visitor vacating Room 9, for Stella said to him : "Our visitor will stop in Room 9 for about a week; I got him to promise that he would not dash away at once, as almost any interesting person is apt to do. Don't you like him, Thad? He looks frightfully like you sometimes, it is clear enough that he is your cousin. Have you talked with him about——"

"My dear Stella, I *never* talk to people about things of that sort. When they want to, they talk to *me*. And *he* has said nothing so far."

"He will of course," Stella said.

That is where the matter ended. The Stranger never referred again to the fact of their consanguinity, and Trunk did not either.

Meanwhile, every morning, Stella and the Stranger would walk away in one direction or another, and not return until lunch-time. He would always say how superb the scenery was, which Stella had been so kind as to point out to him. In conversation in the evening he and Trunk were always clashing, or rather the host always disagreed with anything the guest said, and they would have longer or shorter arguments. The latter was never annoyed and never disconcerted. He did not say, "You always disagree with me." He appeared to take that for granted.

Something very unusual occurred on the fifth day after the arrival of Trunk's strange relative. A number of books were in a large bookcase in the living-room. Trunk wanted a *History of Ferrara*, which he had last seen there. As it was there no longer, he sought out Cobe, who seemed to remember having seen it in Room 9. It was as a consequence of this that Trunk burst into the Stranger's bedroom. As it was the morning, there was no one there, and the intruder planted himself in the middle of the room, and swept his eagle eye around it. It was then that he caught

215

sight of a verse manuscript on the small table with which the room was provided. He walked slowly across and gazed down upon it with a thoughtful look; it was scrawled all over and the central core was almost lost in a cloud of balloons and deletions. He picked it up. He began reading, and at once realized that it was a poem he had started work on a few days earlier. As he read on he saw that the corrections were not his. It was his verse, but all the corrections were the Stranger's, in a handwriting slightly different from his own.

He stood gazing in amazement at the familiar words. Was this a case of a literary theft? If so, how the devil could the Stranger have secured entrance to his writing-room, which he very carefully kept locked, and no domestic had access to it.

There was a shadow across the page, and the Stranger was at his side.

"Ah, you are reading my manuscript," he said, and gently removed it from Trunk's hand. "I have not copied out my first draft," he explained.

"So I see," Trunk said. "Why did you change the word 'mud' and substitute the word 'grit'?"

"I see you have been examining my composition," the Stranger remarked.

"Yes," Trunk told him, "and I find that you are writing, word for word, what I am writing. You, however, are *improving* my composition."

For a moment the Stranger looked embarrassed.

"How extraordinary," he said at length. "It is yet another instance of my telepathic endowment. I began writing quickly, without thinking much what I was doing. *Then* I began correcting—like the schoolmaster I am." He paused. Then he added, "I must stop doing this."

"It would perhaps be better if you did." Trunk eyed him toughly for a moment or two, and was about to leave the room, when he turned at the door, and said "Are you reading a *History of Ferrara*, by any chance?"—"No, sir," he was told, and so took his departure.

Thaddeus Trunk was very much disturbed. He had a thrill of deep apprehension. In the end he decided that it was yet another instance of his amazing powers. This poor fellow was so overpowered by his personality that he had reached the point of telepathic imitation. Evidently he was very psychic.

In spite of his rationalization of this very odd discovery, Trunk was now possessed of a constant uneasiness about this unwelcome guest. Once or twice that day he passed him in a corridor; they did not speak, and as he touched him in passing, realizing that strange silent body so near to his, he experienced a spasm of a kind of eerie alarm. He thought how, in the past, when they had happened to come near to one another in this way, the Stranger had never spoken. The image which he had of him most clearly if he had had to recall him, was one from the first day of his sojourn there. They were standing in the paved court at the back of the main building and suddenly the Stranger spat. Nothing odd in that, but he noticed that what he had spat had blood in it, and he had looked queerly at him as he asked, "Do you often do that?"—"Why no," the other man had answered. "Now and then I have noticed that my sputum has blood in it. A little blood, it is nothing."

Trunk was a few minutes late for tea that day, and arrived in the middle of a conversation between Stella and the Stranger, *les jeunes* listening in. Before he came in, his wife had laughingly referred to the "tough guy" ingredients in Thaddeus; for they had been discussing Hemingway, and she felt that it would have been affected to ignore the fact that there was another "tough guy" not so far away.

The Stranger had analysed this "toughness" in a very clear and sensible way, she thought. He said that since he had been born around the same time as Thaddeus, he thought he could understand the origin of this exaggerated masculinity. "You see, Thaddeus Trunk was born under the shadow of Theodore Roosevelt's 'Big Stick,' he grew up with the Bull Moose symbol under his eyes, the strenuous life ideal inspiring every Presidential utterance."

It was at this point that Trunk entered. The Stranger continued, "But quite apart from that, those were tough times, especially in the West. If you were riding in a lonely place and met another man, or men, you would do well to remember how lawless the nation was in which you dwelt, and give these strangers as hard a look as you could muster."

Trunk realized at once that all this had something to do with him. As he, as usual, dropped into the low easy chair he preferred, his accumulated resentment came to a head suddenly. He felt that he could and should fling this impudent so-called cousin out of the front door. He was a timid man, beneath his veneer of toughness, very averse to showdowns of any sort; but his chest rose as he turned towards the Stranger, and a growl came out of him which his wife had never heard before.

"You had better stop that, Stranger, you had really better not go on in that way. I do not like it. Remember it is the same nation now as it was then, and by hell I will throw you through that door if I hear any more stuff of that kind coming out of you."

There was a heavy silence, and Stella Trunk felt herself trembling a little. Stella was inclined to be "fey," as an English-woman is apt to be. When she was young she believed in Tinka-bell, she was disposed to favour anything which was only half there, or which came down the chimney rather than in at the door. This Stranger had dropped out of the sky, he was a being she had not got to the bottom of, but she was greatly attracted by this cousin of Thaddeus. She felt the rage that was surging in her husband. At any moment, she knew, he might leap out of his chair, and there would be a battle. What should she do? She bit her lip and waited, her eye travelling from the rumbustious form of what she knew to be her gentle husband, and this com-posed but, she realized, more redoubtable figure at his side, almost touching him. Would the spring be released? At every quite harmless natural movement she felt there was about to be an eruption—that this was the first move and the next would be chaos.

But the Stranger spoke softly and soothingly. "I do assure you, Mr. Trunk, that no offence was intended, and I ask you to forgive me, if, by inadvertence, I have been stepping on your toes."

There was again a silence, uncomfortable, but Stella had the feeling that the storm raging inside her husband was abating. Then one of the young poets suddenly said: "Mr. Trunk, may I put on a record—the last Purcell fantasia, the one-note, you know. Mrs. Trunk looks very tired, sir, and I think she would like to hear that music."

"Okay, young man," Trunk gave vent to a critical puff. "If you think the Missus would like that barley water and saccharine."

And so the tension evaporated. But that evening at dinner, half-way through it, it was renewed. That meal was always prefaced by the drinking of Bourbon or gin. And during the meal a full-bodied Burgundy was warming the veins of the party.

As Thaddeus sat down he called to his wife, pointing at the Stranger, who, as usual, was occupying the place on her right-hand side. "Be careful of that guy," he warned as he pointed. "I overheard him conversing with someone who had a tail."

"How amusing," said his wife, with much warmth, "I must ask him about that."

Trunk sat at the end of the table opposite to that of his wife. The Stranger and Stella seemed on better terms than ever that evening; he was filling her glass from a bottle which stood between them; and then he filled his own. Then he would raise his glass and murmur something, and it all looked detestably friendly to the observant Thaddeus. Just as there are thunderstorms which disappear, to roll and flash elsewhere, so there are psychic disturbances experienced by men, which vanish and, after an interval more or less long, once more make their appearance. The sudden inflammatory condition earlier that day had left a great sore bed inside the abnormally provoked host. So it was that Stella shivered as she heard that voice again, which she had heard for the first time when her husband abruptly took fire when he came in at tea-time.

"Take your snout out of that wine-glass, you louse—yes, I mean *you*, Mr. Cousin of my arse! Also stop playing the sucking-dove with my wife, you worm-eaten old charmer! Yes, you, Mr. Cousin of that apology for a bitch slobbered over by my Aunt Jane."

Stella half rose. "Thad! If you don't stop I shall have to leave the table."

"That's okay with me, entirely okay with me. Take yourself off if you don't like my company."

"Mr. Trunk!" The Stranger was glaring at his host.

"What do you want, grease-spot—are you going too? If I don't spik handsome and affable to you? Waall if you *doant* take your suet-face out of my sight pretty soon I shall have to use my boot to you!"

"You old drooler," bellowed the Stranger, "if it weren't for Stella I would be shutting up that dirty old mouth of yours."

Trunk had become very pale, and his mouth was pulled down at the corners as the traditional warriors of Japan look in battle, but his underlip was trembling. Grasping the table in front of him with two hands, he spat hysterically any word that he could find.

"Thieving punk, have you stolen any more of my manuscripts? Why I ever brought a rat like you——"

The Stranger had sprung up. In a moment he had reached the bottom of the table and seized Trunk by the tie, and jerked him out of his chair. The young man sitting on the left of the host had risen and began springing about. He received a blow from Trunk, who was hitting out with aimless fury as he felt himself being prised into the air by his revolted guest. But the next minute the Stranger was battering at his face, and then delivering a haymaker, as the youthful audience later described it, in the centre of the bulging beard, which sent him reeling down upon the floor, where he lay at full length, completely still.

Gasping, Stella rose and ran to the side of the prostrate Thaddeus. The youngest of the poets was already kneeling at the other side of him. Everyone had risen. The Stranger strode very quickly out of the room, colliding with Cobe who was hurrying in, in response to a scream from his wife. She was waiting at table, and was now screaming hysterically.

Half an hour later, the Stranger, fully dressed, and carrying his suitcase, walked out into the court. Stella, who was with him, went over to the chauffeur, on his knees beside a car, and asked him to get the station-wagon ready, as this guest wished to catch the night-train for New York. She then returned to where the Stranger was standing.

"He will not keep us long," she said. They began pacing up and down, the Stranger, in a low voice, explaining how greatly he had been provoked.

Before they left there was a scene. His face swollen, and

striding a little less toughly than usual, Thaddeus came out of the house and walked slowly towards them, his hands in his jacket pockets. In one of these was a gun, which he had brought with him in case the Stranger should wish to repeat his knock-out. Out of his tumefied face looked two very angry eyes.

"Stella, go back into the house."

"No." Stella shook her head.

"This guy beat me up. That's what I get for my hospitality. You reward him for beating me up by being his escort to the station."

The Stranger spoke. "Was I to remain passive, under your filthy abuse?"

Thaddeus went up to Stella, and thrust his hand under her arm. "That drip can go as he came. *Faccia di merda*—yes, you . . ."

"Don't be absurd—at least say what you have to say in your own language."

Stella approved this retort of the Stranger's.

"Don't make a fool of yourself Thaddeus, I will remain with this guest of ours, who is leaving because you insulted him. I wish to make up to him for the bad treatment he has received."

"I insulted *that* . . . !"

"He might knock you down again!" Stella sneered. "You had better go in and have a rest."

At this Thaddeus turned on his heel, and feeling a little giddy, for he had been struck another blow, this time by Stella, went slowly into the house.

While this altercation had been proceeding the chauffeur had had time to get the station-wagon out; he was buttoning up his overcoat. Stella and the Stranger advanced towards him, he held open the car door, and Stella got in, followed by her protégé. So, a minute or two later the Rebellious Châtelaine and the Uninvited Guest rolled away. That was the last Thaddeus saw of his wife. Or, to state briefly what had happened, a second Thaddeus, whom Stella had recognized as the real Thaddeus had made his appearance, and Stella, very simply, changed Thaddeuses, deserting, or, if you prefer it, leaving Thaddeus Number One.

Only a shadow, a shell, remained upon the mountain. In the

221

mountain mists a bulky phantom of publicity like one of those oversize garish posters which are so repulsively familiar continued to milk a goat there, and to spit imaginary blood. But, bit by bit, this advertisement figure evaporated, and there was nothing left at all of the one-time poet who had been devoured by that Moloch, the Public.

What else is there to say? The disembodied instrument will still produce annually, perhaps, a slender volume with verses of the same matchless beauty. But as the Public receives these final perfect messages it holds in its mind the heroic image of the dying poet: for it, old Thaddeus is still milking his goat in the high mountains, and as he does so, with the symbolic spitting, his lifeblood ebbs away. This image is as necessary to it as that of the beautiful ineffectual angel was to the contemporaries of Shelley; as dear as the sadly-gazing eyes of the bearded sage of Craigenputtock was to the generation which venerated Carlyle. There must be a visual human equivalent—if that were all, Thaddeus would be justified. What he did not realize was that the Public supplied its own publicity, and that he must only live, in flawless innocence. It was but a minimal fragment of that Public which was his affair at all. Lastly, and what it is most amazing that he should have forgotten, it was not the part of the Public of his deepest predilection which was concerned with romance. That it was the vulgar who were to have the last word was what his actions signified.